MW01134406

VESSIE FLAMINGO

OUTSHINING THE MOON

A TALE OF SELF-MASTERY AND LOVE

JERELYN CRADEN

Bloomington, IN Milton Keynes, UK

authorHOUSE™

AuthorHouse™
1663 Liberty Drive, Suite 200
Bloomington, IN 47403
www.authorhouse.com
Phone: 1-800-839-8640

AuthorHouse™ UK Ltd.
500 Avebury Boulevard
Central Milton Keynes, MK9 2BE
www.authorhouse.co.uk
Phone: 08001974150

This book is a work of fiction. Names, characters, places, and incidents are products of the author's imagination or are used fictitiously. Any resemblance to actual events or locales or persons, living or dead, is entirely coincidental.

VESSIE FLAMINGO—OUTSHINING THE MOON

© 2006 JERELYN CRADEN. All rights reserved.

No part of this book may be used or reproduced in any manner whatsoever without written permission except in the case of brief quotations embodied in critical articles and reviews.

First published by AuthorHouse 4/27/2006

ISBN: 1-4259-3547-8 (sc)

Library of Congress Control Number: 2006903725

Printed in the United States of America
Bloomington, Indiana

This book is printed on acid-free paper.

Writers Guild of America, west, Inc. Registration No. 878452

To those who illuminate my life —
my son, Omie, my mother, Lee,
my treasured family, friends, and teachers.

VESSIE FLAMINGO
OUTSHINING THE MOON

ONE

A flamingo flew over a sandbar fifty feet from a white sandy shore—the flutter of its wings, the only sound in the late afternoon sky. The sea was a turquoise calm—the sun, warm loving hands.

A young man jumped from a thirty foot cruiser onto a dock then to the shore and along the water's edge past sandcastles and sea turtles—his foot prints filling with the tide.

A young woman stood at the top of a hill in front of a house whose wings stretched out like the wings of an eagle. She looked down and saw him running…running…

New York 1980

Nooooooooooo! Why am I being punished? All I wanted to do was drive to Kennedy and catch a flight to St. Lucia or Eleuthra or any place that's warm and far away from Lou and every moronic jingle he's ever made me write. Okay, so he didn't make me, but I felt like a fly in a jar after the lid's been taken off. You just stay there because you think you have to.

Vessie VanCortland was stuck in her four-seat Thunderbird classic beneath a five foot mound of snow. She couldn't see through the iced windows, couldn't open the doors. She was locked, blocked, filled with anxiety as snow kept pelting down imprisoning her in a living tomb. It was the worst blizzard to hit New York City and for a smart young woman, Vessie felt desperately dumb. She looked at the travel brochures on the bucket seat beside her. Magnificent white sandy beaches. Sun streaming through lush tropical palms. A crystal clear sea.

The car radio belched static as a newscaster's voice kept breaking bad news:

"... even rescue cars need to be rescued."

"Rescue cars?"

Vessie hit the radio with her freezing hands. She had hoped that by blasting it as loud as it would go, it might reach out and touch someone; but it didn't reach and it didn't touch, it just died.

She caught a glimpse of herself in the rear view mirror. "Damn, I'm turning blue. I look *lousy* in blue!"

Vessie couldn't look lousy in anything—goofy, maybe.

The huge rainbow colored earmuffs and matching muffler wrapped around her neck and head stuffed down inside the tall stand-up collar of her faux fur coat detracted from her long shiny auburn hair and emerald green eyes. It was more a Hanna-Barbera look than Vogue.

Frightened and freezing she asked herself: *How the hell did I get into this mess?* But she knew. She just couldn't take it anymore. *It,* being Lou Fields who was proving to be not only a *toxic* boss—he made bi-polar something to strive for.

The recession was unforgiving. Lou was convinced that winning the equivalent of an Oscar for a television jingle would boost business and guarantee the survival of his jingle house, Fields and Friends. For weeks he had been pressuring Vessie to bring home the bacon at the upcoming Geo Awards, and his crazy-making was off the charts. After dealing with ten years of it, she finally had enough. She turned off her electric keyboard, jumped into her Thunderbird and headed for the airport.

Then all hell broke loose.

The sky spit bullets. Wind snarled. Trees snapped. A great gust of swirling white exposed the Chrysler building, Grand Central, the Guggenheim at 5th and 89th. Then white again—a ghostly dream-like white with a big fat hole in it—Vessie stuck in her impending doom.

She tried to shove the word *help* out from behind her frozen face. She was always able to make her body do anything she wanted; but now the simple task of parting her lips begged the aid of a hacksaw.

Lou Fields paced the floor twelve blocks away. He was a ferocious bulldog in a five foot human frame. "Where the hell is she? I'm going to lose the musicians." Everyone had made it to the 6:00 p.m. demo session at Allsounds to record the new Catflakes jingle Vessie had composed, except Vessie.

The recording engineer sat at the mixing console—feet up, eyes closed. The musicians, ten in total, sat on folding chairs in the adjoining "live room" smoking, drinking coffee, discussing real estate and stock investments.

Remy Bartells, Lou's staff producer, sat cradling a phone anxiously waiting to get through to the airport. "I told you to cancel the session," he said. "I told you Vessie wouldn't be here—she *split*."

"Don't be ridiculous," Lou said. "She was working on the final changes. She was going to bring copies like she always does. *Split?* She'd never do a thing like that."

"No, she wouldn't normally do anything but the best for you. But you can't keep making her cancel her vacations and expect her to stick around."

Remy got a busy signal and dialed again.

"What? I'm gonna turn down business? Vessie's my top jingle writer."

"Yeah, who you burnt out."

The absent composer closed her eyes. Paradise was almost hers. She could see it, touch it, feel it. Salt water—buoyant. Her long thin body, floating. Sun caressing, licking, soothing her. A chill raced up her spine. Vessie put her mittened hands to her face. It seemed not to be hers anymore, but a kabuki mask painted white with holes cut out through which her eyes registered panic. *Is this it? Is this how I'm going to die?—Vessie VanCortland, hack composer of tuna fish, hemorrhoid and cat food jingles freezes to death in her car?*

The keyboard player headed for the door. "Hey, thanks Lou. That was the easiest session I *never* played."

The studio lights flickered—Lou flinched. "What the hell?"

"Damn!" said the engineer. "Looks like the power's going."

"Elevator's stuck!" yelled the keyboard player huffing it back to the studio.

Remy slammed the phone. "The airport's shut down. Vessie's plane never got off the ground."

3

Lou saw red. "You mean she's here? She's in town? Then why the hell didn't she show up? The ingratitude—the goddamn ingratitude!"

Remy's heart sank. *Where are you, Ves? Are you okay?* He turned to Lou. "She *drove* to the airport."

"In that meshugana car of hers?"

"I'll try her at home." Remy dialed as Lou stood frozen. "No answer."

The lights went out—the room was pitch-black.

"Damn!"

"Jesus!"

"This is nuts!"

The recording engineer flicked on a flashlight. Remy Bartells' boyishly handsome face was consumed with fear. He made his way to the window and looked out at a sheet of white. "She might be stuck in it somewhere."

Lou forced himself to look. "Goddamnit! I told her to get rid of that car of hers, but no—*'It's a classic, Lou.'* A classic trap!"

A little girl with green eyes and auburn hair dressed exactly like Vessie— rainbow earmuffs, matching muffler and mittens and faux fur coat— appeared in the bucket seat beside her, crying.

"Don't cry," Vessie said. "Your tears'll freeze your eyelids shut." *What am I saying? Who am I talking to?* "Wait a minute!" she said. "Who *are* you? How the heck did you get in here?"

"I'm your inner child."

"My what?"

"Your inner child."

"Then what the hell are you doing out here?"

"Showing you how miserable you feel."

"Great, a cheerleader! Well, don't worry. Pretty soon I won't feel a thing."

"That's what I'm afraid of. You've been out of touch with your feelings for years."

"Oh my god, a Jungian."

The child cried harder.

"Okay, hold it right there," Vessie said. "If you're my inner child, why are you complaining? I walked out on a jingle session because of you!"

4

Her eyes said, *you did?*

"That's right. I was about to take you to an island. A gorgeous, sunny, lush green island far away from Crazy-maker-Lou."

"An island?"

"Yeah, hot sun, blisters on your tush, salt water on your flippers."

"So."

"So? So, here I am freezing to death because you kept yelling, Vessie, get a life. All work and no play, Vessie. You hate your job, Vessie. Write songs you believe in and stop being a sell-out!"

Her inner child wiped the window exposing their ice-covered cell. "Guess we're stuck, huh?"

"We just look stuck. It's really me *un*-sticking myself!"

"I'd hate to see you with a roll of packing tape."

Then the child went ballistic—big ear-crushing sobs.

Diversion, diversion, Vessie thought. She cleared her throat and sang: "Take a Catflake to breakfast, and you'll have a thrill. Take a Catflake to breakfast, and I'm sure you will…"

"Please," said her inner child, "if I puke now you're really in trouble."

Vessie closed her eyes. The air was biting cold and hurt less that way. She heard *om-mani-padme-hum* floating inside her head. Om-mani-padme-hum, her old meditation technique. The mantra yogi Paramahansa Bramananda, Founder of the Spiritual Enlightenment Ashram in Malibu California taught her eleven years ago. Six little syllables from the ancient language of Sanskrit that could help transcend her fears and warm her freezing body.

Vessie grabbed onto them like a life raft. *I've got to concentrate. I've got to make this work, because if somebody doesn't find me soon, this could be my last day as a human and my first as a popsicle. Chant, Vessie, chant girl, chant.*

"Om-mani-padme-hum, om-mani-padme-hum, om-mani-padme-hum, om-mani-padme-hum…" *It's been a long time, too long. Why did I ever stop meditating?*

Her inner child wanted to know, too. "Why did you ever stop meditating?"

"Enough, just do it."

"Om-mani-padme-hum, om-mani-padme-hum..."

Good. Keep it up Vessie, she told herself. "Om-mani-padme-hum, om-mani..." *Wait... you're too anxious. Subtle, Ves, be subtle. Don't pounce on those syllables. Whisper them. Let them take you deeper. You remember... just let goooooooooooooo.* She could feel her muscles begin to relax, her thoughts begin to fade. Then she had a vision.

She saw everyone she had ever loved crowded into the back seat of her car: her father, Reverend Everend VanCortland; her mother, Erlinor Sutton VanCortland; Mrs. Smith, her beloved Jewish surrogate mother; and Paramahansa Bramananda, her guru—his legs wrapped in an Indian-style dhoti of bright orange cloth, chanting, "Om-mani-padme-hum, om-mani-padme-hum."

"Mama! Vessie's a witch!"

Oh, and her older sister, Smoodgie, as a ten-year-old with her hair in a flip and a Pixie Band parting her thick dark bangs. And, as always, Everend tried to stop her from taunting Vessie.

"Don't talk about your sister that way."

"Well she is!"

"Excuse me young lady!"

Vessie turned to Smoodgie. "How can you call me a witch? I'm your *sister*!"

"Are you kidding? You're the weirdest kid in Symington. You speak to angels nobody can see. You know the phone's going to ring before it rings. You even heal hamsters and... and cats' and dogs' paws. You're a freak!"

"A freak? Update your pictures, sister dearest. I haven't done that since we were kids."

Erlinor piped in. "Not since your father made you Church Organist. A clever diversion, Everend."

"Well, it did take her mind off doing those things." He looked at Vessie lovingly. "And what a blessing to discover your God-given talent for music. The songs you write are beautiful, Ves."

"Oh, Daddy, you really think so?"

"Of course I do, darling girl."

Vessie turned and faced the snow-covered windshield. "God I miss you."

She heard Smoodgie stab her in the back. "God I *hate* you."

Vessie whipped her head around. "Smoodgie, grow up! You're my *older* sister, remember?"

Suddenly, Smoodgie, aka Charlene, transformed into her present age: thirty-five.

"And, Smoodgie?" Vessie said. "The phone's for you."

"Very funny." Then a phone rang. "Damn you, Vessie!"

Smoodgie picked it up and Vessie grabbed it away.

"Nobody home," she said, and slammed it down.

"You can't do that."

"Of course I can. This is *my* vision!"

Tucked into the back seat in a full lotus position, Guru Paramahansa Bramananda continued to chant, "om-mani-padme-hum, om-mani-padme-hum."

Vessie and her inner child joined in.

Sirens wailed through the streets of Manhattan. A blur of swirling red light streamed at a snail's pace from the tops of squad cars and ambulances as they crawled through a sea of unrelenting white.

Stuck inside Allsounds, illuminated by a single flashlight's beam, Remy avoided Lou's eyes. He wouldn't allow himself to appear vulnerable to a man whose only concern was himself. He looked away fighting tears.

"I never should have let her go."

"What do you mean *let?*" Lou snapped. "Since when does Vessie listen to *you?*"

"She's my best friend, Lou. She listens."

"You're my producer. She *has* to listen." Lou scanned the room. "Christ, where the hell's the goddamn electricity?"

"Om-mani-padme-hum, om-mani-padme-hum…" Something was interrupting Vessie's focus—an intruding thought, a vision mocking her attempt at survival. She kept repeating her mantra but the vision was overpowering.

Suddenly, it was as if Vessie were looking into a crystal ball dated 1955. There she stood in her rosebud-papered bedroom staring into a shiny new cage at two birds whose faces appeared to be kabuki masks through which their small eyes registered *panic.*

TWO

Before Breasts

Smoodgie peered over Vessie's shoulder. "They look sick to me. Especially the boy bird. He looks like Milton Berle acting like a crazy person."

It was Vessie's fifth birthday and her parents, Erlinor and Reverend Everend VanCortland, had presented her with two periwinkle and white parakeets. Vessie was overjoyed. She loved anything that could fly. And now she had two winged treasures chirping loudly in the cage before her. Ten-year-old Smoodgie wasn't about to let her little sister enjoy them for a minute.

"They're crazy, Vessie, just like you."

"They are not crazy, they want out," Vessie said. "Birds aren't meant to live in cages."

"Smarty-pants. How do you know? You think you know everything." Smoodgie gave Vessie a hug that was meant to crack her ribs. Vessie winced. Smoodgie ran out of the room slamming the door behind her.

"Vessie," she heard one of the birds cry, "please let us go. I know it's your birthday, but we'll die in here."

Vessie's heart sank. She knew what it felt like being cooped up. Closets frightened her, although she wasn't sure why. Smoodgie knew why. She had locked her baby sister in one when Vessie was two. Erlinor, thinking Vessie was asleep in her crib, found her as she happened to look for a photo of herself and Everend taken on the VanCortland senior's Connecticut farm. It was in an album on the shelf of the cedar-lined closet where Vessie lay asleep in a puddle of urine.

"No. I won't let you die!" she told the birds.

"Vessie! Supper!" Erlinor shouted from the foot of the stairs. "Make sure the cage door is shut."

It was twenty days before Christmas and Vessie looked out through her bedroom window at palm trees swaying in the Santa Ana breeze. Symington, California, a community of twenty thousand, seemed always to be swaying. Vessie believed that Santa would fly in on a surfboard as she lay dreaming of Jesus, who was black. He must have been, she figured, from praying for forty days and forty nights in the hot Palm Springs sun. Or was it the Sahara? She never told Erlinor that Jesus was black. She knew how her mother felt about Negroes.

Vessie always did as she was told, but not today. She opened the window, then the cage door, said goodbye to her new winged friends, and shut the bedroom door behind her.

Everend was all smiles as Vessie entered the dining room. He looked handsome in his green and white seer-sucker suit despite his George Gobal haircut that looked like a lawn mower ran across the top of his head. Vessie looked like an angel in the pink ruffled dress Erlinor had laid out for her to wear. A barefoot angel.

"Vessie VanCortland, where in the world are your *shoes*? And your *socks*?"

Vessie was too upset to respond. The long oval cherry wood table was set for the occasion with her mama's prized china and sterling, but her place setting was as usual—a plastic plate embossed with an image of Howdy Doody and a Clarabelle mug. *Where's my grownup place setting? I'm a whole year older.* "Mama!" she cried.

"Don't be a silly-dilly, Vessie, you love Howdy Doody and Clarabelle." Under her breath she whispered to Smoodgie. "Plastic won't show the grease from her fingers." Smoodgie flashed Vessie a mean-spirited grin, enjoying Erlinor's conspiratorial aside. "And Missy," Erlinor said to Vessie, "I want you to march right back up those stairs and put your shoes and socks on. Your special socks with the double-edged pink ruffles."

Everend spoke in a tone that meant, *not now. "Er*linor!"

She rebutted lifting her ski-jump nose in the air. "Ever*end!"*

Then the Reverend opened his arms to Vessie. "Come here my darling girl."

She climbed up on his lap and burrowed her small head of shiny auburn hair into his shoulder. *Vessie, always Vessie,* Smoodgie thought, knocking over a crystal water glass.

"Charlene! Dear Lord" Erlinor yelled. "Go get a towel, no two!"

Everend hugged Vessie gently and close, hoping some of her goodness would rub off on him.

Erlinor grabbed a towel from Smoodgie and pushed it down into the sopping wet table cloth. "Everend, Vessie's been indulged enough for one day." She grabbed the sterling dinner bell and rang for Conchita, the maid, to bring in the roast leg of lamb.

Vessie jumped down as Everend took off his cotton jacket exposing a white short-sleeved Brooks Brothers shirt. Relocating to a high-back chair, she heard him say: "Nearly every one of Cecil Pratt's rabbits got heat exposure. Two of his roosters *died."*

Erlinor rolled her eyes as she took her place across from him. "He needs *fans.*"

"Tried buying fans, but the whole town's sold out. Best to keep inside in this heat."

Vessie felt sick. Her birds would surely die just like the roosters. "May I be excused?" Without waiting for a reply, she ran from the table.

Smoodgie saw this as an opportunity. "That was rude!"

Erlinor agreed. "Vessie, come back here!"

"Perhaps she isn't feeling well," Everend said, heading for the stairs.

Smoodgie shot back. "In the *head.* That's where she's sick."

Vessie ran to her room praying that the birds would still be there; but when she entered, they were gone. All of her blood rushed from her head to her feet and into the floorboards. She sat on the braided rug as tears flooded her pink round cheeks.

"They would have died in that cage. I just wanted them to be happy," she told Everend, who was now towering over her. He quickly scanned the room, realized what had happened and searched for the right words that might console her.

"Vessie, the uh… shopkeeper said the birds were uh .. from *South America.* It's much hotter there, darling girl. Why, this weather would be nothing to them. It's uh… it's *cold* they don't like. They'll be fine… sure they will," he said, hoping the birds would die far enough away from the house where Vessie wouldn't find them.

That night Vessie's bedtime prayer had a new addition: "… and I pray for everyone who wishes they could fly… like me."

That summer Vessie tried to fly. She started by running on the grass flapping her arms, jumping as high as she could. Nothing. The wooden bench was next. She brought it outside to a spot where she knew Smoodgie and Elinor wouldn't see her. She stood on it, flapping her arms, envisioning herself taking off lifting higher and higher. Nothing. She kept trying taller objects until finally—Vessie broke both her legs trying to fly off the garage roof. And this is what Smoodgie said: "She's crazy!"

She's crazy, she's crazy, echoed in Vessie's head, then—*om-mani-padme-hum, om-mani-padme-hum.* She envisioned her guru's face, heard his words. *Do not fight the thoughts that come into the mind. Let them come and then repeat your mantra: om-mani-padme-hum, om-mani-padme-hum.* Yes, Guruji, yes.

Another vision. *Eyes, deep hazel. Hair, thick—sun bleached. Body, muscular, tanned… running… running. "Om-mani-padme-hum, om-mani-pademe-hum."*

Sirens wailed through the snow-blanketed streets of Manhattan as Vessie's mental photo album turned to another page—1960.

THREE

Vessie Learns to Heal

"These are breasts," Smoodgie said, sticking out her B-cup boobies in her new pink angora sweater. "And those*"* she said, pointing to Vessie's chest, "are cheap imitations. Now, the only reason I bring this up is because when I get back from New York, I expect to see that yours are much bigger. If not, I will disown you and pretend you do not exist."

Vessie didn't answer. She knew Smoodgie was just showing off and was used to her off-the-wall manner. "Will you write to me, Smoodgie?"

The teenager swayed her aquamarine felt skirt from side to side making the chain collar on the cloth poodle jangle. "Oh, I'll probably be too busy. I'm sure Uncle Carl will spoil me just like Daddy does. And you know Aunt Helen. She's just got to go everywhere and do everything. Maybe a postcard. Maybe not."

It was June and Smoodgie's sweet sixteen wish had been granted. Erlinor and Everend would send her back east to visit her sister, Helen, and brother-in-law, Carl.

New York didn't interest Vessie. She loved the spaciousness of Symington. The yard, the wide tree-lined streets, the sun that never seemed to set. Tall buildings didn't interest her, and the fragrance of the lemon and grapefruit trees, now in bloom, was something she just wouldn't want to miss. Besides, who would feed the Bordman's, the VanCortland's elderly next-door neighbors? Vessie believed they were desperately poor because of their extremely old furnishings. That's why she had been sneaking eggs, peanut butter and bread from her house to the elderly couple's for years. Everend didn't have the heart to tell her that the Bordmans owned some extremely valuable antiques and were far from destitute. He insisted that

12

Erlinor keep it "our little secret" as he didn't want to discourage Vessie's extraordinary generosity. Besides, the Bordmans enjoyed Vessie's visits and regarded them as *treats.*

Palm trees swayed and Santa Ana breezes swept through the open windows of the white wooden filigreed church in the small town of Symington, as Reverend Everend VanCortland continued his Sunday morning sermon.

> "Our Lord meant for us to shine His light on all
> our brethren.To allow His presence to express itself
> through every man, woman, and child of every color
> and religion. To heal the world as we heal ourselves."

Everend, born to a minister father and school teacher mother, yearned from an early age to experience the presence of a Divine power. He wasn't sure what it meant back then, but he knew it clear as day when he recognized the connection between a Higher Force and his youngest daughter, Vessie. His strongest personal experience of connecting with universal energy or Divine Intelligence came when words flowed through him during his sermons. Words he didn't write.

> "To allow His presence to express itself through all
> our deeds. And to shine His light within us.
> May the light in your house be you.
> And let us say… amen."

Vessie sat transfixed. She had heard her father's sermons hundreds of times before, but today his words struck a chord that made her whole body vibrate. She ran them through her mind again. *To allow His presence to express itself through all our deeds. To shine His light within us. May the light in your house be you.*

With Smoodgie in New York, she was able to concentrate more fully in church. She wasn't being jabbed in the arm and told: "That's Colin Beaton two pews down, just broke up with Betty Johnson," or, "Look at Johnny Page… not bad since his zits cleared up." She was even able to see colors around Everend's body. She had seen people's "colors," she called them, since she was little. Nobody told her they were *auras*. And nobody took her seriously when she tried to describe them. So she just gave up.

"Vessie! Vessie dear, we're waiting for you." Erlinor shook her head looking through the church which was empty except for Vessie. *She's lost again. That child!* She straightened her navy blue pill-box hat, frustrated that her youngest daughter didn't hear her, or *wouldn't* hear her, but instead stared at the pulpit as if the sermon were still in progress.

The power of Everend's words catapulted Vessie straight through the chapel roof. "Oh oh ohhhhhhhhhhhhh!" she sputtered. Her arms became wings. Her hair—long magnificent feathers. She felt totally and unequivocally free. She looked down and saw Everend greeting members of the congregation just outside the church entrance surrounded by waves of pink, purple and green. She saw Erlinor calling to her from the church foyer, surrounded by warm yellows and golds. And, she saw her own body still seated in the first pew surrounded by light.

"Vessie, Vessie dear, let's go!"

Vessie snapped back into her body and obeyed.

What a summer.

While most girls her age spent time playing with dolls, Vessie began playing with angels. She made them out of old nylons, cotton padding, and embroidery thread. And when she finished sprinkling three angels' wings with glitter and sat them side-by-side against the rosebud pillow Erlinor had made, they spoke to her.

"It's time you learned to heal."

Vessie's emerald eyes grew with excitement.

The lessons began.

Every morning right after breakfast Vessie excused herself and headed down to the basement where she knew she could be alone. It hurt her to see people and animals in pain. And because she didn't want to risk being ridiculed for her "odd behavior" by Erlinor or even Everend, she decided to keep her lessons with the angels exclusive to Curlie-hamster and Max-the-rat who lived in the basement.

In an old baby buggy that Erlinor stored with every article of baby clothing that used to be hers and Smoodgie's—Vessie made room for the angel dolls on a small yellowing cushion. She did what they told her, and after many rehearsals was ready for her first attempt.

One sunny afternoon as she swung back and forth in an inner tube that hung from a tall birch tree in the spacious backyard, Vessie noticed a neighborhood cat lunge at a sparrow in the sunburnt grass. She jumped off the swing and ran to free the bird from the cat's grasp. "Shoo! she yelled. "Shoo cat!" It scampered away. The bird lay stunned, shivering, one wing displaced.

Vessie kneeled beside it remembering what the angels taught her. She raised both hands to the sky and closed her eyes. *Please help me heal this bird. I want to heal this bird.* She lowered her hands as close to it as it would allow, and repeated silently: *His love goes through my hands to your wing, through my hands to your wing.* She gently placed her hands on its tiny body and restated her intention. *Please help me heal this bird.* She lifted it onto her lap and lightly placed her hands on its wing. *His love goes through my hands to your wing, through my hands to your wing.* She could feel the bird become still.

Moments later the palms of her hands tickled. She pulled them away and saw the bird flutter its wings, lift off her lap—and *fly.*

All that summer, Vessie practiced the healing technique on birds, hamsters, dogs and cats. Now, all she needed was a human.

FOUR

Hands On

The last Saturday in August, the Santa Ana winds forced the back screen door to slam a fright into Conchita. All two hundred and fifty pounds of her jumped one way and the serving dish she was holding jumped the other, hitting the stone floor and smashing to pieces.

Erlinor burst into the kitchen. "What in the world?"

"I... I pick up all the pieces, Missus... I put it back somehow."

"Conchita... you... you... you *pig*!" Erlinor turned and crossed herself, hoping Everend hadn't heard her natural inclination to sarcasm expose her practiced pious façade.

As Conchita hunched over trying to clean up the mess, a sharp piece of porcelain slit her hand and blood ran all the way to the sink.

Later that night, when Erlinor and Everend's bedroom lights went off, Vessie snuck into Conchita's room.

"You sleeping?"

"No," Conchita said. "Why you not sleeping?"

"Does it hurt?"

"Si. *Boinga, boinga,*" which Vessie took as meaning—it throbs like hell.

The room was dark except for a burning candle illuminating a picture of Conchita's son, Real, who had died of pneumonia two years before. Vessie took Conchita's bandaged hand and held it gently. She wanted to heal her, to take her pain away. She had grown to love this woman who was always there—before school, after school—with kind words and sad eyes.

"What you do, Vessie?"

"You'll see. Now, just relax. Close your eyes and relax."

16

Conchita sank down beneath the covers. Vessie lifted her hands and silently said: *Please help me heal Conchita. I want to heal her.* She lowered her hands just above the wound, closed her eyes and concentrated on the words the angels taught her:

> His love goes through my hands to your hand…
> through my hands to your hand.

She gently moved her hands onto the bandaged palm and kept repeating the words over and over until Conchita's snoring broke her focus.

The next morning, Conchita was gone—her bed made, closet empty, and the photo of Real just a memory. Everend gingerly confronted his wife.

"Perhaps you were a bit rough on her last night, dear."

"Me? But, dearest, all I did was tell her she was a… uh… to clean up. It's not my fault she cut herself."

Vessie was perplexed. *What happened? What did it mean?* Nobody knew until a week later when a letter arrived addressed to Everend.

> *Dear Mr. V -*
> *My cut. She took my hand. Said words.*
> *In morning no cut. No mark.*
> *Vessie friend with devil.*
> *Conchita*

My little girl is a healer, he thought. *Dear Lord, help me.* He was thrilled, but devastated—afraid that Vessie's special abilities would cause her ridicule and isolation in the small unsophisticated community of Symington. Everend did something he had never done before. He kept the letter from Erlinor. He knew that if he showed it to her she would over-react and cause Vessie anguish she didn't deserve. So, he crumpled it, took it into the yard where the incinerator stood, and burned it to ashes. The next thing he did was buy Vessie an organ. *Music will be a great diversion,* he decided. *Best to dissipate this energy with something she will love.*

"The organ is so big."

"You're a big girl, now, Ves."

17

"But, why, Daddy?"

"Because I need an organist who won't be late for services. Mildred Angsley is always late."

"But, won't she be mad?"

"Oh, by the time you're ready to take over for her, she'll be begging to leave. Besides, this will be fun for you."

It wasn't just the incident with Conchita that concerned Everend. Vessie had become psychic.

"Don't you go doing that now," Erlinor would tell her. "If you know the phone's going to ring or somebody's at the door before they get a chance to ring the bell, you just keep it to yourself. I want no hocus-pocus in *this* house, young lady!"

Everend prayed that Vessie's interest in music would grow as her *unusual* abilities diminished. He did everything he could to protect his darling girl from becoming a social outcast. So, at the early age of ten, Vessie slowly began to overcome her handicap of being *special*.

Hocus-pocus, Vessie thought. *Mama called it hocus-pocus. Smoodgie called me a freak. My god, these thoughts, these memories.* A chill ran through her. *My mantra. I'll focus on my mantra.* She took a long deep breath. The cold air made her cough. *I'm not afraid, I'm not afraid,* she told herself. But she was. She was terrified, and clung, once again, to her only hope: *om-mani-padme-hum, om-mani-padme-hum.*

Lou Fields and Remy were playing bumper cars without the cars as they awkwardly made their way in pitch darkness down the fire stairs from Allsounds recording studio with a group of disgruntled musicians. It was definitely a case of the blind leading the blind.

A few penlights shone and a couple mini-flashlights. Some small accessories lit up, but nothing serious that would lighten fears and enable greater mobility. It had been hours since the power went out and Manhattan had grown substantially humbler, except for Lou.

"I want a Geo, damn it. I want that jingle award."

"You're unbelievable, Lou," said Remy. "We're on the goddamn Titanic and you're worried about your trophy shelf? What the hell about Vessie?"

"Of course she'll write it."

FIVE

Daddy Love

"Om-mani-padme-hum, om-mani-padme-hum…" Vessie juggled her mantra with visions of the past trying to be her own best coach: *Keep meditating, Ves. Keep meditating and you'll survive.*

November 1963.
She was standing on the crowded Abraham Lincoln Junior High School lunch court wearing a green polished cotton pencil skirt and matching top when Jenny Wright, a chubby thirteen-year-old classmate, ran toward her.

"President Kennedy's been shot!"

Vessie was outraged. "That's not funny!" she shouted.

A bell rang calling everyone back to class. "Did you hear?" "Is it true?" "Can't be." "Oh no!" The horrifying news was then broadcast over the school P.A. system.

Later that day, the Bordmans sat with the VanCortlands glued to their neighbors' new color television. Not a word was said as they watched footage of their President being shot as he sat beside his pretty young wife in the back seat of an open-air car that moved through the downtown streets of Dallas, Texas.

Erlinor fell limp against Everend's chest. Smoodgie stomped out of the den and ran to her room. The Bordmans crossed their hearts and closed their eyes. Vessie sat frozen, feeling more alone than she had ever felt before.

Images of the event continued to plague her until her tear-soaked pillow begged to be replaced. She couldn't understand how a thing like that could happen or why? John F. Kennedy and Jackie were the perfect couple, the perfect parents, the handsomest and smartest pair. They *were* the bride and groom on top of the wedding cake. Who in the world would want to ruin that? Vessie kept envisioning the biggest most beautiful cake in the world with John and Jackie standing on top, and then, BANG! his head gets blown off.

Way down deep inside a sadness grew in Vessie—a stain of broken trust that splattered across her teenage soul. She felt her innocence taken from her that 23rd day of November. She didn't know how to explain it, but she shared her feelings with Everend the best she could.

He shared *his* feelings with her. "I feel like something was taken from me too," he said, "...and millions of Americans whose motivation for getting up in the morning has always been *hope*.

Hope, hope. "Om-mani-padme-hum, om-mani-padme-hum."

More visions came—then more.

Vessie sat at the organ playing a song she had just composed.

"Good as any Beatles' tune," Everend told her.

The Beatles? Oh my gawd! To Vessie, that was like having a benediction made over her keyboard. From the first time she heard them sing: "I Want To Hold Your Hand" and "She Loves You"—she felt *yeah, yeah, yeah* in her heart.

Vessie was consumed with melodies and lyrics. She was now fourteen and an avid organist and songwriter. She was too busy to think about the lessons the angel dolls taught her. Rarely noticed people's "colors" anymore. She still knew when a phone was about to ring and when someone was approaching the house from blocks away. And she still felt a kinship with her father that she was grateful for, without realizing that he had purposely guided her away from abilities he was afraid would one day bring her harm.

Everend always knew what to say to encourage Vessie. He knew her better than she knew herself. Erlinor knew that even in the privacy of their own bedroom, she was unable to penetrate the depth of love he felt for their youngest child. And right now, in the sweetness of her meditation, Vessie longed to see her father again on a typical Sunday morning in church.

She saw Smoodgie flirting with an acne-ridden teenager in the next pew over. Erlinor fighting sleep. Reverend Everend proudly nodding to her to play the next hymn.

The pipe organ, whose enormity had inspired her to name it Big Moose, dwarfed her, exaggerating Vessie's youth and honorable position as Church Organist.

> Have you had a kindness shown?
> Pass it on!
> 'Twas not giv'n for thee alone?
> Pass it on!

Everend was right. Mildred Angsley was glad to pass on her position as Church Organist, and Vessie was proud to take it from her, even though it meant having to play required music at Sunday services, weddings, christenings, and funerals instead of her own preferred compositions. But she made sway, especially when it came to playing music for children. She loved their playful innocence and always looked forward to choir practice and the annual Nativity play.

It was a warm Saturday morning in December. The sun beat down on tall pineapple-etched palm trees offering no clue that Christmas was two days away. Vessie and Everend sat on the leather-tufted bench in front of Big Moose, the pipe organ, discussing a hymn he chose for the midnight Christmas service. A voice shouted: "Excuse me!" Jenny Wright, Vessie's chubby school friend, ran toward them excited and out of breath.

"Excuse me for interrupting, Reverend," she yelled, moving closer. "Vessie, if you don't leave now you'll be late—the competition starts in twenty minutes."

Everend was bewildered. Vessie's heart raced. "What's this?" he asked.

"The Greenbriar Junior Song Writing Competition," Jenny said.

Vessie's face flushed. "It's not important, Daddy." She turned to Jenny. "Sorry, Jen. You'll have to go without me. I didn't know we'd be rehearsing this long."

"What's this about, Vessie?" Everend asked.

Now *Jenny* looked surprised. *What? She didn't tell him?* she thought. Jenny being Jenny blurted: "Vessie's song made it to the finals. Hundreds of kids will be there. It's the biggest junior song writing competition in the county."

"Jen!" Vessie shouted. "I said, go *without* me."

"Jenny, would you excuse us please? I'd like to have a word with Vessie," the Reverend said. Jenny found a pew and sat down. He turned to Vessie. "Why didn't you tell me you entered the competition?"

"You know about it?"

"Of course I do. This is a small town." He looked at her gently. "So… Vessie?"

"I didn't tell you because…"

"Yes?"

"I didn't… want to *disappoint* you if I lost.

"You could *never* disappoint me, darling girl. Don't you know that?"

"It's not important Daddy, you need me here."

"No, *you* need to be *there*. It's a tremendous opportunity. I didn't want to put any pressure on you to enter, but since you have…" He called to Jenny. "She'll be right with you, Jenny." He looked at Vessie. "You have to be there to find out what happens… especially if you win. And if you don't win, it won't matter. I'm already proud of you."

I once knew a man, or so I thought
who bought me a ribbon and a rose
I once knew a man who loved me
'Til he left me
I don't know why he left me
Did I forget him?
No, I didn't want to
Do I regret him?
No, he loved me
Shall I cry him out of my mind?
I cannot do that
He is the only happiness I can remember

Vessie's song placed second. It had a haunting melody and she wasn't sure why she wrote it until she got back from the competition. Everend was found dead in the vestry from a coronary heart attack. She was devastated. She loved her father more than life. He understood her—accepted her unconditionally. She admired him—loved his humanity and depth of heart. Losing Everend was like losing a part of herself. And the worst of it—she believed his death was her fault.

Vessie was always able to tell if someone was sick—their colors would be somewhat jagged, out of alignment. Like the time she saw the colors around her fifth grade math teacher's body. Not knowing that Miss Evans had just been diagnosed with cancer, Vessie felt compelled to tell her that she hoped she felt better. That incident cost her a three-week after-school detention. Afterall, nobody believed *how* Vessie got the information. All they knew was that her behavior was totally unacceptable.

Now her guilt was massive. In her irrational young mind, she believed that if she had stayed at the church with Everend instead of going to the competition, she would have seen evidence of his impending heart attack and he would still be alive. *If I stayed. If I saw his colors.* If if if if if. But Vessie hadn't seen Everend's colors for some time, or anybody else's. Not since music had become her focus.

She knew she had to stop carrying this guilt. It was making her miserably unhappy, and she knew Everend wouldn't want that. She also knew what he would want—for her to keep playing and composing music. So, rather than take on the responsibility for everyone's state of health and risk another mishap—Vessie vowed never to see people's *colors* again. But the pain of their separation shook her to the bone.

Erlinor was unable to help Vessie—*she* was trying to cope with her own loss by taking medication behind locked doors. To cope with losing a man she never felt worthy of. Who she knew married her only because he got her pregnant. Who tried to provide a respectful role for her in the community—a home, family. Who tried to love her only to be disappointed by her lack of interest in his spiritual passion and sensitivities. Now she had nothing. Without Everend—who was she?

Smoodgie distanced herself from her mother and Vessie. She was angry. There would be no chance to ever be close to her father. She threw herself into learning to be a dental hygienist and, on the weekends, meeting eligible bachelors. She forced herself not to think about Everend's death and how it caused her family to fall apart. She dismissed inquiries from church members into why Erlinor had become reclusive; why they never saw her in church anymore.

"The new minister's quite good, don't you think?" a congregant whispered to Smoodgie in church one Sunday morning. "But there was only one Reverend Everend."

Smoodgie was in pain and wore a soldier's mask.

Vessie felt cold. The loss of her father had left a hole in her heart so big and deep that just the thought of it made her shiver. She couldn't afford to feel any colder, not when she was being forced to look at her own mortality and the possibility that she could actually freeze to death before she was found. Sheets of snow pelted down, burying her beneath an ever-growing hill. There was no physical way of getting warm.

What a concept, she thought. *I could be a stiff before rigor mortis sets in.*

"Stop it! Stop it!" shouted Vessie's inner child. "You're alive, you're breathing, and your toes still hurt. Stop your sniveling and keep us alive! Wriggle those toes," she implored, "wriggle 'em!"

"Wriggle! Wriggle!"

They *wriggled* like hell inside their faux fur lined boots, when... *Roy? Roy Thatcher? My god! My first boyfriend.*

It was nineteen sixty-six and Vessie had tits.

SIX

Vessie & the Fly Boy

Smoodgie looked through the pane glass window as a grey Volkswagen pulled curbside in front of the VanCortland house. "Is that him?"

Vessie didn't get up—she already knew. "Yep, that's him."

You'd think he was Smoodgie's date, the way she flitted and preened in the hallway mirror—straightening her skirt, hiking up her brassiere straps.

"My Lord! He's six foot two if he's an inch. Where'd you meet such a hunk?"

Vessie just smiled.

"Well, where'd you meet him?"

"The phone's for you."

The phone rang and Smoodgie ran for it grumbling. "Nut case... nut case."

Vessie was sixteen and looked twenty. She was tall, slender, had almond shaped eyes the color of emeralds and shiny auburn hair, thick and wavy to her shoulders. Smoodgie could no longer tease her about her *cheap imitations*—she wore a C-cup brassiere and had a waist that looked like a child's wrist.

Smoodgie was engaged to Edward Kleig, a young intern at Symington General, but it didn't stop her from getting into a flap over a good-looking hunk.

Since Everend's death two years earlier, Vessie had taken no notice of males of any age. Her father's loss was too deep and consuming. She spent so much time composing fugues and death marches that Smoodgie was shocked Vessie *had* a date.

As for Erlinor, she had become an old woman overnight. Her hair turned grey and so did her attitude. She never bothered to question the girls' activities anymore. When asked her opinion she would lethargically reply, "Whatever's best."

Just beyond the Symington city limits, the grey Volkswagen made a U-turn into the gravel parking lot at the Buttonville Airport.

"Ready for your first flight?" Roy asked.

Roy Thatcher was handsome. He had a strong jaw, deep blue eyes, and jet black hair. He looked like a model for a Camel cigarettes ad in his red and black checkered shirt and khakis. Vessie felt lucky to have met him while playing organ at his niece's christening. She was told he was studying for his Instrument Rating and planning on being an airline pilot. Vessie was happy to accept Roy Thatcher's invitation.

Fly, wow! I've always wanted to fly, she thought. She still wished she could just start running and flap her arms and... whoosh... lift-off. Just like in her dreams and her visions where she'd fly high above the streets of Symington... above the Post Office, the Variety store, the John F. Kennedy Community Center. She'd wave to everybody... and the wind would blow through her hair... and ohhhh the feeling... the freedom... the power... the bliss.

"That's it over there. That Two Fifty Cessna." He pointed to a four-passenger plane. "It's a beauty. Just like you, Ves."

Vessie wasn't used to being flirted with and simply recognized it as a friendly way to break the ice. But no ice was on the horizon that day. The sky was blue and the clouds could be counted on two fingers. Vessie was in heaven before they left the ground.

Roy proceeded to fly his *beauty* like its wings were his shoulders. The higher they climbed the more they shared a free unrelenting gush of giggles. At two thousand feet, he couldn't hold it any longer. He said something in a way Vessie had never heard that something said before. Roy Thatcher closed his eyes and said, "Ooooooooooooooooooooo!" Then he lit a cigarette. It was beautiful.

26

"How about next Tuesday? We can fly to Joshua Tree for lunch and a swim. My aunt and uncle are expecting me."

"Nobody home?"

Vessie was surprised that she and Roy weren't being greeted by his Aunt Susan and Uncle Marley. "It's all right," he said reaching into his pocket. "I have a key."

He opened the door of the rambling ranch-style home and headed straight to the refrigerator. A note was waiting beneath a plastic cactus magnet:

We're at the club. Food's in fridge. Pool's warm.
Love, M & S

The sun was hotter than in Symington and so was Roy.

"I'm dying for a swim. Wouldn't you like to cool off, Ves?"

"Those turns you were making, wow!"

"You brought a bathing suit, didn't you?"

"One day I'm going to fly. Think you could teach me?"

"Everything I know."

Roy wasn't used to being with a girl like Vessie. He was a hunk and, like most hunks, was used to getting his way.

"So, let's go swimming and then have lunch."

"Lunch will be great," Vessie said. "But then I really have to get back. Besides, I can't wait to get back up there in that beauty of yours." Vessie flashed her green eyes and Roy became butter.

Okay, he thought. *I'll fuck her next time.*

But, next time came and the time after until the days wrapped themselves around months and the farthest Roy got with Vessie was a day trip to Tiajuana.

Vessie wiped guacamole from her mouth. "My mother would die if she knew I was here, even if it's just for the afternoon."

Roy couldn't hold it in any longer. "Vessie… I love you."

"I love you, too, Roy," she said, patting his arm like a poodle.

"No, I mean, *really* love you. Like, *in love.* I am in love with you, Ves."

27

Vessie didn't know what to say. In love? No one had ever said that to her before. She didn't know what *in love* meant. She may have looked like a woman, but her experience was that of a child. She had never even thought about being in love, and that's what Roy realized when he read Vessie's face.

As for Erlinor, she had no idea Vessie had spent the past three months twenty thousand feet above her head. Vessie had told her about it the first time Roy asked her out, but in Erlinor's advanced state of depression, it just hadn't registered.

"Mama, Roy Thatcher asked me to go flying with him."

"Drugs? The boy's on drugs?"

"No, Mama, he's not on drugs."

"Oh... I guess he must like you then."

"I don't know. I guess so."

"These new expressions."

"Mama, can I go?"

Erlinor's eyes glazed over. "Whatever's best."

So, Vessie went, again and again. But, when she arrived home that day, Erlinor was waiting for her on the front veranda waving a carving knife and screaming at the top of her lungs: "You blasphemous harlot! Damned child of Satan!"

What's going on? Vessie was shocked. *Has Mama gone completely off her nut?* Erlinor kept screaming, waving her arms, losing her footing on the wooden slat porch.

"If the Lord meant for you to fly you'd have wings! Jesus said..."

The knife was so big and sharp, and she was striking the air so wildly that Vessie ran next door and pounded for the Bordmans to open up. The door opened and she flew past Mrs. Bordman toward the phone. "Mama's in trouble. Gotta call Doc McVee." But, by the time he arrived it was too late. Erlinor had gone for the porch post with the blade, missed, and fallen into a compost heap impaling herself.

"It's all my fault," Vessie cried to the tune of, Pass me Not, O Gentle Savior. "I never should have gone flying." Tears fell onto the church organ keyboard as Vessie played the hymn and the congregation walked slowly past Erlinor's flower-laden casket.

For tearful weeks, she tried to make sense of the events leading up to her mother's death: Everend's fatal heart attack, totally unexpected. It didn't seem to matter that Erlinor was a minister's wife and an avid church-goer; she was terrified of death. She was also totally dependent on Everend. Then poof! he was gone. Rather than reach out to friends for support, she withdrew from everyone, including the church. She wouldn't answer the door or the telephone. Mail kept mounting up. She couldn't make a decision to save her life. And *then* the phone call from Roy Thatcher's mother who she hadn't seen since Everend's funeral.

> "So, Erlinor. What do you think of our kids'
> wild afternoon flight to Tiajuana? Those
> crazy Mexicans sticking Bayonets into the
> backs of bulls just for fun. Never did anything
> like that when *I* was a kid."

Finally, weeks after beating herself up, Vessie reconciled that her mother's passing may have been a godsend. *Mama was so lost without Daddy, now they're reunited in the big pulpit in the sky.*

"Om-mani-padme-hum, om-mani-padme, hum." *Mama... Roy.* She could see him, but with somebody else's eyes—deep hazel. With somebody else's hair—thick, sunbleached. "Om-mani-padme-hum, om-mani-padme-hum."

SEVEN

The Big Kiss

Black flowers, grey parades
Days filled with hours ticking away
Time that goes nowhere
except to your grave
This is what life means to me

You'd think that with all the hours Vessie spent morosely transforming her despair into writing songs, her fingers would have whittled down to pudge stumps. But she was finding her way by *ear*, so to speak, through a challenging maze of events.

She was now an orphan, sixteen years old, two years away from her high school graduation, and in the care of the one person who never really cared for her: Smoodgie.

Smoodgie was now an orphan, twenty-one years old, engaged to be married, and not thrilled about being Vessie's legal guardian. But she dug in her heels and was doing her best to assume the roles of both mother and father, which proved especially difficult as her unwed belly continued to balloon. By spring, Smoodgie was married to young intern, Edward Kleig, and busy tending to their first-born, baby Everlyn-Gene.

The first thing Smoodgie Kleig did was change Vessie VanCortland's future. She sold the organ, bought an electric piano, and upon its presentation told her: "You can plug yourself in day and night with these ear phones, so the only person who has to suffer through your music is you!"

Suffering was not on the agenda. Vessie was *ecstatic*—filled with unbridled creativity. She had never experienced anything like it with Big

Moose, the pipe organ, or the smaller one it replaced. This new instrument seemed to guide her fingers to play the songs she used to play when Everend was alive and told her, *You're much better than the Beatles, darling girl.*

"You're much better than the Beatles, Ves," Roy Thatcher said. She looked at him as if God spoke to her at the well. "Much better."

Vessie threw her arms around Roy and kissed him so hard his lips swelled like inner tubes. Then his libido, which he had trained to do a sleeping dog act at her request, jumped up, rolled over, and wet his pants.

Roy Thatcher's parents spent most of their time in bed. They ate there, wrote letters there, worked jig-saw puzzles there, read, watched television which was suspended from their bedroom ceiling, and occasionally received guests there, like Vessie. They did everything but make love there, which according to the Thatcher's was for the *young people.*

Roy Senior extended his large hairy hand that stuck out the sleeve of his silk paisley pajamas. "Charmed," he told Vessie.

Thelma Thatcher patted *her* side of the mattress and waved the girl over. "Come child, sit down… the Beatles are on Ed Sullivan."

Vessie didn't want to see the bottoms of Roy's father's feet or his mother's chest bones protruding above a low nylon negligee. She wanted to be properly greeted at a church function or tea or funeral. But by the time Ed said, "That's our show for tonight," she had curled up against the hand-carved cherub headboard shoulder-to-shoulder with Thelma, Roy Senior, and Roy Junior eating Raisinettes and wondering how in the world Everend and Erlinor had overlooked such wonderful earthly delights.

Roy Junior whispered to Vessie. "Let's go to my room."

He took her hand and led her out of the room, down the long narrow hall of dark wood floors and beige stucco walls that bore a mounted photo of Roy Senior accepting a gold watch for selling gold watches. Roy's room was at the far end of the hall and had a sign on its door that read:

Fly Boys Do It

Roy locked the bedroom door behind them.

"Won't they wonder what we're doing in here?"

"They know what we're doing. We're doing what they're doing."

31

He led Vessie toward the bed, then stretched his long lanky body across the bedspread pulling her down with him. She could feel the warmth of his body, smell the sweetness of his aftershave. It felt strange but good, especially when he began stroking her hair.

"Ooooooooooooo," she purred. *Oops! an audible leak.* "Excuse me, something in my throat."

Roy met her excuse with a kiss. That was it.

> They kissed and they touched
> They turned and they squirmed
> He grew and she knew
> It meant big fat trouble

Lyrics flashed through Vessie's head as her blouse came away in Roy's hands. He rubbed his smooth tanned chest against hers. *So close so gooooooooodd!* They were no longer in a room but in a space that was hot, humid, and filled with hormones.

Vessie whispered as she pushed him away. "Uh-uh." It was wonderful, *but.* They could touch each other and go crazy, *but.*

Roy rolled onto his back and groaned. Vessie had never seen a boy's *thing* before and Roy's was so long and stiff pointing due north like that, she didn't know whether to salute it or paint it silver and fly a flag. But, it was going to have to stay pointing away from her. Some things were sacred and the entrance of a man's privates into a woman came only after marriage. So it was written. So she bit her lip.

His hand found hers and its innocent touch bridged the gap between their legs. Vessie felt an energy and trust surge from her to Roy and back again. Their eyes met as their blood cells did a rumba Kathryn and Arthur Murray would have died over. It was puppy lust and the wonderful thing about it—it was free, non-fattening, and had no mortgage.

EIGHT

Diamonds & Saddle Shoes

"God Roy! How many rings are there?" It was ten p.m. the third Thursday in November, 1966. Roy had come straight over from his fat friend Charlie Evan's fat father's jewelry store clutching a manila envelope that he shook upside down on the VanCortland's kitchen table.

"I wasn't sure which one you'd like so I brought a dozen of 'em."

"Roy! Diamonds! But, the bikini and the stuffed dead chicken you gave me were beautiful gifts." Vessie loved teasing Roy. She knew this was his way of broaching the subject of marriage, but she wanted to hear him say it.

"Whatever did I do to deserve all these rings? Let's see... it isn't my birthday... and Christmas isn't 'til next month."

Roy scratched his head and cleared his throat which Vessie had seen him do every time he felt less than uncomfortable.

"Waaaaaaaaaaa-waaaaaaaaa!" wailed baby Everlyn-Gene, interrupting her recently married parents who were in bed halfway to orgasm.

"Ves, I, uh...can we go into the living room?"

Vessie could hear Roy's heart pounding from four feet away. He led her to the green and gold embroidered love seat and became Robert Redford.

"Ves, I want you to be the mother of my children," Robert told her. Roy sat there half-believing what he just said. Vessie sat there half-believing what she just heard. She knew it was coming, but to actually hear him say it brought a feeling she hadn't known since before Everend died—*security.* Roy loved her and wanted her more than ever, despite the frustration that his *thing* had to endure.

Vessie stared into the eyes of the young man who aimed for her to be his wife. "Yes, Roy. Yes, yes, yes, yes, yessssssss!"

"You're too young," Smoodgie told her. "You're a child, Vessie. I'm sure if Mama and Daddy were here they'd tell you the same thing. Isn't that right, Edward?"

Edward Kleig feigned agreement. As far as he was concerned, Vessie was big enough to eat as much as he did and on the little money his parents allotted him until the completion of his internship at Symington General, it was just fine if she no longer ate at his table.

Roy explained that he and Vessie wanted to extend their engagement until she graduated high school. By that time he would be earning the wage of a professional airline pilot and they could be married.

"That's different then, isn't it Edward?" Smoodgie received a less than positive glare, but ignored it. "Ves, let me see the ring."

Ooo's and ahhh's and chit-chatty excitement began with Smoodgie and continued with Vessie's high school classmates.

"It's a beautiful ring," one girl said, then whispered to another as Vessie walked away, "I bet she's pregnant."

All of Vessie's classmates eye-balled her in gym. Bets were made, cosmetics put up as collateral; but, weeks passed and still no tummy. "Aw, heck, have to kiss that rumor goodbye." But some were beguiled and believed that Vessie was the luckiest girl in the world and hoped that one day they too would be swept off their two-tone-saddle-shoed-feet.

NINE

One Strike & You're Out!

"Induction notice? What do you mean, induction notice?"

Roy told Vessie not to worry, that it was his turn to go, but Nam wasn't going to come anywhere near him. In one respect he was right. He would fly for the United States Air Force *over* Vietnam, dropping napalm and other sundry items on men, women, and children. But now was now, and Vessie didn't want to part with her best friend and fiancée in just three short weeks. She had had enough partings in her sweet and sour sixteen years. She was also terribly disturbed that the loss of life in Vietnam was being reported by television newscasters in the same manner as baseball scores: *Today's casualties: Vietnamese 60; Americans: 54.* She remembered what her father had told his congregation: *When man realizes that war is in his own soul, he will know where to go to establish peace.*

Roy tried to cheer her. "We've been invited to a party near the airport. It's just for pilots and their wives. We'll get to see what our future'll be, Ves."

"Our *future*?"

Suddenly Vessie's stomach jumped to her throat. She felt flushed, nervous. It was one thing to wear Roy's ring and *dream* about their future—another to be *in* it.

"Welcome! Oh, 'scuse the hair rollers, I didn't have time," said their twenty-year-old hostess, Mrs. Willie Williamson.

Introductions were made as Vessie looked around the living room at all the young wives and all their young hubbies and all their young crying babies. It looked like a photo session of "Queen for a Day." Whose story was the worst? Who sacrificed the most for a tract house near the airport, polyester evening clothes, Kraft dinners, and Maybelline? Her hostess shoved a cold dripping can in her hand.

"Vessie, have a beer."

"Thanks, but I don't drink beer."

The room hushed. Heads turned.

"You don't drink *beer*?"

Vessie may as well have said, *I don't breathe air.*

Their young husky host appeared. "Roy! Glad you could make it." He grabbed Vessie, his eyes glazed with drink. "This your girl?"

The evening continued and with it, Vessie's nightmare. The crying babies, the diapers hanging in the kitchen, the hallways, the overburdened bathroom. The beer slugging and cheap jokes. The cigarette-stained twenty-year-old teeth. *This is going to be my future? My life? But, it can't be. Daddy wouldn't have wanted this for me. Where's the beautiful music? The manners? The space to breathe, to create? No yard out back of this place—just a place to hang more diapers. And those planes zooming over head. It's one thing to choose your flying times, another to have them choose you. No. This isn't right. This isn't marry-me-have-my children. This is marry-me-have-my-life!*

Vessie clutched her stomach.

"Roy, I feel sick."

Roy was guzzling with his flying buddies. "Huh? Wha? Whaz dat?"

"Ever try eatin' a Ritz cracker and chewin' gum at the same time?" said one of the wives to Vessie, chomping on a wad of gum and popping a Ritz cracker in her mouth. The woman's purple eye shadow was so thick, Vessie was sure she had melted one of her kid's crayons and dripped it on. *I've got to get out of here*, she thought. After much persistence, she peeled Roy away from his party.

Roy's car was noisier than their conversation. It was an old car and Vessie had something new to say which she didn't know how to say, so she said nothing.

Days passed and she still couldn't find a way to tell Roy that she had made a mistake and never should have accepted his ring. She loved him, but realized that love wasn't enough. Not when it came to marriage. There were so many things that needed to be considered. Things she realized she wasn't ready for and really didn't want—like being one of the young wives-of-the-fly-boys' community living just off the airport tarmac. At the time, it was more of a strong intuition than anything; but, strong enough to let her know she wanted out. How could she hurt Roy? But, then… how could she hurt herself? Finally, Roy pulled it out of her.

"You're seeing somebody else, aren't you?"

"What?" She was flabbergasted. "Of course not. Why would you even think a thing like that?"

"Vessie! When we're together it's like you're not even here. You're like this ice queen. I mean, what the hell am I supposed to think?"

Roy was verging on tears.

"Oh Roy, I'm so sorry. I… I…" She couldn't look him in the eyes. She lowered her head and took off the engagement ring. "I'm sorry." She held it out. "I can't marry you. I just can't."

"You're giving my ring back? But you can't! I'm the *guy*."

Roy flushed with anger. He paced and shouted: "If anyone breaks this off it should be *me*. Jesus, Vessie, what am I supposed to tell my folks? My buddies? How the hell am I supposed to go to Nam without a girl to write home to? You can't do this. You can't, you… you can't!" He raised his big log of an arm to hit her.

White hot steel shot straight through Vessie's spine stretching her body 'til her head hit the ceiling. "Do it and I call the cops!" she said.

"Jesus!" He was totally freaked out. She looked down and saw Roy in diapers sucking his thumb. At least that's how he appeared to her. He blinked his eyes. She was back to her normal size. *I'm losing it*, he thought.

Vessie couldn't believe it. Five minutes ago he was Mr. Almost Perfect.

"Nobody raises his hand to me," she said, "noooo-body."

Roy threw the ring on the carpet and stormed out of the house.

Smoodgie raced into the room.

Vessie picked up the ring and forced a smile; but, sadness besieged her Superwoman pride. She fell limp against Erlinor's satin sofa. She could still smell her mama's perfume, still see her daddy looking at her lovingly. *Hug me*, she thought, *be with me*. Vessie felt utterly and completely alone.

From a bottomless place she had never known before came primitive uncontrollable sobs. Smoodgie couldn't bear it. She ran to her sister and embraced her for the first time.

Wind howled. Freezing cold air and the distant screams of sirens menacingly forced Vessie's attention back to her present claustrophobic cell. *"I hate this car! I hate this blizzard."* Smoke waves escaped from her nostrils and lips. Her inner child cuddled closer, raised her head and shuddered. She searched Vessie's eyes hoping to find comfort; but, found fear staring back at her.

Remy couldn't stop thinking about her. He had to find Vessie, needed to know she was all right. He stopped on every floor as he and Lou came down the fire stairs in darkness, making his way by touch into empty offices, locating a phone, dialing numbers he couldn't see, then finding zero and praying for operator assistance. But time and again, he couldn't get through.

TEN

Hello L.A.

"Say cheese!" Edward shouted. Vessie held out her high school diploma as she stood on the veranda of the house she grew up in. She looked beautiful in her new moss green graduation suit. Her reddish-brown hair, now inches longer, hung gently down her back and shoulders.

Smoodgie stood proudly beside her husband, soothing baby Everlyn-Gene's gums with hanky-covered ice. It was a Kodak moment attached to an unhappy memory—a shiny brass plaque nailed to the same post that Erlinor had attacked with a carving knife two years before.

DR. EDWARD KLEIG, M.D.

"C'mon, Ves… say cheese! Cheese!"
Vessie smiled and announced. "I'm moving to L.A."

Dinner took a backseat to Vessie's news.
"That's where the music publishers are," she said. "You know how busy I've been writing new songs. Well, now I have over thirty and I want to get them published."

Edward was concerned and had a lot to say. Now that he had his own practice he felt he could be more generous and help support his young sister-in-law.

"It's crazy in L.A.," he said. "The drugs are rampant, the hippies are trouble makers, the music business is nuts. I think you ought to stay right here in Symington. Give yourself some time. You can go to L.A. later…when you're older."

"Older?"

Edward locked eyes with Smoodgie for support. "Don't you think so, dear?"

"One thing Vessie's always known is her own mind," Smoodgie said. "I think we should encourage her to go. Otherwise, we'll have a very unhappy young lady on our hands." She emphasized the *young lady.*

Vessie sprang from her chair, raced around the oval table and gave Smoodgie a big warm hug. Surprisingly, she hugged Vessie back. That was the 2nd hug in a lifetime. *Headline material:*

BIG SISTER DOESN'T HATE LITTLE SISTER ANYMORE

She never did, really. It was just a mixture of love and intent to kill. The belief that since the day Vessie was born, she had to take a back seat to a spotlight that would never again be hers. But now *Smoodgie* felt special. She was married to a man who loved her, was the mother of a beautiful baby girl, enjoyed a respectable position in the community, and had a bed that bounced around at night. What did Vessie have? She pulled her close and whispered.

"You need some birth control pills?"

June 1968.

Martin Luther King and Robert Kennedy had just been assassinated within three months of one another. The air hung thick with anger and horror, especially at the corner of Melrose and La Cienega, Vessie's first day in L.A.

Edward was at the steering wheel of his two-tone Buick hardtop. The trunk was filled with Vessie's belongings—the electric piano held in place with bungee cords. He stopped at a red light and hoped they would soon arrive at Vessie's newly rented room because it was hot.

"Ninety-five degrees," reported the radio weatherman.

Smoodgie was asleep beside Edward, glued there like when they were dating. Vessie was in the back seat with baby Everlyn-Gene, taking in everything there was to see on her new turf.

"Then, four big black guys," Edward would later recount, "came up to the car, two on either side, and started yelling, 'yo killed him, yo killed

40

King, Muthafucka,' and they shook the car so hard I thought they'd turn us the hell over. Well, Smoodgie woke up and looked out and started screaming, and the baby started crying, and I don't know what Vessie was doing, but I'll tell you, there was no way I was going to stay there, no way at all. The light was red, but I felt safer going through it than sitting there, so I shot the shit out of the gas pedal and took off."

What he wouldn't recount was what he didn't know happened. Vessie was crying. She was upset that because she was white, she was the enemy. She cared about Negroes. She knew what it was like being part of a minority. She remembered being the only kid in Symington who spoke to angels.

Jeanie C. Riley sang "Harper Valley P.T.A." over the car radio as Edward drove through Vessie's new neighborhood rife with men dressed in black satin coats, big black hats, ringlets at their ears, Klezmer music blasting out of sidewalk speakers, and posters of J.F.K. and Robert K. hanging in every shop window.

"Jews live here!" Edward announced. "Vessie, do you know what that means?"

"Sure. I can get great pastrami at affordable prices."

Smoodgie was feeling a bit less faint after driving away from the car-shaking incident, but when she saw the men in black satin..."Jews!" she sputtered. "Daddy never would've approved." Down she went again.

Vessie was on fire. "That isn't true! Daddy had a great respect for Jewish teachings. He preached brotherhood toward all races and religions every Sunday. You were there. Weren't you *listening?"*

Vessie's new landlady's cake and strudel body stood poised in the doorway of the lower duplex on Orange Street. "I'm Missus Smith, come in, sit down, you'll have some nice fresh danish... *prune...* I made it myself, and some tea, the water's hot."

It was too much for Edward to bear. He needed to get into white meat country. Why did Vessie have to rent a room through the L.A. Times? Why didn't she check into a motel for a couple days and look around first like he suggested? Was she really going to live here in Mrs. Smith's house?

"Missus Smith, ha!" Edward whispered to Smoodgie and Vessie. "She must have changed it from Goldsmith or Smithstein. Those Jews are all alike...sneaky, petty, all for themselves."

41

"Here… gorgeous prune danish. Have some Mister… Mister…"

"It's *Doctor* Kleig," Edward said, "and no, we really can't stay. My wife is ill and my… my daughter, uh… has a dental appointment."

"She has teeth already?" Mrs. Smith laughed warmly. "Sure, go if you have to, but take some danish with you." She wrapped it in a white paper napkin and sent the Kleig's on their way. They almost forgot to say goodbye to Vessie.

"So, did you come here to be a star? I did," she told her new young friend. "Oh sure, I was in lots of movies. If you blinked you'd miss me, but who cared." She held up a photo of herself with a man in period costume. "Even Solly, my late husband, may he rest in peace, did some walk-ons. That's us in Hello Dolly."

Vessie's eyes glowed. "You worked with Barbra Streisand?"

"No. Melba Bromberg. It was the Hadassah version. Melba squeaked, we screeched. It was like Sunday morning in a deli only with bustles on."

She led Vessie past the kitchen to a room that had been her son's before he got married. "I can use the company. Solly, my husband, passed away two years ago. Mrs. Swartz, who lived upstairs, moved out last month. We would talk and we would talk. But now… now I have you."

A built-in grandmother, or mother, Vessie couldn't decide which. She had never felt such warmth from Erlinor. Were all Jews like this? Vessie hoped so and looked forward to eating all the prune danish she was offered.

First thing the next morning, she walked around the corner to Factor's delicatessen on Fairfax, ordered a buttered bagel and tea, and wrote these lyrics:

> Something newish
> I am Jewish
> At least a Jew in my heart
> Tell you boyish
> I was goyish
> But now I've found a new start

ELEVEN

Vessie the Working Girl

FARMERS-STYLE INSURANCE was etched in stone on the Wilshire Boulevard building. The entire eight story structure was filled with insurance offices. Vessie was dressed appropriately for her interview: beige pleated skirt, white short-sleeved blouse with a Peter Pan collar, and two inch beige heels. She scored high on her typing test and was creative when asked about her secretarial experience.

"I worked for Robert Kennedy's sister's cousin, Blanche McDermott Kennedy, who passed away shortly after his death. Oh, and I'm twenty."

The day Vessie met her first boss, Bruce Menken, would be etched in her mind forever. He had a horrible cold—more like the allergy from hell. The whites of his eyes were pink and his nostrils, crusty from blowing too hard. He sat her in a small cubicle surrounded by a sea of stenographers and gave her dictation to transcribe. She put on the earphone device and anxiously explored the speed regulator. Fortunately, she would be the only one who could hear the tape as it played back Bruce's lisps. She tried them all and settled on her favorite speed—the slowest.

Deeeeeeaaaaarrrrr Mmmiiiisssttttteeeerrr
Mmmmmuuuuurrrraaaayyyyyyy.

It was the lowest baritone she had ever heard and it made her laugh, *hard.* Like *wet*-yourself-laugh, which was not okay because it attracted stares.

There she was typing her way to her first week's paycheck, amused by the absurdity of being hired as an Executive Secretary with no experience or talent, when a lyric formed in her head:

Dear Mister Murray
tell me you care
that I'm in a hurry
with no time to spare
Gotta fly higher
than any old tree
Gotta be free
Mister Murray
watch me

Vessie imagined herself flying high above the Farmers-Style Insurance building past bumper-to-bumper traffic to music publishing companies up on Sunset Boulevard. And now with a steady job to pay the rent, she was ready to go there on her lunch breaks with the hope of getting her songs published. Entitled to thirty minutes, she would stretch them to ninety with the aid of excuses.

"Bruce, it's probably nothing, but, my doctor needs to run tests." Or, "Bruce, they think they've found it, but they've got to make sure that what they didn't know it was isn't what they didn't think it could have been."

Vessie surveyed the directory in the foyer of the twenty-three story building at the corner of Sunset and Vine: Angel Storm Music, Clearwater, Montgomery Music, Persona, Raintree, Sass—all major music publishers renting space in the terrazzo and granite tomb. She was ready. She had fifteen songs on reel-to-reel tapes and accompanying lyric sheets. Now, one deep breath and off to Angel Storm—one of the hottest music publishers in the business.

The doors opened at the nineteenth floor and Vessie got out. A black girl, five eleven in heels, slinked past. Her full afro, pants tight enough to have been painted on, and her formidable jiggling breasts reminded Vessie how conservative she must look for a songwriter, unless she were peddling hymns.

44

"No, I'm *not* peddling hymns!" she told Rick Stratton, assistant to John Milton, General Manager of Angel Storm. "They're pop tunes, and if you've got time to listen, I have tapes with me."

Stratton thought it would be a waste of time but that she was pretty and he might get lucky. So, he listened to the first song, then the next, and then stopped the tape and called in John Milton, his Ken doll look-alike. They both wore blue jeans, cowboy shirts, boots, dark glasses, and Sebring haircuts ala Fabian. At first, Vessie couldn't remember who was who. Then Stratton said:

"All your songs as good as these?"

Vessie gushed. "Well, thank you. Thank you very much. Yes they are. I mean, well, yeah."

"You know, most songs I stop four bars in. You know why?"

"Because they..."

"Because they stink! Because if someone heard them on the radio they'd skip to another station faster than they could score more dope. You dig?"

Vessie nervously smiled as Milton picked up a lyric sheet.

"Rhyme scheme's good, chorus is catchy. Let me see your legs."

"What?"

"Your *legs*."

"My legs?"

"You want to get published? Show me your legs. You can show Rick your tits, he's the tit man. Lock the door, Rick." Vessie had to think fast.

"Your phone's going to ring. It's... it's headquarters. I'm Detective Sergeant *Kleig*, and you are both under arrest for sexual coercion of a prospective client." Then the phone rang. The Ken dolls did their imitation of two corpses standing as Vessie picked up the receiver. "Kleig here. I've got them. Come on up." She backed away toward the door, unlocked it, and ran out of the office like her ass was on fire. "Oh my god, oh my god, oh my god, oh my god, oh my god," she repeated all the way to Mrs. Smith's house.

"Oh my god, oh my god, oh my god, oh my god, oh my god," Mrs. Smith repeated upon hearing her shocking tale. "Roots should grow from their kneecaps and tzimmas on their insides should shmush out like a squished knish!"

Vessie could make no sense of this whatsoever, but it didn't matter. She was home safe and sound in the kitchen of her darling surrogate mama, water was being boiled for tea, and fresh cherry peroshkies were being brought to the table.

"Bruce. I've got to call Bruce! I should be at work now." But Mrs. Smith would have none of it.

"Vessella, you sit down and listen to me. Tomorrow you go see more publishers. You get right back out there or you'll stay a secretary the rest of your life."

That's all she needed to hear. The thought of typing memos and inhaling stale air all her life was too much for her to bear. She made two appointments for the following morning and, once again, was on her way.

The reaction at Lightning Music: "Your tunes are good but I don't hear a hit." At Treason Music: "Your tunes are good but no better than our staff writers'. If you're going to compete off the street, you'd better have songs that are going to blow people away, otherwise, take up embroidery."

Vessie hated embroidery. No. She wasn't going to give up that easily. There were other publishers in L.A. and she intended to find them.

"It sounds like a Sinatra tune, but we don't deal with his people. Peggy Lee might do it, but she isn't hot right now. Sorry."

> Baby, I see you clearly now
> Baby, I hear your name in the wind
> And my life is beginning
> I can feel it beginning
> My life is beginning to begin

Vessie felt like her life was beginning to end. Her idealistic lyrics were beginning to reflect a part of her life that had become endangered. She couldn't eat, couldn't sleep. She got on a bus and headed back to where her idealism sprang from: Symington.

TWELVE

Bumps & Blessings

Vessie could see that what the stranger sitting beside her was writing
were lyrics:

> Buses
> My life's like buses
> Coming, going,
> getting no place in the race against time
> I'm just like
> Buses

"You're a songwriter."

Pete Dreyer's eyes popped like someone goosed him.

"Shit! I thought nobody would recognize me on a *bus.*" He reached
into his briefcase for his dark glasses.

"I don't recognize you."

Pete relaxed. So did his pock marks.

"Sorry, but ever since my last three songs went platinum and those
damn magazines started printing my face everywhere, it's been rough." He
took out two magazines from his briefcase and showed them to her. There
was Pete standing beside Rod Stewart and Tina Turner.

Poor baby, why don't you spread your crisis over here?

By the time they reached Symington, Pete had given Vessie his business
card, told her he would listen to her songs and if they were good he'd try
to help her. She trusted Pete not to try any funny stuff; he had shown her
photos of his girlfriend, Arthur.

They waved goodbye as Pete continued on to Palm Springs to hide out at his publisher's villa, and Vessie stepped off the bus back into the small town she used to call home.

Smoodgie stood on the front veranda with her arms opened wide looking prettier than ever. The sun backlit her straight dark hair and streamed through her green voile dress. She seemed happy, at peace with herself. She reached out, grabbed Vessie close and whispered in her ear so that baby Everlyn-Gene wouldn't hear: "Have you gotten laid yet?"

They spent much of the weekend discussing sex, although Vessie really didn't want to. Smoodgie forced the issue, feeling it was important.

"If you don't use it, you'll lose it. It'll just close up."

Vessie knew Smoodgie was teasing like she always had, but thought maybe there was some truth in what she was saying. *Maybe the longer I'm a virgin, the greater the chance that my attitude about sex will close up.*

"Are you suggesting I hop into bed with a guy as insurance against becoming frigid?"

"No no no. We're not talking insurance," Smoodgie said, "we're talking *fun*!"

"Fun is not what Daddy said about the begat routine. Fun wasn't mentioned in the bible, *sin* was. So was hell and burning in the mire of self-deception. Fun was something you had at circuses and parades, Easter hunts and birthdays. Fun was never said in the same breath as... *fucking.*"

"Bers gunkrow pills," gurgled baby Everlyn-Gene.

It was early Sunday morning, and as Vessie entered the empty wood frame church where Everend had preached for twenty-six years, a wave of melancholy swept through her. She looked up and saw him standing on the pulpit—a vision of light with grey beginning at his temples. His eyes, deep blue and warm, welcomed her. His velvety voice said:

> "Vessie, *you* are the house of God.
> This church is simply a place to remind
> you that heaven and hell are wherever
> you are. Read the bible, but read between

48

the lines. Listen to your inner voice.
What comes easy to you is God's will —
His blessing. Let Him express through you
and you will always be happy.
Let Him express through you and you
will always be happy."

*Happy? I don't know, Daddy. If this is God expressing through me,
then please tell Him to stop! I can't turn a corner without a lyric popping
into my head. Everything I do becomes a lyric. If I feel lonely, I think of
words about loneliness. If I feel optimistic, I write things like Up, up, away
from gloom, away from heartache. If I wake up at two in the morning,
I write a lyric about waking up at two in the morning. I can't go to the
bathroom without thinking up a song about taking a poop and wiping
myself. I'm sorry Daddy, but it feels more like a disease than a blessing.
Sometimes I wish I were happy just staying home, baking cookies, and
polishing silver. Why do I have to be special? Why do I have to have a
path? Why can't I just have babies, live in a tract home, and be satisfied
counting cat hairs and cigarette butts? Or go to college and get excited
about learning the origin of the word etu? Huh? Tell me, Daddy. Tell me,
why can't I be normal like other girls?*

Suddenly, Vessie heard the voice of her dearly departed mother.

"Everend, Vessie's been indulged enough for one day!"

Then Everend disappeared.

*Noooo. I need to know what to do. Daddy, please. Please give me a
sign.*

A flamingo flew in through the open window and landed beside the
keyboard of Big Moose. Its graceful pink wings folded along its sides.

Oh my god oh my god oh my god. Vessie raced to the organ.

"Play Vessie," she heard the bird say. *"Play for me."*

She sat on the tufted leather bench, her fingers trembling on the
keyboard, and sang Everend's favorite song:

"I believe for every drop of rain that falls
A flower grows
I believe that somewhere in the darkest night

A candle glows
Every time I hear a newborn baby cry
Or touch a leaf
Or see the sky
Then I know why
I believe"

The flamingo flew high above the organ and disappeared. Vessie whipped her head around toward the opened window where she had seen it enter. It was closed. All the windows were closed.

Vessie sat for a long time thinking about what had happened. A vision? Her imagination? No matter, she decided the song had meaning. *I believe for every drop of rain that falls, a flower grows. I believe that somewhere in the darkest night, a candle glows.*

Yes, Vessie thought. *I've got to believe that somehow, somewhere this thing I'm driven to do—this passion for writing songs—will be supported.* The lyric repeated: *I believe... I believe.*

Vessie determined never to let rejection shut her down again.

That afternoon, on a bus back to Los Angeles, Vessie ate a piece of homemade apple pie, a roast beef sandwich, and a thermos of soup from Smoodgie's care package. At the bottom, wrapped in plaid preppie cloth and tied with a bow were more birth control pills and a note that read:

> Take one and call me in the morning.
> XOX Dr. Sis

The blizzard was relentless and not about to blow itself out any time soon. The power grid that was hit caused the blackout to extend across most of New York State. Lou and Remy finally reached the ground floor of the art deco building—its pitch-black lobby, ominous and foreboding. It was hard to see exactly what was going on, but a couple things were certain: the keyboard player was having trouble breathing and was in need of urgent medical attention, and an attempt was being made to calm people stuck in all three elevators as their muffled cries echoed off the marble walls.

Vessie held her inner child, desperately trying to hold onto life itself in a long overdue attempt at self-caring and self-love. She forced herself to think of good things, happy things: the image of the man with hazel eyes and sunbleached hair. His strong muscular body running along a white sandy shoreline. She embraced the memory of Mrs. Smith welcoming her back to L.A. after a weekend with Smoodgie in her warm, ever-swaying Symington.

THIRTEEN

Vessie and the Pop Star

"Vessella dahlink, thank God you're back. I found just the break you need, but you gotta grab it before somebody else does." Mrs. Smith showed Vessie an advertisement in the Free Press that read:

WANTED: PIANO PLAYING WAITRESS
Yoyo's
105 Sunset Boulevard
Drop by.

Vessie proceeded to satisfy her greatest supporter by eating four of her finest, greasiest potato latkes, a baked apple, and sugared tea. Then she changed into an East Indian tie-dyed skirt, t-shirt and sandals, and let her long hair do a Cher.

Waiting for a bus in Los Angeles was like waiting for the Second Coming, but eventually it came so, perhaps so will He.

The night lights shone through the bus windows. The only thing that came close to the multitude of neon in Symington was at Christmas when the houses blinked on and off like landing fields. Everything here was so vivid, so graphic. Donut Heaven, a neighborhood donut stand was shaped like a thirty foot donut. The Dog, a hot dog stand, was shaped like a bun with a wiener inside. People munched at a metal mustard counter. And on and on. Disneyland had spread to the streets of Hollywood.

So, as Vessie reached her destination, she was not at all surprised to find that Yoyo's was shaped like a shocking pink fifty foot spinning—*yoyo.*

Outside of the two story club, a lineup of people were waiting to get in: hippies, mostly, and the occasional three piece suit discreetly sharing marijuana packed into filter cigarettes.

Vessie made her way through the crowd and into the club flashing the newspaper ad with determination.

The place was packed, noisy, and filled with smoke. Iggy Sand, its owner—thirty-something, stoned, blonde hair to his shoulders and black and white striped bell bottoms to the floor—stood breast high to Vessie and remained fixated there.

"So like I'm trying to change the scene here, 'cause like man, we're stuck next to the Wyatt Erp Hotel and we want their customers, too. So, like we don't want our image to say, hey, we're stoned man, even if we are, you dig? So like the music, man, has got to be where the *shirts* and the *sandals* can hang together. If you can play what they'll both dig and not spill drinks between sets, you got the gig."

"I write songs."

"Groovy, let me dig it."

"You mean, now?"

Iggy grabbed Vessie's hand and led her through the crowded club to the piano at the far end of the room. The *shirts*, as Iggy called them were nibbling Brie and fruit and getting fuzzy-eyed on wine, martinis and margueritas. The *sandals* sipped apple cider and munched sunflower seeds and dip. And as marijuana fumes trailed from the restrooms into the club, the disparate patrons eyed each other wanting to know what the hell they were doing in the same place?

Iggy grabbed a hand mike and announced:

"Okay, everybody, it's Tiny Talent Time." He turned to Vessie. "What's your name, babe?"

"Vessie."

"Okay. Chiquita Rialto here, is gonna do her thing. So be nice, even if she stinks. Alllllll riiiiiiight, *Bessie*!"

Iggy walked back through the crowd as Vessie nervously began to play a soulful song amidst boos-soaked catcalls.

> "I once knew a man or so I thought
> who bought me a ribbon and a rose

once knew a man who loved me
'til he left me
I don't know why he left me"

A big bruiser sitting at a front table yelled, "He hated your singing, that's why!" The woman beside him gave him a nudge. She seemed to know what Vessie's lament was about.

"Did I forget him?
No, I didn't want to
Do I regret him?
No, he loved me
Shall I cry him out of my mind?
I cannot do that
He is the only happiness I can remember"

Some patrons were too occupied to notice Vessie in the darkened corner or hear her above the chatter, but most put their hands together and applauded until she played the next song and the next.

Iggy smiled as he leaned against the bar. He didn't notice a sloshed customer flick ashes in his belt buckle thinking it was an ashtray. *This chick just might be the answer,* he thought, *might be the answer.*

No one had ever applauded Vessie's music before. Church was church. This time she was exposing her thoughts and feelings to an unbiased crowd.

"To a girl who is blind
Sweet man of mine
You're my window with a view
To a girl who can't see
sweet destiny
You're the colors I have dreamed
You are every place I've ever been
and everybody I've spoken to
Sweet man of mine
You're my window with a view"

54

It was a song she had written sometime between kissing Roy Thatcher and kissing him off. As she began to play another, a white stretch limousine honked for cars to clear a space curbside in front of the club.

Foot, an enormous hulk of a man, parked the car, jumped out and quickly opened the back door for Bobby Rich, formerly with the pop group Mention, and his two female companions. Despite the fact that he was known to surround himself with beautiful women, he had earned the reputation of "nice guy"—a celebrity who ate Kellogg's Special K and meant it.

He looked just as he did on his album covers: handsome chiseled features, penetrating dark eyes, long dark hair topped with a black leather cap, and his signature black leather bell bottoms.

Fans immediately buzzed around him for autographs. Objects and pens appeared.

"Autograph, Bobby, please my name's Brie, Jamie, Sam."

You name it, they asked him to sign it: brassieres, jockstraps, belly buttons, butts. Foot grabbed a jockstrap and snapped it at the crowd, clearing the way.

Vessie was coming to the end of her song.

> "My life is beginning
> I can feel it beginning
> My life is beginning to begin, baby…"

Bobby Rich entered with his entourage and autograph hounds.

> "… now…"

Iggy Sand spotted him and ran over. Vessie recognized him and stopped singing. *Wow! Bobby Rich? I listen to his album "Over and Over," over and over.*

Bobby stared at Vessie as if the Virgin Mary had appeared.

She finished her song:

> "… nonowwwwwww!"

The audience applauded. Bobby whispered in Iggy's ear and Iggy yelled out—"Vessie! Sing another song for..." He made sure everyone would hear, "... *Bobby Riiiiiiiicccch!*"

The rest of the crowd saw Bobby and went nuts. Whistles, applause.

Someone shouted, "*You* sing, Bobby!"

They stomped, clinked glasses and chanted, "Bobby! Bobby!"

Bobby shouted, "I'll do it if it's okay with Vessie. Is it okay with you, Vessie?"

Oh my god oh my god oh my god! Vessie popped out of her body and back again. She couldn't believe Bobby Rich was pushing his way through a crowd of fans toward *her.*

The next thing she knew, he was sitting beside her on the piano bench gazing into her eyes and whispering in a soft velvety voice. "Vessie, this one's for you." His fingers owned the keyboard as he sang.

> "Long ago I had a dream of you
> And now that dream of you
> is really coming true
> In my soul, I hold you close to me
> You mean the most to me
> Say you love me, too."

Vessie's heart raced. Bobby Rich was singing straight to her. *How can this be happening? All I did was get off a bus and answer an ad.*

Bobby finished to wild applause and aggressive fans. Foot could see possible trouble and with three giant steps was at the piano.

"Back off!" he boomed. "Back the fuck off!"

Bobby asked Vessie more questions in two minutes than she'd been asked her whole life. "Where are you from? What sign are you? Do you like to cook? Where did you learn to play keyboard like that? Whose songs were you playing? Who holds the publishing on them? Do you have a boyfriend? Can I drive you home?"

Vessie looked at Bobby's two female companions. "I think you're already occupied."

"I'm Rita, one of Bobby's back-up singers," said the brunette. "We're just buddies."

"I'm with Rita," said the blonde. She put her arm around the singer and licked her neck.

Bobby asked again. "How about I drive you home?

Vessie wasn't being asked a question of a rocket scientist, but by the time she replied Bobby could have grown white hair and worn a pacemaker. "I can't. Thank you. I'm busy."

She wasn't busy. She didn't know anyone in Los Angles to be busy *with* other than Mrs. Smith, but she had never been asked out on the spot like that before and it threw her.

"Then, tomorrow night. I'll see you then, Vessie." Bobby got up from his chair not waiting for an answer. Foot, his two hundred pound security blanket, cleared the way. Vessie was unable to move as she watched the closing of a scene she never dreamed would take place with her in it.

How bizarre. How dream-like. Symington was never like this. L.A. was new and exciting. But somehow Vessie knew that her Pollyanna view of the world was about to change.

FOURTEEN

Vessie & Bobby & Smoodgie & Edward

The night was cold. Ocean breezes blew damp air all the way from Santa Monica to Sunset Strip. But inside the white stretch limousine, Vessie and Bobby were in heat. He held up a surprise gift: a large bulky object draped with fine silk which he proceeded to unveil.

"Voila!"

A magnificent gilded cage with two grey birds appeared.

"Cockatiels? Bobby, they're beautiful!"

What they were was noisy and messy, but Vessie was thrilled.

"How did you know I love birds?"

"You love anything that flies. You said so last night. You think maybe if *I* grow wings?"

Over the next six weeks, Bobby Rich proceeded to sweep Vessie off her small town feet. He took her everywhere: celebrity parties, private clubs, dinners at Chasen's. He introduced her to mega stars, minor stars, gonna-be-stars, his band, his manager, his hair stylist, his massage therapist, his psychic, you name it. They danced and laughed. Roses came, dozens and dozens. Mrs. Smith couldn't believe it. She thought for sure Bobby had wiped out an entire crop. There were Godiva chocolates, endless love letters, shopping sprees, moonlit drives in his Maserati, and the promise of a publishing deal. *That* scored *BIG* points.

One night as they walked barefoot along the Malibu shore, the sky bright with moonshine, Vessie asked: "Why me, Bobby? You can have anybody."

"I tried it with Ringo, but his bangs got in my eyes."

"C'mon, seriously."

"I mean it. I'm allergic to hairspray!"

"Bobby!"

"Well, you don't wear hairspray."

"You're impossible."

He stopped walking and pulled Vessie close.

"You're unspoiled, Ves, untouched. You're like snow before it hits the ground." Then he blurted: "I don't want to lose you, live with me, I love you Ves."

Vessie never knew she had an ego. Now she had to carry it in a suitcase. As for living with Bobby, she wasn't sure. She had never committed to a non-commitment before. But there was so much she loved about him that her hesitation hesitated.

He was thoughtful, caring, imaginative, fun. He told hilarious insightful stories about some of her favorite recording artists. She loved hearing him sermonize on the importance of listening to all types of music—classical, jazz, pop, rock, country, theatrical. He would play her recordings of ethnic music that she never knew existed. Bobby was making her life richer, more colorful, and Vessie felt grateful.

He pulled out a blueprint of his Beverly Hills home and pointed to an area marked 25' x 30'. "This can be your room, Ves. I won't even touch you if you don't want me to. His eyes said: *please.* "How about it? Will you live with me?"

Oh my god, oh my god, oh my god. He wants me with no strings? He must be an angel. She remembered the angel dolls she made the summer Smoodgie was in New York. She remembered the healing lessons they taught her. And she remembered that she was stuck in her car trying desperately to survive.

"Om-mani-padme-hum, om-mani-padme-hum."

"Om-mani-padme-hum, om-mani-padme-hum..." echoed her inner child.

"We can drive to Symington this weekend and celebrate with your sister and brother-in-law," Bobby said. "C'mon, Ves, say yes."

For weeks, glitter journalists had been hounding Vessie for interviews at Mrs. Smith's, Yo-yo's, enroute to Yoyo's. She welcomed a break from them, and from Bobby's fans crowding the sidewalk every night waiting for him to come pick up his *working girl.* As for living with Bobby, she couldn't think of a good reason not to, so she told him:

"Okay."

Vessie was looking forward to spending a quiet weekend with Smoodgie and Edward. But as they pulled up to the house in the long white Bobby-mobile, the two lovebirds were greeted by a local television crew, newspaper reporters, a crowd of locals, and a fifteen foot banner that stretched across the front porch and read:

WELCOME HOME VESSIE AND SUPERSTAR
BOBBY RICH

Vessie could have died. She wanted to crawl under the floor mat. How could Smoodgie do this? It was a circus out there. Bobby Rich fans, six to sixty, jumped up and down waving and shouting. Symington hadn't known this much excitement since the dam overflowed and the schools shut down. And why did she have to write *superstar* in front of Bobby's name? Vessie looked at him and was surprised to see Bobby not only laughing, but loving it. He said he felt like they were in a Bing Crosby movie without the snow.

"Darlings!" Smoodgie shouted making sure she got the cameraman's attention before slinking dramatically toward the car. "Welcome to the home and *office* of... " she looked straight at the camera, "... Doctor Edward Klieg, M.D., twenty-seven West Palm Drive, Symington."

Foot's eyes rolled up like window shades, partly from the acid he dropped five miles back, but mostly because of Smoodgie's over-ripe performance.

Vessie remembered when Everend and Erlinor would greet her upon arriving home from school and how, instead of holding her hand, Smoodgie would be twisting it.

Bobby gave Vessie a reassuring smile and lowered the car window as he waved to his fans. Vessie thought surely Edward must mind the way Smoodgie was fawning all over her boyfriend. But, there was Edward, fawning all over her boyfriend.

When the last of Bobby's fans had left their property, Edward led his guest out to the veranda. The warm night air which usually calmed him, now made Edward extremely anxious. "I wanted to get some... some... *weed*." He had a hard time saying it. "Ya know, for you to smoke... to make you feel at home, but my wife said we couldn't handle the scandal if we got caught."

"It's all right. I never smoke the stuff."

"You never smoke *marijuana*?" Edward was shocked. "But, all superstars smoke marijuana."

Bobby made Edward promise never to tell anyone that his only addiction was his sister-in-law. He didn't want his image tarnished. Edward promised but couldn't hide his disappointment. Bobby was not supposed to be *normal*.

Smoodgie proceeded to make every moment count. She would stand up to pass the butter or water or salt or to stretch, moan, and swish her hair around. At one point, she slinked over to a light switch and flicked a light that was already on.

After supper, Vessie said goodnight and went upstairs into one bedroom as Bobby disappeared into another. The Kleig's sat up until dawn trying to figure out why. Edward was the first to comment.

"They must've had a fight."

"They were sitting right in front of us. There was no fight. Maybe Vessie's still a virgin."

"Maybe, he got it shot off in Nam."

And on it went while Vessie and Bobby slept like lambs.

At six a.m., Vessie slipped into Bobby's room. He was sound asleep. She had never seen him sleeping before. She had never been in a bedroom with him before but she had to talk.

"Bobby," she whispered. "Bobby Rich, famous pop star person. Wake up, pleeeeaaassee, wake up."

Bobby turned over exposing his buffed chest. He was surprised to see Vessie standing there. *Is she ready for me now? Does she want me here in her sister's house?*

"We've got to get out of here. I adore my sister, but not when she acts like a moron."

There went that dream. "But, Ves, she planned a dinner party for us."

"Right. It'll probably be televised. Lord knows what she's up to. No, please Bobby. If we stay, it'll just get worse."

"What'll we tell her?"

"I don't think we'll have to tell her a thing." Then she told Bobby her plan.

The breakfast table was set with Erlinor's finest china, silver, and cut crystal champagne glasses. Everything was ready to be served: French toast, strawberries, chilled bubbly, ready and waiting… and waiting… and waiting. Smoodgie finally broke the silence.

"It's eleven o'clock. Don't you think we should wake them?"

"No. Let them sleep."

"But the *food*, Edward."

"I told you not to cook until they got up."

"Well, I was excited."

Another half hour went by. Then Smoodgie heard laughter coming from Bobby's room. It grew louder and the Kleig's flew half-way up the stairs wanting to hear more. Bed springs boinged and banged louder, faster. The Kleig's were pleased. Then they heard something being thrown around the room. Smoodgie gasped.

"My Lord, it's Vessie!"

Vessie screamed and moaned. Bobby cackled and snorted. Whipping sounds, screams—louder and louder.

What the Kleig's couldn't see behind Bobby's door were the two lovebirds throwing pillows at walls, smacking chairs with belts, feigning el grande de kinky-ola.

Edward was shocked. Smoodgie felt her old bible studies rise inside her like a Phoenix. Sure she loved rubbing shoulders with a celebrity, but not like this. The Kleig home was a good home. They were young leaders in the community. Who were these deviates and how could they get them to leave before their neighbors found out?

After five minutes of silence, Bobby came out of the room buckling his belt. Smoodgie and Edward scurried back to the dining room. Vessie appeared at the top of the stairs covered in Band-Aids.

Bobby raised his champagne glass. "To Vessie… who makes all my *fantasies* come true." Smoodgie fell faint in Edward's arms.

That afternoon, Vessie and Bobby had no trouble leaving the Kleig's. Before they could finish saying: "I'm sorry, but we really have to be going," Smoodgie and Edward blurted: "Fine, goodbye!"

FIFTEEN

All Caged Up and Nowhere To Go

San Ysidro Drive wound its way behind the Beverly Hills Hotel up a mountainside stopping where Bobby Rich's house sat perched overlooking tennis courts, swimming pools, and dream houses with seven digit mortgages.

Electrified barbed wire lined the iron fence that sheltered the A-frame dwelling Bobby called home. If the house could talk it would have said, *I may belong to a superstar, but I'm really just a nice, simple house—two bedrooms, cozy enough to be almost humble.* But behind it, further back from the street, was its mate—another three bedrooms that housed Bobby's chauffeur Foot, his housekeeper Rainbow Sunshine, and his younger brother Lester who was heavily into yoga and spent most of his time levitating and getting bruised a lot.

A stream ran beneath a wooden moat leading to the front door which stood twenty feet high between two walls of glass.

Bobby opened the door for Vessie as the cockatiels fussed in the hand-held cage. A barefoot woman with long braided hair and a t-shirt with an eagle on it raised her eyes and smiled.

"Ves, meet Rainbow Sunshine, the coolest housekeeper this side of the Smokies."

The woman smiled warmly. She had worked in the Rich home for eight years and seen it all—the women, the parties; but never anyone like Vessie—sweet, innocent, girlish. She took the cage and led the way in.

The sunken living room was surrounded by glass windows forming an A-frame where the stone fireplace climbed to the ceiling. The stream beneath the moat at the front of the house flowed under the glass walls down to the lower level of the living room and then out beneath a window to the swimming pool. The bedrooms sat side-by-side off to one corner of the four thousand square foot house. A Jacuzzi dominated the master bath, marbled here and sunken there and mirrored just about everywhere. Mexican blankets and brightly colored clay figurines and candlesticks warmed the sharp angles of the modern structure. And, resting on the mantel-piece in the master bedroom was a display of Grammys that Bobby used as bookends.

Three weeks later Vessie showed up at Mrs. Smith's, sobbing.

"Vessella, what's wrong?"

Vessie sobbed harder.

"Oh my god! What did this monster do to you?"

She put her arms around her young friend.

"He calls me... Barbie Doll."

"The pervert."

"He reads to me."

"Trash monger."

"When he kisses me... he kisses me on the... on the..."

"He'll do time for this."

"... on the forehead."

"The *forehead*?"

"He's gentle and kind and never comes into my room. He never takes advantage of me in any way!"

Mrs. Smith straightened her back.

"I was right. The man's a schmuck! Vessella, dahlink, I don't understand the meshugana arrangement with the bedrooms, but a blind man could see the problem. He adores you, you adore him, and you're horny and need to get shtuped!"

"But Missus Smith... it's wrong to... you know, *do it* before marriage."

"It's wrong if you get pregnant, dahlink."

Vessie told Bobby she was moving out. "I'm sorry, I can't explain it. I... we..."

Bobby couldn't bear it. He grabbed Vessie and kissed her hard. "I've been holding back from you. I thought it would give you time to love me… to prove how much I care. Please Ves, I have so much to offer… so much."

If Mrs. Smith could have seen her nice goyisha Vessie braid herself around Bobby like challah bread—and, just how much Bobby *did* have to offer.

Vessie flew that night like she had never flown in a plane. She and Bobby became their own super jet soaring through space, laughing and crying and *doing it* over and over.

Morning came and so did Vessie, thrice. The cockatiels cooed. The air smelled sweet. Vessie felt born again and wanted to start a new religion. She would call it:

IN GOD WE FUCK

Climbing all over Bobby seemed the natural thing to do. Why had the act been so badly publicized? Why wasn't it being offered in school instead of Social Studies and Home Ec.?

Weeks passed. Vessie and Bobby were like newlyweds. Foot rarely saw them. Rainbow Sunshine cleaned the house, left food, and disappeared before she could be shooed away. The only time the lovebirds saw Lester was when he levitated right through one of the windows, smashed into the cabana, and had to be taken to the hospital.

Vessie stopped working at Yoyo's, much to Iggy Sand's chagrin. It was Bobby's idea. He told her she didn't need to be somebody's freak show. That her music was good but people weren't packing the club to hear her songs, they were coming to see Bobby Rich's lady. It was true and it hurt.

Bobby's *people* were the only ones allowed visiting rights: his agent, manager, producer, accountant, publicist. And that's strictly because it was necessary. Especially when he turned down a European concert tour which they strongly objected to.

"You need this tour. An album doesn't just sell itself. You know that."

Bobby stood firm. Especially, when he ravaged Vessie's thigh and told her, "European men are animals. They'd eat you alive. And I'm the only one who's going to do that."

At first Vessie loved the attention and loved giving it back. But soon she came to realize that she had become Bobby's obsession. Nothing else mattered to him. Life did not exist beyond the confines of Casa Rich. He no longer wanted to do anything or go anywhere. There were no more moonlit walks, no dinners out, no people, no parties, no fun. She had become as caged as her cockatiels, and began having recurring dreams.

> Vessie's in the kitchen trying to get Erlinor's attention.
> "I'm busy, Vessie, can't you see that?"
> Suddenly, Vessie's body lifts five feet above
> Erlinor's head. "Look Mama, I can fly!"
> What does Erlinor do? She screams:
> "Get down from there right now young lady.
> We'll have no hocus-pocus in this house!"

In another dream:

> Vessie's lying in bed with a man beside her.
> Her feet are chained to the bedposts and she's dying.
> She rises up above her body and flies away, past
> the man, past the house, over treetops and power
> lines to the other side of the ocean.

Vessie woke up in a sweat. Bobby was lying beside her, always beside her wherever she was, whatever she was doing. Her heart raced. She was drenched in dread. She was a fly in a jar—Bobby, the Fly Keeper. Vessie told him her dreams hoping to break through to him, to rally his compassion, but he just laughed. "You're horny, baby." He grabbed her and took her, believing that was the cure-all that would *right* all that was wrong. *Fly in a jar. Fly in a jar.*

The baby grand was now her savior. She played it for hours, dredging up songs she had composed years before. And there was Bobby, hovering over her, his eyes burning into the lyric sheets—and every time, he'd head for his room in a huff, warm as Frusen Gladje. Then, after nine or ten "nothing-is-wrongs," he'd do variations of, "That guy in your song. You never told me about *him*. How many other guys haven't you told me about?" It got so out of hand, Vessie didn't know what to do.

She stopped playing piano. She stopped singing. And, finally, she stopped thinking in lyric form. She spent most of her time staring at the caged birds and crying, or sleeping all day avoiding her new religion.

Foot, Rainbow Sunshine and Lester couldn't help but notice Vessie's changed behavior. Her smile was gone. The piano remained untouched. The poolside chaise lounge was empty. So was the house—of her laughter and sweet hellos. She rarely came out of her bedroom. And from the other side of the door, instead of singing, they heard her cries.

Concerned, they drove to Mrs. Smith's, told her that Vessie was troubled, and were sent back with a picnic basket. When they told Vessie it was from Mrs. Smith, she immediately removed the hand embroidered doily expecting to find wonderful homemade treats and, instead, found a Cosmopolitan magazine and a note that read:

Turn to page 108.

The article was about victims of depression. Vessie read it and sure enough, there she was on pages one hundred eight to one eleven: always on the verge of tears, always wanting to sleep, unable to make decisions, no desire to eat.

Suddenly, her old self snapped back. *There's no way I'm going to be a cliché in Cosmo!* It worked. Mrs. Smith, once again, had the wisdom of a saint.

> "I gotta get away today
> Gotta get off by myself far away
> Gotta leave my man behind
> Seems today we're running on different time
> And at times like this I gotta say
> I gotta get away today"

Vessie sat at the piano singing and playing, hoping that Bobby would hear the words that would make saying goodbye easier, but all he said was:

"New song?"

"Goodbye, Bob."

"Goodbye? What do you mean, *goodbye*?"

"I'm dying here." She got up and headed for the door. He grabbed her hand.

"What's going on?"

She was choked up and didn't know where to begin.

"You caged me. You opened the door and locked me in." She pulled away. He stopped her.

"Please, talk to me."

"We never go out. You're always right on top of me—moody—sulky. You go crazy when you read my lyrics." She mimicked him: "*You never told me about THAT guy. Who was THAT guy?* Jesus! You're jealous of people who don't even exist. You saw how depressed I was, and what did you do about it? You screwed me. You made me feel like a whore. Shall I go on, Bob, or do you get it now?"

Bobby did something he had never done in front of Vessie before. He farted. Then, totally embarrassed, he fell to his knees and cried:

"Don't leave me, please Vessie. I'll be good, I promise."

"It's got to change. You can't cage me like this."

Bobby promised, crossed his heart, and sprayed the room with Lysol. Then he planned a party in Vessie's honor.

SIXTEEN

The Deal Breaker

The house was packed. Foot proudly acted as doorman, Rainbow
Sunshine supervised the traveling food trays, Lester levitated and flew
out the window landing in the pool where Bobby's back-up singer, Rita,
was busy playing doctor with a Lolita look-a-like. Mrs. Smith sat at the
piano playing Jewish love songs only she loved, and the rest of the guests,
sardined together, breathed each other's Halston, Aramis, and Acapulco
Gold.

Some guests were sober enough to realize they just saw someone fly
out the window. They ran to meet the amazing man with Vessie in the lead.
She offered her hand and with two others, fished Lester out of the pool.

He looked like drenched drapery. His Ghandi style *dhoti* wrapped
around his waist and legs—and his Nehru style *kurta* shirt that hung down
to his knees, seemed to have sucked up all the water.

Lester's slight build, short-cropped blonde hair, soft blue eyes, and
pleasant but indistinguishable face offered no clues that he was in any
way related to Bobby Rich. The tabloids, however, had a heyday with the
"brother of the pop star's bizarre yoga exploits," so Lester's reputation
preceded him.

Although they rarely spoke, Vessie felt a secret kinship with him.
Lester was the brunt of his older brother's jokes: "… the weird one in the
family," Bobby would say time and again, which always brought back the
sting of Smoodgie's torments: "You're crazy, Vessie. You're crazy."

"You're amazing, Lester!" she told him.

"Where'd you learn to levitate, Oh Great One?" a guest asked.

Lester smiled shyly and retreated to his room for the rest of the night.

Vessie looked radiant. Her long auburn hair hung down the back of her long white dress. Wherever she walked, Bobby's eyes followed. So did a face from the past.

"Vessie!"

"Pete!" It was the songwriter she had met on the bus to Symington.

"Hey, babe, I won't ask how you're doin' 'cause everybody knows you're a hot item. Even if your songs were rotten, I could get them published. But, I'm sure Bobby's taken care of that."

"Actually, he hasn't. I kept hoping he would. That's why I didn't call you. I guess he just doesn't believe in mixing business with pleasure."

"You still own the publishing rights?"

"Yep."

"I know I can work a deal." Pete took her hands and kissed both her cheeks.

Vessie was ecstatic and, wanting to share her joy with Bobby, searched the crowd with her eyes and found his staring at her.

He called for everyone's attention.

"Once in a lifetime some of us are fortunate and find our soul mate. Well, I've found mine and I'd like you all to meet her."

Vessie tripped over two composers, a bass player, and a recording engineer on her way across the smoke filled living room to where Bobby was playing host.

"Vessie, this is for you."

He held out a ring—an eighteen carat gold band with a gold ball and chain dangling from it. In the center of the ball was a six carat canary diamond.

Later that night, when the cigarette butts had been wiped off the walls and the house was put to sleep, Vessie and Bobby made love. And all the while she tried to convince herself that things would be different. He would honor her creativity, her privacy. They would have a life outside of Casa Rich. He'd get rid of that matching toilet he had installed next to hers. But her gut wrenched. What did *it* know that she was about to?

The phone rang as the sun came up. It was Pete Dreyers. "Your old man said if I get you a publishing deal I'll never work in this town again. Sorry."

Vessie left the ring on Bobby's pillow, picked up the bird cage, and slipped out the side door. She was halfway down San Ysidro when the Maserati pulled up along side of her. Vessie kept walking.

"A little upset are we?"

"Pete Dreyers phoned."

"It's for your own good."

"I'm the only one who knows that."

"How can you let a few songs come between us?"

"Ask yourself that question."

"If you don't come back, you're finished in L.A."

"I haven't even *started* in L.A."

"I'll make sure you don't get hired in a dive!"

Bobby continued to yell threats mixed in with a few, *C'mon back baby's*.

"Leave me alone, Bobby, or I swear, I'll call the police."

"I'll never leave you alone."

Vessie saw a Beverly Hills police car, flagged it over, and made her first citizen's arrest.

She was relieved to be back at Mrs. Smith's. She could breathe again, think again, create again. How did she ever lose herself in that relationship? How did she allow herself to get sidetracked from her goals, her *path*? From now on she would refer to events in her life as B.S.—Before Sex, and A.S.—After Sex. B.S., in high school, she could *see* boys in an instant: He's a friend… he's a possible date… he's a nerd. But, A.S.? Much trickier. Now she was afraid she'd be blind as a bat, eyes clouded with lust; hands groping for that six inch pacifier.

"Sex isn't a sin," she told Mrs. Smith. "It's a sin what it can do to you."

She thought about her time with Bobby as a form of temporary insanity. Now that it was over the entire experience felt alien to her. How could she have been in love with him only weeks ago and now just thinking about him made her skin crawl? She was frightened by her over-exposure to exposure. *Sex isn't good for me. I moved to L.A. to get my songs published and that's what I'm going to do.*

It was Sunday. Vessie stood before the Church of the Truly Holy of Hollywood looking at what appeared to be the *Twilight Zone*. Smog hung low around the steel and glass structure as people crowded in looking like anything but church-goers. She entered and made her way to the organ. It was the first time she had been inside a house of worship since leaving Symington and her position as Church Organist behind. Thoughts of Everend and Erlinor stung at her heart. *Will I ever stop missing you? Longing to see you? Touch you? Hear your voice?* Three deep breaths and she dove into playing the first hymn as the Church of the Truly Holy of Hollywood's new wholly un-Hollywood organist.

This was no ordinary church, no ordinary preacher. One hundred and fifty out-of-work actors, retired actors, working actors, could-have-been actors, and wish-I-had-never-been-an-actor actors waited to be blessed. The set looked authentic but the flock, totally miscast.

Reverend Dave stood at the pulpit dressed in a white three piece suit, sky blue shirt, and a scarf tied around his neck like Gene Autry. His haircut cost thirty dollars and his manicure fifteen. He spoke with a southern twang and a Colgate smile.

"Brothers and sisters… as the palm trees sway and you and I sit here as Jesus did in the land of Canaan… don't believe that the Lord has forgotten you. Don't believe that the Lord doesn't *know* how much you love Him. How much we *aaaallllll* love Him."

The congregation responded, some with Clint Eastwood deliveries, others with Kate Hepburn.

"We love Him. We love Him."

"And don't you believe that the Lord won't answer each and every one of your prayers. He will. He will."

The worshippers echoed: "He will. He will."

"That's right, brothers and sisters. He will answer your prayers… right after you put your dollars in this basket. That's right, just pass it down, pass it down. Now, as soon as He is witness to how much you will part with in His name, He will bless you and answer those prayers. After all, it's better giving your money to the Lord than to the I.R.S."

"Amen, brother!"

Vessie figured, why should a church be any different from any other place in Hollywood? Reverend Dave was simply a reflection of his environment. She knew that Everend would have made room for this shallow attempt to connect with the Almighty. *It's better than nothing,* Vessie thought as she heard the preacher exclaim:

"Brothers and sisters… you *are* who you hang out with, yay-asssssss!" The fervor grew. "And when the Lord spoke, the doors of hell flew open and Satan shouted…"

"Vessie VanCortland, where the *hell* are you?" Bobby shouted from the doorway spooking the entire cast. He reached out to Vessie who sat frozen. Then he passed out.

Congregants ran to him demanding autographs. He was unconscious but they insisted. One wizened fan kicked him and walked away. Vessie pushed them aside as she and Reverend Dave played paramedics.

When Bobby came to, he was lying in the Reverend's lap who was lapping it up.

He immediately asked where Vessie was and was handed a note:

Please let go. It's over. Let it be over.
Vessie

The incidents continued and Bobby's instability grew more profound. He shoved threatening notes under Mrs. Smith's door. At other times, love letters. Bobby stalked Vessie in restaurants, grocery stores, cleaners. And always following *him* were reporters. A constant audience surrounded their confrontations.

"I know I was a schmuck. You were right and I'm sorry.
Please come back, Ves."

The reporters would write this down verbatim. Some pushed microphones at the couple wanting to record every nuance.

"No. It's too late. It's over."
"But it'll be different this time. I promise."
"That's what you said *last* time. No!"

Vessie wasn't flattered by Bobby's attention; it wasn't ego-building. In fact, being hounded by a crazy ex-boyfriend scared her. She thought about Roy Thatcher and his big log of an arm about to hit her, and her mama waving a knife like a loon. *Passions. Irrational behavior. Irreversible damage.*

A long black box was left at Mrs. Smith's door. Vessie opened it and found a dead lily and a note that read:

If you don't come back I'll kill myself.

That was it. How dare he be so selfish as to give her a catch twenty-two! *I can't go back to him,* Vessie thought. *That would kill ME.*

Vessie left the box in front of Bobby's iron gate. Rainbow Sunshine found it the next morning. *She's coming back!* she thought, and ran with it into the house. Bobby got excited by her excitement. But when he opened the box he found his note with an addition scrawled across the bottom:

Fart all you like. I'm not coming back.

To spite her, Bobby slit his wrists.

SEVENTEEN

Return of Healerwoman!

Just outside Bobby's hospital room two police officers shooed reporters away. Foot and Rainbow Sunshine, puffy-eyed from crying, blew into each other's hankies. Vessie and Mrs. Smith chatted solemnly, both wearing dark glasses—Mrs. Smith's rimmed with rhinestones. Suddenly, the door to Bobby's room flew open and Lester motioned for Vessie to come in.

Why did this have to happen? It started out so innocently. The sweetness, the fun, the intimacy.

Bobby was asleep, tubes dangling from his nose, intravenous feeding into his veins, his wrists wrapped with gauze and tape.

Lester assumed a full lotus position and closed his eyes.

Vessie sat beside her ex-lover on the edge of the bed feeling compelled to do something she hadn't done since she was a child—the healing technique the angels taught her.

She closed her eyes and grounded her energy. She imagined a silver cord running from the base of her spine, anchoring to the center of the earth. Then she raised her hands and repeated silently: *His love goes through my hands to your wrists, through my hands to your wrists.* She kept repeating it over and over as she moved her hands above Bobby's wounds.

As the morning light streamed across his face, Vessie tip-toed out of Bobby's life. He awoke with a surprised feeling of well being. "Good morning!" he sang to the nurse who was changing his bandages. She looked at his wrists.

"Aaaaaahhhhhhhhhhh!" Her face went gauze white. She backed away as if she'd seen a ghost, then turned and ran from the room.

What the? Bobby was afraid to look. *Surely, she's used to seeing such eye-sores,* he thought. *This can't be the worst she's seen. Or can it? Jesus! What did I do to myself?*

What Bobby saw were two perfectly healed wrists that looked like nothing had happened to them other than having been washed. There were no marks where the blade had parted the skin. No hint whatsoever that anything abnormal had happened to him within the past thirty-four years. He sat up in bed and fainted.

Lester smiled and flew into the door.

Two days later he found Vessie at Mrs. Smith's. As much as she liked Lester, Vessie felt compelled to tell him: "I've got to cut off all ties with your brother."

"This isn't about Bobby. *You* healed him, not the doctors like the papers are saying. I was there. I saw you."

Vessie was shocked. "Really? It worked? The healing technique worked?"

Lester's eyes said, *yes.*

"I knew it worked on birds and small critters... but a *human?* Wow."

Before Vessie knew it, they were in the back seat of the limo. She couldn't believe it. After all those years of wondering what happened to Conchita—the healing technique worked.

"You have great things to do with your life, important things," Lester said. "My yoga master will show you how."

The limo headed north along the Pacific Coast Highway past bikini beaches, hot dog stands, and houses blocking the ocean's view teasing that glamorous lives were being lived that you weren't privy to. On the other side of the highway stood a wall of mountains where houses nestled like eagles staring out at the sea.

"Lester, where *is* this ashram?"

He leaned across her and pointed straight up. The car veered to the right along Heavenly Drive, a winding road lined with flowers the likes of which Vessie had never seen before.

"Yoga is a spiritual practice not a religion. Devotees from all faiths all over the world send flowers to Guruji. They hope to make his outer world as beautiful as he has made their inner worlds."

Vessie smiled thinking of her father and how his words always elevated her. But was Lester speaking the same language? She wondered if she was crazy going to this *ashram*. But then, this *Guruji* did teach Lester to do something she had always dreamed of doing. Although he kept bumping into things and injuring himself, Lester could fly.

Fly, fly, I wish I could fly! Vessie opened her eyes. "Damn!" She was back in the reality of her nightmare —a prisoner inside her frozen car.

"You swear a lot," said her inner child.

"Oh, for Christ's sake."

"See? I thought you were this *SPIRITUAL* person."

"What's vocabulary got to do with it? And stop judging me. I'm doing the best I can." So was Remy. He was on a mission to save her.

The art deco lobby was in chaos. Paramedics were strapping the keyboard player to a stretcher, and firemen were forcing the elevator doors open with crowbars. People kept bumping into each other. Remy wasn't sure who he just bumped into but was relieved to discover it was a policeman.

"Please officer, my best friend is stuck, probably freezing in her car somewhere and you've got to help me find her." His failed attempts to reach her by phone and his torturous imagination had gotten him wound up in a frenzy. The man in blue turned a flashlight on him and could see the pain on the young man's face.

EIGHTEEN

Vessie & the Guru

The ashram was a New England style structure: wood frame, salt-box shape, except for the veranda that flounced around it like a teenager's skirt. It looked warm and inviting—a great place to find a shady spot, curl up with a good book and dream, or sit in the sun and be a nuisance to a fly.

"It's where we live and study," Lester said. "It's our temple." He pointed to a narrow path trellised with multi-colored flowers that curled off to one side. "Master lives down there in a small house. I'll tell him you're here, although I'm sure he already knows. Guruji knows everything. Go to the main house, Ves. You'll be welcomed there."

Vessie watched Lester disappear through the vines. Then, suddenly, the sound of spinning tires spun her head around. She could see the tail lights of the limousine disappear as it left the parking area and descended out of sight. Foot was gone. *Oh my god. What the hell am I doing here?* She felt her heart race and took several deep breaths. *You'll be alright,* she told herself. *Lester's here. Lester? Lester's a flake! Relax, be present.* Another deep breath. *Okay, temple,* she thought. *The only time I heard the word temple was when Daddy spoke about the Jewish church, uh, temple. What kind of temple is this?*

Vessie climbed the wood stairs past several men and women who were busy sweeping, but not too busy to offer her smiles. On the veranda others were washing windows and tending to flowers that grew in deep pots. The women were draped in saris of unstitched cloth that flowed neatly over a blouse with a scooped out neckline. The men wore dhoti-kurtas, the same fashion as Lester wore the night he levitated into the pool. They were all dressed in white. They weren't whistling, but Vessie thought they should be, for their lilting presence radiated a happy weightlessness.

A strong fragrance permeated the air. *Rose incense,* Vessie thought, breathing it in like ambrosia. She followed the sweetness inside. There, a large entry hall, wainscoted with rich reddish-brown maple, led off in three directions.

Vessie was fascinated by what she might find behind each door. She chose door number one, the center door, and opened it. There was no bedroom suite or trip for two to Hawaii. Not even an air conditioned Cutlass Supreme with sunroof and power-steering. There were pews and a center aisle, like in Everend's church; but no wooden effigy of Jesus bleeding all over his feet.

She walked cautiously to the altar. There were framed photographs and paintings of men she had never seen before, except for Jesus. He was smiling, not all cut up like meat. The other men had beards and mustaches. They looked serious, but jolly, and were dressed in an orange dhoti draped over their chest like Ghandi. An urn filled with sticks of incense burned beneath the gallery. Vessie felt compelled to sit down and close her eyes.

Seconds later, a man stood beside her. She didn't hear him come in, but felt his presence and opened her eyes. He was tall and dark skinned, dressed like the men on the altar. His nose was long and aquiline, jaw strong and jutting, lips red as plums. Black hair fell in ringlets on broad shoulders. Black penetrating eyes stared at her.

Suddenly, electricity flowed from him to Vessie forcing the release of walled up tears.

"There has been much sadness," he said. "Let the sadness go. Let the anger and frustration go. Lose that which clutters and covers who you really are. You are not the mind. You are not your thoughts. That is illusion."

He zapped her with more energy.

Instantly, Vessie's tears felt like warm gold.

"Welcome, I am Paramahansa Bramananda."

She didn't know what was happening to her. She just knew it was wondrous.

He turned, walked softly to the altar and pointed to the photographs. "This was my Master, and he... his... and he... his."

Vessie had heard East Indian accents before, but now every lilting syllable seemed to be a song on the cosmic hit parade.

"Ah, you're wondering about the men and women on the veranda. They are acolytes...my disciples."

His extra sensory perception is awesome, she thought. *Sort of like knowing the phone's going to ring.*

"Yes, it's like knowing a phone is going to ring."

Vessie realized she was no longer alone. There were others like her, other oddballs.

"If you are an oddball, then all here at the ashram are oddballs," he said.

A wave of excitement, relief, *hope* filled her. She wished her father was there. She watched the powerful man in the orange dhoti lead her from the sanctuary to his dwelling. He seemed neither man nor woman, but a delicate blending of the two. Now it was her turn to walk down the trellised pathway. She felt oceans away from Los Angeles. The air was scented with pungent jungle flowers, and the trees and shrubs grew at their own pace. Everything was natural, unlike the manicured gardens of Beverly Hills where hedges looked like bowling balls and storage boxes, and flowers grew in predictable placements like colors on a paint-by-number canvas.

Vessie watched Bramananda remove his sandals before entering, and followed suit.

"We remove our shoes to keep the vibrations of the outside world, outside," he told her.

The little house was the size of a hut—its one room separated only by the arrangement of a futon at one end and a small altar at the other. He sat down on a gold silk cushion and folded his legs in a full lotus position, then closed his eyes.

Inside, beyond the retina and vessels of blood, he was transcending the outer world, letting go of all that was material, experiencing that which is beyond pizza, under arm deodorant, and taxi cab receipts. Vessie didn't intend to, but again was compelled to close her eyes. She felt like Alice falling down the rabbit hole, but, the hole was filled with *light*.

"Oooooooooooo." Vessie could feel her breathing slow to a snail's pace and a rush of energy bubble from her belly to her toes. Bramananda was causing her to experience pure energy. He was giving her a sneak preview of what was to come if she chose to study with him. She felt like everything delicious: chocolate, black forest cake, hot buttered challah, Dijon mustard on chips, honey on apples, and whipped cream on everything. Nothing was going to drag her away from this experience. Nothing.

Just as he had caused her eyes to close, he opened them. Her body was a marshmallow calm—her mind as clear as Mrs. Smith's chicken soup.

"You have been under much stress. That is the greatest hindrance to enlighten-ment. You must recharge yourself. I will show you how, if you choose for it to be so."

Vessie chose to be sewn into the hem of his dress if it was okay with him. *But, why me?* she thought. *How come I'm so lucky?*

"Because, it is your karma," he said. "Nature's law of cause and effect. Nothing in life is luck or chance. You get what you deserve and you deserve to learn from me."

NINETEEN

Once Upon an Ashram

Vessie's room was part of a converted attic. The peaked ceiling sloped low over a single cotton mattress. The window stood knee-high to the bed where a cubby-hole pretended to be a closet. The room was large enough to get in and out of without bruising if you were careful.

Lester backed out slowly. "See you in the sanctuary at sundown."

Vessie was alone for the first time since she got up that morning in Mrs. Smith's back room. She sat down on the bed and looked through the window at the grounds below. A magnificent flower garden was lush and pregnant with bloom. A vegetable garden grew rich and full in ribboned rows of sumptuous delights. And in the distance at its base, the ocean, vast and milky blue, seamlessly touched the sky. Vessie knew that upon this canvas she could dream, her soul could thrive.

She lay down, stretched her body like a cat, and listened to the silence. Its high pitched hum and the pungent aroma of incense reeking through the floorboards hypnotically drew her into a sleep closest to death—closest to life. She dreamed that Bramananda was calling to her: *Vessie, come to the main sanctuary. It's sundown.* She struggled to wake up and won.

It was dark in the room and she realized that the evening meditation must have started without her. She tried to get up but was held back by the weight of her extremely relaxed body.

The area just outside of the sanctuary was lined with sandals. Vessie remembered what Bramananda told her about keeping the vibrations of the outside world outside and quietly slipped hers off. She entered on tip-toe not wanting to disturb the thirty acolytes and monks who were deep in meditation. Bramananda faced them, seated in a full lotus on the podium. Again, incense burned wafting through the room. Vessie found a space at the end of a pew and sat down. She could feel energy in the air that was so powerful it caused her to close her eyes.

Seemingly moments later, actually thirty minutes, Bramananda said with a quiet musical lilt: "We have a new acolyte with us."

Vessie was snoring.

"Let us do our revitalization technique and direct pure energy to her," he said.

Moments passed and she opened her eyes. *What happened? What did I miss?*

"Sleep often comes to those at the beginning. The nervous system needs to repair itself from the stresses of the outside world. Then, one will be ready to receive instruction."

Vessie and Lester stood in the cafeteria-designed dining room around stainless steel pots of food. "We don't eat meat, fish or poultry," he said. "Nuts, legumes, soy products, vegetables and fruit are our mainstay. Guruji says we eat food that won't fight our bodies when we sit to meditate. After all, the intention is to transcend thought and go beyond matter."

Matter? Vessie thought. "Sure, Lester, whatever you say."

"Oh, and Ves, Master has given us all different names. So, from now on, please call me *Anil*."

"Anil?"

"It means, *of the wind.*"

"Welcome, Vessie, I'm Jyoti." A pudgy woman about fifty stood before her with the smile of an angel.

She looks like her name should be Grace or Beth Anne, Vessie thought.

"You're right," Jyoti said. "My given name is Grace."

Vessie's heart raced. She threw her arms around her, not caring if it was inappropriate.

"Yes," Jyoti said. "It's good to be with kindreds." Her pale upper arms hung like taffy from the short sleeved blouse she wore beneath the many yards of white cotton draped around her. "Tomorrow I will instruct you on your duties here at the ashram." She left like a breeze, faintly brushing Vessie's arm.

"Lester, I mean... Anil? *I don't say wat to now.*"

84

Lester laughed and said not to worry, that Vessie was just overwhelmed by it all and would soon learn to talk again. And she did, on the one telephone that connected the ashram to the outside world.

"Vessella, is that you, dahlink?"

"Yes, I think so." Vessie explained that she wouldn't be home that night and might not be home for awhile. "I'm going to study with Lester's guru. He's an amazing man."

There was a long silence. Then Mrs. Smith said, "Is he single, dahlink?"

Vessie loved ashram life. Everyone had duties to perform and Sister Jyoti made sure they did them. The new acolyte tended to the vegetable garden, swept the floors, did the laundry, and cleaned the toilets all the time humming or singing a Buddhist hymn:

Rāma raghava, Rāma raghava, Rāma raghava
Raksa mām
Krishna kesava, Krishna Kesava, Krishna Kesava
Padhi mām

The melody was beautiful, but there was something magical about the words. Whenever Vessie sang them she felt *high*, like the first day she worked in the garden.

The overcast Malibu sky had burnt off its low cloud cover and was dotted with a few puffs of cloud. Seagulls swooped in the distance over early morning surfers in black rubber skin suits as they sat atop multi-colored surfboards waiting to catch a wave. The garden was a peaceful calm.

Vessie was on her knees with a sprinkling can in hand feeding newly planted tomato seeds like babies. Around her in neat rows were the green tops of carrots and corn and bean stalks that stood half-way to picking. She breathed in their subtle fragrance—felt the rich earth beneath her feet and under her finger nails. "Rāma raghava, Rāma raghava, Rāma raghava," she sang, "Raksa mām."

Suddenly, a rush of energy shot through her body and lifted her higher and higher above the tallest stalk, the highest tree where birds flew around her confused at what they saw. "Krishna Kesava, Krishna Kesava, Krishna

Kesava, Padhi māṃ," she sang. One bird said to another, "Ah, it's that weird yoga stuff again," and flew off.

She looked in the distance at the mountains with mansions on acres of land—*Is that Barbra Streisand?*—at horses in corrals—tanned bodies in swimming pools—workers on ladders pruning trees, on land sites constructing new houses. *That IS Barbra Streisand.*

She looked down and saw acolytes, like a squadron of birds, pretzeled in a full lotus levitating, hovering over an unplanted patch of field. She saw herself still standing beside the tomato patch below.

Oooomppphhh! She snapped back into her body with sprinkling can in hand.

Nobody saw what happened except Paramahansa Bramananda. He appeared beside her. "Oh, Guruji," she said. "I just had the most amazing experience."

He smiled. "I now know what your Hindu name will be," he said. "Gita. It means *song.*"

Every morning in the "common room," a couple dozen uncommon men and women wearing dhoti-kurtas and saris, legs pretzeled in a full lotus, performed kundalini quick-breathing exercises and silently repeated a mantra that generated so much energy in their bodies that they lifted several inches off the floor, some, as much as a foot. Then there were a handful that could lift off several feet and travel short distances—twenty to thirty feet. But most of the acolytes hopped around on the floor making "cooing" sounds.

Vessie stood beside Sister Jyoti watching a morning levitation session. Her mentor wanted to explain what was causing the *cooing* and began by telling Vessie about *chakras.*

"Chakra in Sanskrit means spinning wheel of energy. There are seven chakras in our body and they directly correlate with different parts of our physical form. Imagine Gita—seven spinning wheels of energy stacked together in a central column from the crown of your head to the base of your spine. When we open them and align the centers, our vital life-force flows through freely. The technique they are practicing opened their chakras and released so much life-force energy, it forced this cooing sound."

"Wow. Sign me up for *that!*"

"When you are ready…" Jyoti said, "when you are ready."

Several weeks later as Vessie kneeled beside some thick green vines in the vegetable garden, an acolyte named Vyasa, aka Marvin Nusserbaum, a drop-out accountant from New Jersey, levitated out of the large common room window in a full lotus cooing and cooing and landed right on top of her new crop of tomatoes. *Fantastic! He can fly!*

Two days later, she and Sister Jyoti were in the garden and heard: *"Cooooo. Cooooo."* Brother Vyasa and two other acolytes, who were also yet to perfect their technique, flew out of the ashram window and landed on the rest of Vessie's crop. She looked down at what was now tomato sauce. "Awesome."

Bramananda appeared. "Tomorrow at dawn, Gita, I will give you your first technique. Sister Jyoti will tell you what to bring." The older woman smiled and nodded. Then as quickly as he appeared—he was gone. Vessie, wide-eyed, turned to her mentor.

"Yes, it really happened," she said. "You'll get used to it."

That night, Vessie wrote to Mrs. Smith and Smoodgie:

> I wish I could explain what I'm feeling,
> but I think you'd have to experience it yourself.
> All I can say is—every day when I wake up
> and every night when I go to sleep, my heart
> feels love for the whole world. Sri Bramananda
> says I'm ready for my first technique.
> I'm so excited and can hardly wait to
> experience transcendental consciousness again,
> like the first day I was here when he zapped
> me with pure energy.
> I love you as always, and send you white light
> and blessings.
>
> *Gita*

P.S. How do you like my new name? Sri Bramananda gave it to me. It's Sanskrit and means: song.
P.S.S. You can still call me Vessie, but isn't it a great name?
P.S.S.S. Sri Bramananda can actually de-materialize in one place and re-materialize in another. I saw him do it today.

87

Home in Los Angeles, Mrs. Smith cut off a big hunk of challah bread, made herself a nice cup of tea and sat down and read Vessie's letter. This is what she thought: *That's my Vessella—my female mench!*

Home in Symington, Smoodgie took time out from preparing for one of her many charitable events and sat down and read Vessie's letter. This is what *she* thought: *My poor baby sister. She's fucking NUTS!*

TWENTY

Vessie the Yogini

Bramananda and Vessie sat together before sunrise in his small hut. "Anil told me you can heal people. Tell me, Gita, why do you do this?"

Vessie was dumbfounded. She never questioned *why?* She was just drawn to do it.

"Indeed, you are drawn to do it. Anil told me you healed his brother. I know you also healed many small creatures and your parent's maid."

"You know about Conchita?" *Of course you do,* she thought. *You know everything.*

"I know not everything, but many things—enough to ask you more questions. Do you know why you are able to do this? Why you leave your body without effort? Why you know certain things will happen before they occur? Why you feel *high,* as you say, when you sing devotional hymns?"

Vessie's eyebrows were in a knot. "I... I don't know, Guruji."

"It is because you are a conduit for pure universal energy. Energy that is in all that is. I am that, you are that, all is that. And in *that,* all things are possible."

"Yes! I've seen you appear and disappear. I couldn't believe my eyes at first. That's how you do it? You connect to pure energy?"

"Yes, Gita, in a very specific way. There are many things you can do when you attain higher states of consciousness."

"That's a state *I* want to live in," she said.

"There are many techniques I can teach you, but you must begin by strengthening your nervous system, your physical vessel. I will give you a mantra taken from the ancient language of the gods, *Sanskrit,* the classical language of Hinduism. It is the oldest and most systematic language in the world. Each syllable has a powerful effect on the person who recites it. The ragas you sing are composed of Sanskrit words. That is why you feel so *high* when you sing them. That is why your soul-body left your physical body that day in the garden."

I knew that hymn was magical.

Guruji smiled. "For your mantra, it is not important that you understand the meaning of the words. In fact, it is best that you do not. The goal is to go beyond thought. When you let go of the mind-thoughts, the emotions will lose their power. When you let go of thought, you make room for new possibilities."

New possibilities.

"You see, Divine Intelligence is within you as it is within everything. When the mind takes control and dominates, you cannot hear its voice. You may call this *intuition.* It is your Higher Self that knows what you need and how to get it. When your mind is cluttered and busy you cannot hear the smartest part of your *self*—that is when you lose your way and make poor choices."

Bobby.

"The truth is: You are always connected to Higher Consciousness. To access it, you must quiet the mind."

Quiet the mind.

"By repeating your mantra, your thoughts will become fewer and fewer and eventually you will reach the source of all thought—the *transcendent* or pure energy consciousness. Do not be afraid to let go. Your body will feel more and more relaxed as the stresses and tensions attached to the thought-problems release. Do you have the things I asked you to bring for the puja?"

Vessie's eyes glowed. "Yes, Guruji." She had waited weeks for this day to arrive. Now she sprang to the straw mat where she had laid the snap dragons and azaleas from the flower garden, dried apricots and a small container of spring water, all wrapped in a shiny piece of gold silk cloth.

Bramananda took the contents and placed them on the altar. He poured the water into a small bowl, and placed the flowers and fruit before the photographs of his guru and his guru's gurus. He lit sandalwood incense,

90

poured water into his hand and drank a bit, then quietly chanted Sanskrit words that Vessie had never heard before. He offered fruit and flowers to the souls of the Enlightened Ones. More chanting followed and silent prayers were said.

Vessie felt a sweet calm embrace her like a thousand hugs. Bramananda opened his eyes and saw that Vessie's were closed. He began his instruction.

"Focus your attention between the eyebrows at the cosmic consciousness center and repeat after me... om-mani-padme-hum, om-mani-padme-hum."

"Om-mani-padme-hum, om-mani-padme-hum."

"Continue this. When thoughts come in, let them come and go, and then bring back the mantra: om-mani-padme-hum."

At first her thoughts were of every day concerns—*Is Sister Jyoti pleased with my flower arrangements? I feel so bad about spilling bleach on Brother Prakash's orange dhoti-kurta.* But Vessie held firm to her guru's words and continued to bring the mantra back into focus, repeating over and over—"om-mani-padme-hum, om-mani-padme-hum."

Eventually, mundane thoughts slipped away and she was alone in the transcendent, aware of her body but feeling no attachment to it—conscious of her guru's presence, but unaffected by it. She experienced a level more subtle than the atom. She was no longer Vessie, just pure energy—one with everything that exists. At that level, she just *was.*

Vessie just *was* for a good thirty minutes.

"Gita," Bramananda said softly.

She opened her eyes. She felt a wave of well-being she had never known before—a feeling that wasn't attached to a person or thing. She also saw her guru surrounded by light.

"The light around my body is called an *aura,* Gita. You've been able to see auras since you were a child."

Tears filled her eyes. "I told my mama and sister what I saw but they didn't believe me." Everend's death flashed through her mind.

"Let the guilt of your father's passing go. It was his time, Gita. You had nothing to do with it. Do not allow life's experiences to make you less than you are. Embrace your connection to the universe. Let all that you are shine through."

Yes yes.

"You are with kindreds now. Everyone here can see auras. Everyone here knows when a phone will ring." He laughed. "In order for the mind to reach its fullest potential, to know and experience all possibilities, it needs to tap into the pure universal energy field. One day Gita, when you feel more comfortable with this experience, I will help you fulfill your greatest desire: to *fly.*"

Vessie was shocked. She had never spoken of her secret wish to anyone. She thought it would sound silly, childish. Bramananda, once again, had read her thoughts.

"You mean, I'll be able to levitate like Anil and Brother Vyasa?"

"Yes. That is where you will begin. But you will fly, also. I have seen you leave your body. I know you have done this many times. One day you will be ready to have your physical body travel with you. There is still fear within. When you totally believe and know that you are one with pure universal energy and not separate, you will be able to fly. I will show you how to teleport by de-materializing and then re-materializing wherever you wish to be. But first, you must prepare your nervous system for this powerful energy to flow through you. Deep meditation, Gita... much deep meditation."

"Om-mani-padme-hum, om-mani-padme-hum." Crack! A tree limb fell on the roof of Vessie's car. The weight of the snow came with it causing a dent above her head that forced her to sink down in her seat a good six inches. *Oh my god oh my god oh my god.* She hugged her inner child tightly. "Sometimes, God has a lousy sense of humor."

Vessie meditated on the highest peak of the mountain behind the ashram, on the tiny bed in her converted attic, in group meditations in the temple, and at the feet of her guru. Images would float across her mind—snippets of events that had already taken place and some that would occur a day or two later. Small things like when Sister Jyoti gave her a beautiful white sari, and when Brother Nanumi saw her heal an injured bird. But there was one image she couldn't place and had no reference for. Vessie envisioned a flamingo flying over a sandbar just off of a white sandy beach, and a man running naked along the shore.

92

Weeks turned into months. A year passed. Vessie was given new mantras and new techniques. She could hop around the common room with the best of them, see auras around everyone, and feel so much love in her heart she thought it would burst. Vessie missed Mrs. Smith terribly, and now with her intuition in high gear, she knew how much Mrs. Smith was missing *her.*

"Of course she can come," Guruji told her just as Vessie was about to ask him if she could invite Mrs. Smith to attend their upcoming Christmas celebration.

The ashram had the feel of silk. Everything and everyone seemed to be floating. If there had been a major earthquake and mountains cracked and the sea rushed in, it wouldn't have seemed impossible for it to rise up out of harm's way hovering like the toupee on a great giant ghost. It was sensual and erotic. It said, *Come, you are welcome to experience me. Enjoy all I have to offer; but before you enter, leave your bullshit at the door.*

Clusters of flowers adorned tabletops and bookshelves, and were braided into banisters that curled to the floor. Female acolytes wore blossoms in their hair—males, around their necks in leis.

This was not a religious celebration—it was a celebration of life. Vessie and Lester Anil as she called him, and Sister Jyoti and all of the acolytes and monks were celebrating their connection to their guru, his gurus, each other, those who shopped at Safeway and Thrifty's and Bloomingdale's and the open air markets of Tel Aviv and London, and those who had no money to shop and no food to eat and were given no right to celebrate anything at all. It was a celebration of spirit which they all experienced each time they dove into the subtle sea of *being.*

Mrs. Smith yelled from the car window. "I didn't know what to wear, Vessella. What do I know from Christmas? I know Fairfax Avenue and the May Company, and that's it."

Foot parked the limo and opened the door for Mrs. Smith. Vessie hardly noticed the green, red and white striped dress that looked like a swirl of a new Baskin Robbins' flavor of the month as she flew into her arms and held her closely. *I've missed you so. I love you dearly, you precious, precious soul.*

"So… this is Ten Downing Street. I'm honored."

That night, Mrs. Smith was the most colorful person in the group. The populated pews looked like this: white, red/green/and white fiesta.

Bramananda could see that Mrs. Smith was as special as Vessie had said, and wanted to give her a gift. He closed his eyes and caused her vanilla pudding body to feel as light as a bowl of feathers—her mind to see scenes more beautiful than her favorite picture calendar of Miami. She could even see her dearly departed Solly. He wasn't in a pine box buried in the earth at Mount Sinai Cemetery. He was there in her vision romping toward her along the ocean shore.

"*Solly! Solly!*" she called. He looked so well, so happy and fat. He was the Pillsbury Doughboy with character. Mrs. Smith ran to him and he tried to lift her but couldn't and fell to his knees. They kissed and laughed. Then he disappeared.

Vessie heard the wind howling outside of her frozen tomb. She wanted to breathe deeply, knew it would help calm her, but the air was too cold and bit at her lungs. She drew her attention between her eyebrows at the cosmic consciousness center. Her inner child followed suit.

"You doin' okay?" Vessie asked.

"I don't know. I think I'm going cross-eyed."

"You doin' okay?" a voice asked in the art deco lobby. Light flared from a cigarette lighter and Remy could see the face of its owner—a handsome young man with warm intelligent eyes.

"No. As a matter of fact, I just finished filling out a missing person's report on my best friend and I'm a mess."

Jacques Bisset offered his name and a handshake. He had a calming air about him that Remy felt immediately. There were no taxis to be flagged—the city had ground to a halt. Remy explained that Lou was next door drinking his blues away, waiting for him.

"Join us?" he asked the stranger.

Vessie's inner child cuddled close.

Christmas at the ashram, Vessie thought. *Christmas at the ashram.*

Three large men: Brother Nanumi, alias Leonard Jule, an ex-condom and cigarette paper manufacturer, Brother Salu Abneb, alias Casey White, a wallpaper designer and ex-hedonist, and Brother Lahiri, alias Leonard Washington Jones, the first American to successfully repeat rubber-baby-buggy-bumpers two hundred times while eating a banana, carried an electric piano, amplifier and speakers into the room. The piano had a large red bow tied around it and a card with Vessie's Sanskrit name: GITA.

Mrs. Smith beamed. "Go, Vessella, uh, *Gita*lla. They're calling you."

Vessie couldn't believe it. Someone was giving her the gift of an electric piano? But who? Why? She walked hesitantly, but excitedly to the shiny black Yamaha. One glance at the handwriting on the card and she knew the identity of her mystery benefactor.

Because music is a part of you, my darling Vessella.

Vessie's heart swelled. Tears swamped her eyes as she blew Mrs. Smith a kiss. She hadn't touched a keyboard in over a year. Brother Salu Abneb rushed over with a chair as Vessie sat down. She touched the ivories as she would a newborn babe. It was as if the piano began to play *her.* Every tone sounded clear and sure as she sang.

> "Oh yes, the butterflies are pretty
> Oh yes, the butterflies are pretty
> Oh yes, the butterflies are pretty
> But they once were caterpillars"

The melody was as hypnotic as a raga.

> "See them flying up upon the wind song
> Never crying, in command of what is wrong
> Flying free on wings so sure from falling
> Once they were contented crawling"

Something was guiding her hands to play certain notes, her voice to sing certain words.

"I was just a caterpillar
Who became a butterfly
Shedding darkness full of glitter
Now I have no need to cry"

The last note Vessie sang was so sweet, Bramananda gained a pound. Mrs. Smith was relieved. She hoped Vessie was connecting with the one thing that would get her out of this guru-ghetto. She believed Bramananda meant no harm and was probably doing good by her Vessella, but she was young and all meditation and no play would make her sweet Vessie prematurely grey.

Vessie finished playing her song as her fellow acolytes applauded. Several approached her with delighted surprise:

"Gita! I had no idea!"

"Did you make that song up?"

"Does Guruji know you can play like that?"

Suddenly, all heads turned toward their master.

"No, I did not know that Gita's dharma is the path of music."

They were aghast. *Music*? Did this mean she was, *out*? Did this mean Guruji's favorite acolyte was to leave the ashram, head in hand, ashamed, degraded, thrown to the mercy of the negative forces to spin like a leaf in the nether?

"Absolutely not!" Bramananda said, group-reading their minds. "Gita will stay here until she is strong enough to resume her path in the outside world. Gita, come with me."

Vessie sought Mrs. Smith's eyes. Mrs. Smith gave her the same reassuring smile she gave her every time she fell down emotionally. It didn't make her feel any better, but it did let Vessie know that if she couldn't get up, someone was there to complete the funeral arrangements.

Bramananda led Vessie to the sanctuary and down the aisle to the pew nearest the altar.

"Do you think that going into the world is a punishment?" he said. "There are many ways to heal, to give love. Music is love. It is your true mantra. You are blessed, my child. And you must know this: I will always be with you wherever you go. When you meditate you will be joined with me and all teachers, all saints. You will benefit from their blessings always. By the time you leave the ashram, you will slide into the transcendent like Willie Mays slides into home plate."

"But, Guruji, I don't want to leave. I want to stay with you. I'm so happy here. Please! Let me do your work here at the ashram. In the outside world, love does nothing but hurt."

Bramananda smiled into Vessie's eyes. "That is because it wasn't love that you experienced but attachment to the senses. Love nurtures the soul, Gita. The hurt you knew, the loss of loved ones. You only have to look in your heart to find them, to talk to them, to see them. Tonight, the Divine expressed itself through your hands and your voice. I know you could feel it. We all could feel it. It is your dharma to share love through music. In doing so, you will attract that which is your like."

"You mean, a *man*?" An image flashed across her mind—the man she had seen running… running…

"Go now. Enjoy. Mrs. Smith is waiting for you and the celebration has just begun."

As Vessie walked back up the center aisle of the sanctuary, Paramahansa Bramananda telepathically sent her an extra dose of what he called his Cosmic B-12 Shot—a concentrated wave of pure energy that filled her with a feeling that life was a bowl of cherries *without* the pits.

Time didn't exist for Vessie, until now. Now there was no time to lose. She levitated like a house on fire. She wanted to perfect the technique— strengthen her nervous system before going back into the outside world. Maybe she would even be ready for the advanced technique of flying. *When will I get the chance to do it out there?* she thought. *I'll be too busy looking for work—trying to get my songs published—playing in clubs and wherever else I can find an opportunity.* She kept trying to encourage herself with her guru's words: *Music is your mantra. Music is your path.*

At first she was thrilled that Mrs. Smith brought the piano to the ashram. Then she was sorry. Everything was perfect until then. She knew what she was to do every day, where she was to go—and it was all sweet, fulfilling, and mindless. But she soon realized that her beloved Mrs. Smith knew her better than she knew herself. And so did Guruji. They knew the ashram was a stop-gap: a place for her to heal and recharge, to prepare for experiences yet to come.

The truth was obvious. As soon as she had touched the keyboard of the new Yamaha, Vessie felt connected to the same energy she experienced in meditation. And in that place, time disappeared.

Several weeks later, Vessie was in the common room having beaten the other acolytes to their early morning levitation. She was used to hopping six inches off the floor across the length of the forty foot room. But now energy shot through her chakras like rocket fuel.

"Cooooooo. Cooooooo." Her body lifted higher and higher—three, four, then five feet above the floor hovering around the empty space. She was no longer separated from her body like when she was chanting in the garden and flew high above the ground or when her whole body resonated from hearing Everend's words and was catapulted straight through the church roof.

Her eyes rolled up in her head. She was having… an *ORGASM*. "Coooooooooooooooooooooooo." She flew out the window into the vegetable garden over the bean stalks, over the corn stalks and *fooooomph,* landed right on top of a new acolyte's baby tomato plants.

It was a success.

Weeks later, Vessie was finally able to control her landings, and Bramananda was pleased. "You are strong enough, Gita. It is time."

TWENTY-ONE

Sari but It's Time to Go

Vessie packed her saris and photographs into a large cloth bag. She would leave behind what had been her home for the past eighteen months. She would say goodbye to a tall dark skinned man who wore an orange dhoti, flowers around his neck, smelled of sandalwood and patchouli, and whom she loved like a father. She would be going home to a woman whose front door wore a mezuzah and whose candles burned at sundown on Friday nights.

Vessie walked down the stairway, bag in hand. All the acolytes and monks stood holding candles and chanting one of her favorite Sanskrit ragas. She had seen others leave to go back into the outside world, but never were they given such fanfare. For eighteen months she had heard Bramananda teach:

> *These experiences we believe to be real*
> *are simply illusion, God's drama. Once*
> *we realize this, we are free to move*
> *within the drama, unattached to the peaks*
> *and valleys of emotion.*

Now it was time to hear his parting words.

Vessie entered the sanctuary and found her guru sitting pretzeled on the podium. She never got to say goodbye to her father and thought this might help heal the loss. But how could she say goodbye? Where would words she didn't want to say come from? *There's nothing sweet about the sadness I feel,* she thought. *It rates somewhere between acne and fever blisters.* A baseball of emotion stuck in Vessie's throat.

"You know better than that," Bramananda said. "This scene is merely illusion and should be taken with a grain of bicarbonate of soda and tossed on the sea of the Eternal."

She would miss hearing him weave contemporary sayings with Eastern philosophy. She would miss his unconditional love and rock-steady support.

The tall dark man held out a gold cloth covered book tied with a silk cord. "Everything I have taught you is written here. Also techniques you will one day be ready to practice."

Vessie began to cry. The baseball in her throat scored a home run.

"Meditate regularly and continue to practice the levitation technique. It will prepare you for the advanced technique of teleportation through dematerialization."

Vessie looked up.

"Yes, Gita, as you have seen me do."

"But you won't be there to teach me. Can't I stay here and learn it? Please, Guruji, just a little longer?"

"Gita… you have a schedule to keep. Experiences you must go through. Do not fear. I will be with you always. And my teachings will be with you." He held up the cloth covered book. "The instructions are in here. Now remember Gita, as it is most important. There are four elements that will enable you to teleport your body through dematerialization."

Vessie closed her eyes. *Four elements,* she thought.

Bramananda continued. "Intention, lack of fear, connecting to pure energy, and the belief that you can do it."

Vessie repeated silently. *Intention, lack of fear, connecting to pure energy, belief that I can do it.*

"When you know the 'I am'—that you are one with all that is and not separate, when you truly know and believe, then you will be able to perfect this advanced technique and *fly.*" The corners of his eyes curled like the ends of a moustache. "Practice regularly," he said. "Ask for guidance. If you need me, close your eyes, tune into my station, and I will come to you. And remember Gita, it is your dharma to share His love through music. In doing so, you will attract that which is your like." His eyes rolled up in his head. His body vibrated like a hummingbird's, filling with light. Rays of energy shot into Vessie, straight up her spine, and spun her like a top.

"Cooooooo. Coooooo." She landed back on the pew and opened her eyes. She wanted to hug him and wear him like a mustard plaster. The strength he had promised was hers.

Vessie gently took the book from her guru's long slender hands, bowed before him and walked back up the centre aisle for the last time.

The foyer was filled with all those she had grown to love during her stay at the ashram: Brother Salu-Abneb, Brothers Vyasa, Nanumi and Lahiri, and Sister Jyoti who embraced her tenderly, then slowly backed away.

Vessie slipped into her sandals as her eyes met each of her sisters and brothers whose hearts begged: *Remember me.* Her heart felt full-to-bursting and she forced herself to look away. She walked straight through the open doorway, across the veranda, and down the wood steps where Lester-Anil was hovering in place. There was so much he wanted to tell her, but his eyes said it all.

"Yes," Vessie said, "me too."

She walked past Foot who had come to take her back to town, past the white limousine, and down Heavenly Drive along side of the International Garden of Flowers toward the Pacific Coast Highway where beer bottles, crumpled Sheik wrappers, and torn parking tickets lined the sand encrusted pavement.

She walked past beach houses as jocks sanding surfboards and changing spark plugs whistled and shouted catcalls. It was the first time in close to two years that there was anything other than earth or grass beneath her feet and the fragrance of meadow flowers in the air.

Foot followed in the limo a safe distance behind until he saw Vessie reach a bus stop half a mile down the highway. He pulled alongside, opened the back door, and she got in.

Vessie was back at Mrs. Smith's—this time, wrapped in silk, wearing sandalwood beads, leather sandals, and a glow that couldn't be bought in any psychedelic shop. And again, Mrs. Smith was showing her a way back into the world. With a supportive smile, she handed Vessie the Classified section of the Times. Vessie couldn't bear it. She wanted to be back at the ashram. She wanted to look into Guruji's eyes and know that life was more than just survival. She wanted to plug into nirvana and out of the race.

Mrs. Smith took Vessie's hand. "How can someone who is glowing have tears running down her cheeks? You're smiling, glowing and crying all at the same time. I saw that once. When my great Auntie Hester died and her husband, my Uncle Moishe, knowing he'd be rid of her kvetching forever, did the same thing. He smiled, glowed, and cried. But Vessella, dahlink... nobody died." She put her big comforting arm around Vessie's shoulder. "You'll visit your teacher, you'll do your meditations and maybe while you're doing them you'll feel him with you, like me and Solly, may he rest in peace."

Vessie laughed. What would she do without Mrs. Smith? She was so wise, so supportive. She finished her tea which she had learned to drink like Mrs. Smith: sipping it through a sugar cube held between her teeth until it completely dissolved. *From my Russian roots,* Mrs. Smith had once told her.

Vessie's room was as she had left it: the bed tucked against the back windows, her small ensemble of skirts, blouses, and slacks neatly hung in the open closet. And resting on a narrow night stand—a photograph of Everend holding her on his knee.

She opened her cloth bag and took out a picture of her beloved guru. She also pulled out a piece of silk cloth and laid it across a chair that she would meditate on. He had told her that by separating one's self from worldly vibrations with a piece of cloth made of natural fibers, the body had less pull toward the material world, allowing the mind to transcend thoughts more easily.

Passing a mirror, Vessie stopped and stared at herself. She had changed. She was no longer a girl, but a woman. No longer her father's child, but her *Father's* child. She sat down and closed her eyes. She repeated her mantra over and over as the little room in the back of Mrs. Smith's duplex on Orange Street began to fade away.

TWENTY-TWO

Back in the Saddle

"Yeah, but can you dance?" asked Arnie Jackman, still in the habit of asking a question he knew would receive a negative response.

"The ad said nothing about dancing."

"Just kidding, baby. Listen, if you can play keyboard as good as you look, you got the gig, but the toga's gotta go. What are you, a runaway Hindu or something?"

Vessie was in the Hole, not a hole, but *the* Hole, although it really was a hole—but that's a hole other story.

The club, unlike Yoyo's, was low-key, dark and quiet, and drew regulars who wouldn't want it any other way. They were an older crowd who liked to sit at the bar or in quiet corners and nurse a Daiquiri or whisky and soda, or anything straight up.

Its new owner, Arnie Jackman, won the Hole in a craps game and didn't know the first thing about managing a club. He just knew he liked to drink, liked hanging out with his cronies, liked to gamble which he still did in the back room on Thursday nights, and that it really didn't matter who he hired to play piano because he'd probably fire him or her in a week or two because he knew he liked doing that, too.

Vessie walked over to the piano. *Runaway Hindu*, she thought. It would take a lot more to provoke her than a little ribbing from a forty-five-year-old ten-year-old. She claimed the piano keys and sang:

> "Time, there is no such thing as time
> It's simply just a sign, a way to measure
> every treasure"

Arnie listened attentively.

> "Mine, there's no such thing as mine
> Love is everything divine
> and travels on the wind forever
> Fly, let love touch the sky
> Let love take you high
> on its magic wings of wonder
> You are love
> You are the way
> Everything grows
> Everything stays...
> when there is no time"

Vessie's voice, though never strong, clung to the air like saran. Jackman would have cooed if he knew how. Instead he told her: "Yeah, yeah, that's great. But, do you know any Top Ten stuff?"

Vessie got the job and was delighted. It felt good to be playing again, especially now that she had something to say through her songs. But the customers at The Hole echoed Jackman: "Top Ten stuff, okay baby?" So, she played background music to the clinking of glasses, the occasional brawl, and the low drone of regulars who wanted their alcohol to sober them up from their drugs.

A week and a-half into the job, Vessie was not happy. *Is this following my path? What good am I doing here? I'm not enhancing The Hole, and all I'm getting in return are headaches from the smoke and offers to get laid from sloshed men and women.* She knew she had to leave, to find her niche, but where? How?

It was twelve-thirty a.m. and two customers were left whispering in a corner. Vessie was ready to give her notice and decided she had nothing to lose by performing one of her songs.

> "Time, there is no such thing as time
> It's simply just a sign, a way to measure
> every treasure"

She didn't notice her future boss come in; and if she had, she never would have guessed what their relationship would become. He looked like anything but a music producer. More like an aluminum siding salesman. If she had looked at his feet—penny loafers without socks—she would have guessed he was from the East Coast and somehow associated with the Upper East Side or show business. What really surprised her was when he brought over his five-foot-two rotund body, leaned against the piano and said: "I'm Lou Fields and I'm going to make you a star."

There were a few catches.

Number One: He was referring to an area of the music business that she had no knowledge of: the *jingle* business—the musical part of television and radio commercials. Lou Fields was the owner of Fields & Friends, although no one who worked for Lou was his friend. It was one of the top jingle houses in New York.

Number Two: Vessie would have to move there.

"I'll make you a star jingle writer. Teach you everything I know. You got talent kid. I could see that right off. I'll teach you the hook of a tune, the honing of a fifteen, thirty, sixty second spot. You'll start at the bottom, but you'll soar, my dear. You'll soar and soar as long as you keep putting those rhyme schemes and melodic phrases down on paper where they belong. Products need to be sold. The economy needs to be boosted. And we need to do our part by keeping it all moving. This is one area of the business where you not only *can* be, but *must* be crazy, silly, dramatic, romantic, absurd, always looking for a new way of saying the same old thing. You want a challenge? You want a job that'll pick your brains and force you to think harder, freer, more creatively? You want to fly on the wings of an idea and have it float through televisions and radios to millions of Americans coast to coast? Be in my office Monday morning at eight."

It was already Saturday morning, but that was the deal. "There'll be a ticket waiting for you at American Airlines." Vessie was flabbergasted. She had been asking for a sign and believed this had to be it.

It is your dharma to share love through music. That's what her guru told her. She believed in his foresight. *In doing so, you will attract that which is your like.* What did he mean: *that which is your like?* Did he mean people? Situations? A *man?* The music she would write for Lou Fields would be jingles not songs. Was Vessie following her intuition or being led by superstition and blind faith? Was she about to travel in an airplane or float like a leaf on whatever current took her? It would be easy saying goodbye to Arnie Jackman and the smoke fumes, but not easy saying goodbye to Mrs. Smith.

"Flight three sixty-seven to New York is now boarding."

Mrs. Smith wrapped her great pulpy arms around her precious young friend. "Vessella, I know the hot dogs on the street taste good, but don't eat them. I wouldn't ship a dog in the crates they come out of. And, if you want good latkes and blintzes go to the Upper West Side. Downtown's too expensive and all the cooks in the Jewish delis are Italian. Oh Vessella, I miss your sweet face already. If you need me for anything, you call collect. Understand?"

Vessie understood. She understood how much she loved this woman and would miss her desperately.

"If you need *me* for anything, I'll come back. I love you."

They held each tightly, then let go.

Vessie grabbed her shoulder bag, pulled out her ticket; and as she turned to join the lineup of passengers, she saw Mrs. Smith choke back tears and offer her biggest smile.

Thirty thousand feet above the only world she ever knew, Vessie was on her way to one she had never dreamed of. *This is A.S. and B.N.Y.C.,* she thought. *After Sex and Before New York City.*

TWENTY-THREE

The Big Apple Game

Blue jeans and high heels are what Chrissy, the receptionist, was wearing the first day Vessie stepped into Fields & Friends. Her makeup was the latest Vogue had to offer and her hairstyle, Sassoon. Geo awards, the highest international honor given for commercials lined the walls promoting the company's first class reputation.

The office was on Madison Avenue at Forty-ninth. Around the corner was a coffee shop where homemade pies and muffins twirled on automated lazy-susans. Street vendors selling hot dogs and shish kebobs slapped hot mustard on steamy buns and wrapped napkins around meat filled sticks. Other vendors offering sunglasses, umbrellas, ties, belts, and radios sold their wares on spread out blankets that quickly disappeared when warned that the cops were coming.

Taxicabs and limousines created bumper-to-bumper traffic. Architecture climbed to the skies with deco windows, rococo filigree. Never in Los Angeles had Vessie seen such craftsmanship. New York had everything heaven and hell had to offer. Burnt-out buildings the poor created to force the city to provide adequate housing. The Upper East Side adorned with marble sinks and shiny doormen. The rummies and the elite mixing in the same dance, the same uncensored song. New York New York, tempting the child in every man and woman to decide what it was they wanted and to go for it, or go back to Missouri.

"Would you tell Lou Fields that Vessie VanCortland is here?"

Remy Bartells overheard the announcement. He was Lou Fields' number one flunky. Almost twenty-five, almost tall, almost stunningly handsome, his deep-seated insecurity cast an almost awkward tinge to his presence. He was still doing the odd jobs he did for Lou when he began working at Fields & Friends five years ago: ordering lunches, picking up sheet music, sorting through musicians' contracts. He rarely got a chance to write jingles, but then he was never very good at it. He would come up with a line or two that was usually changed or an idea that was almost good enough; but never the hook, never the *magic.*

Now, his goal was to become a jingle *producer*; and Lou would dangle that hope whenever Remy asked for a raise. He would remind him of the number of talented people who played their tunes in the street with opened instrument cases at their feet. He would hammer home the day he discovered Remy doing just that, at the corner of Forty-second and Fifth; and, how he saved him from having to lie to his parents in Washington that he was doing well in New York. Lou reminded Remy that even at his salary, which wasn't much more than Vessie's would be, he was lucky to be a part of the Big Apple Game.

Remy believed something fortuitous would happen. He would grab the spotlight and prove to Lou Fields, once and for all, that he could hire the musicians, conduct the band and singers, produce the final mix, and put an exceptional product in the hands of the head honchos at Benton and Bowles, Footcone Belding, J. Walter Thompson, Young & Rubicam. *Gimme the Jello account, or Fritos, McDonalds, Cool Whip... I'll give those other jingle companies a run for their money,* he'd tell himself, but was never able to tell Lou.

So she's here! The girl Lou found in L.A. Hungry for his chance to shine and knowing that Lou was about to focus his attention on this *stranger,* Remy was ready to hate her. But as days passed, their ideas clicked, their rhythms clacked. They were immediately best friends forever. He could see why Lou imported her. Vessie's ideas were fresh, her confidence strong, and damn! she was gorgeous. Was that skin or alabaster? Eyes or emeralds? Lips or rubies? Remy was enamored and did everything but wag his tail.

He would suggest corned beef over turkey, seltzer over coke, which movies to see, places to shop. It took him three weeks before he realized that Vessie was a vegetarian, drank only decaf or herbal teas, couldn't afford movies, and bought her clothes second-hand. He thought it was so precious that she ate carrots and crunched granola, that her vitamins cost as much as his groceries. And when she told him about her ashram experience, that she meditated and hopped around her alcove via a levitation technique, he was truly enamored. Wasn't she wonderful, and hadn't she better keep that last bit of information from the ears of Lou-Blinders-On-Your-Brain Fields?

"Okay, you're outta here!" Lou snapped, verbally swatting Remy like a fly.

It was Vessie's turn.

"Here, you'll need this. We've got lots of work to do." He shoved a cup of coffee in her hand as Remy deflated out the door. It was just another day at Fields & Friends and Lou was being his normal nasty self.

"Lou, you know I don't drink coffee," Vessie said.

"You do now."

She was in Lou Fields' Boot Camp.

He played her twenty-five reels of jingles by noon, and for each and every one he played judge and jury: "That's great," or "That's pathetic," or, "A real scum catcher." The latter, naturally, was created by his biggest competitor..

Lou grabbed a black felt marker, drew a diagram on a white board and scrawled:

LOU FIELDS' HIT JINGLE FORMULA

For forty minutes he pontificated on the philosophy, psychology, and ingenuity behind it, around it, in it, under it, and how it all must go into the creation of any jingle worth... "Worth what, Vessie?" He leaned over her, his flushed blowfish face blowing out: "One that sells product!"

Lou's words were big—his ego bigger, which left no room for anyone else in his self-inflated universe. As for the "Formula on the Mount"—it was as profound as fruitcake. But he was definitely a genius at one thing: *con.* If given the chance, Lou Fields could sell life insurance to a dead man.

"I'll tell you a secret," he told Vessie, his voice breaking into a whisper. "It takes more than just coming up with a great idea. It takes *selling* the damn thing." He pulled back. "Yes, SELLING it!" His eyes flashed, his hands spun around. He moved and strutted, expounding whatever. It didn't matter what he said, the man was *electric*—the Super Svengali of *Trite.*

Then he stopped. It was as if a director had yelled, *Cut!* He seamlessly shifted into casual body language, sunk one hand into his pants pocket, the other into a deep bowl of M & Ms, and popped them into his mouth.

"Vessie, did you notice how I lowered my voice, almost whispered when I said, I'll tell you a secret? And how it forced you to lean forward in order to hear what I said? *That's* how you sell an idea. *That's* how you get your client to say: *Yessssss!*" His teeth were full of chocolate. "Good trick, huh?"

Lou was full of tricks, which Vessie would become the brunt of over the next too many years. She felt grateful to have Remy in her life, especially now that she wasn't going to *have* a life working for this complex, Madison Avenue self-proclaimed Creative Guru.

It was winter. The most colorful part of the city was the pavement. What few trees could be found looked ready for burial. The sun appeared only to tease. Faces were held down against the wind. Clothes were dark. Streets darker. Hats hid eyes. Gloves hid hands. Coats hid bodies wrapped in woolen tombs. Sixty-story buildings shadowed it all warning that someone was about to get hurt.

"You will have tests," Bramananda told her. "They will come in the form of situations. You will have opportunities to grow from these experiences. Accept them as blessings."

"Boy, am I blessed!" Vessie said one afternoon after being accosted by a fifteen- year-old, then watched him run off with her purse. "Am I blessed!" The only thing she learned from that experience was to carry her money in her underpants.

Panhandlers lined the streets of Manhattan: blind men, legless men, women who begged openly, others with glazed eyes who sat in dirty torn clothes too lost to beg. Vessie's heart went out to them. Not all of them. To some, her gut screamed: *Liar. Liar. You've got a house in Scarsdale.* To most, she gave what she could. To the handicapped, she *healed.*

Whenever Vessie could peel herself away from the office she would head to Grand Central Station. She knew she could always find street people just outside its doors or inside on the long high-backed wooden benches in the waiting area, sound asleep with newspapers over their faces.

She knew the power of pure universal energy could heal the spirit as well as the body, and she was going to give it her best shot—*anonymously.*

Vessie would sit beside a sleeping street person, close her eyes, take deep slow breaths and visualize a long silver chord connected from the base of her spine to the center of the earth. If there were people sitting across from her, she would lift her hands above her head pretending to stretch, and silently state her intention: *I wish to heal this person in body, mind and spirit.* Then she would lower her hands and hold them just over their foot or arm or head, depending on where she was sitting, and repeat: *His love goes through my hands to you, through my hands to you.*

She improvised. Whenever Vessie would see a physically handicapped person and wasn't able to go through the healing process the way the angel dolls taught her, she would *mentally* send them healing energy. Or give them a hug, silently stating her intention. She never told anyone about her healing attempts. Never knew if they did any good. Vessie only knew she had to try.

Her tan faded the first few weeks she was in Manhattan. She was used to looking pan fried and toasty, and hardly recognized herself. In Symington Vessie had taken the sun for granted, swimming in a neighbor's pool on a whim, sharing a picnic blanket with a cat. Even in Los Angeles on Bobby Rich's patio as tears licked her, so did the sun, painting her terra cotta. At the ashram, meditating in the sunshine, working in the garden. Now the wintry days were dark and sunglasses were obsolete.

She would sit sardined in a bus or subway en route home with strangers hovering over her holding on to metal loops that hung from the ceiling, and try to imagine the pale blue horizon from her ashram window; but she felt cold and closed in… cold and… closed in.

"Om-mani-padme-hum, om-mani-padme-hum." *Is anybody going to rescue me from my frozen car or is this really the end? No, no, I won't think that. I won't die in this snow bank!* Her inner child agreed: "Lousy thought. Everybody now… om-mani-padme-hum, om-mani-padme-hum."

Although she knew to repeat the syllables gently, Vessie machine gunned them, spitting them through her mind until finally, miraculously, she began to relax, to forget her freezing body and the sub-zero temperature.

An animated tube of hemorrhoid preparation wearing a top hat and dancing with a shiny black cane opened its mouth and sang:

"No more ouchy
No more grouchy
Now you can sit all day on your couchy"

It plopped down on a purple and red striped couch and sang:

"You-know-what will feel so ooey
Like when you're in love, all gooey gooey"

Suddenly, a female tube appeared and planted a fat kiss on his lips.

"It's so soothing, you'll feel like mush"

Then they belted out: "SIGTOID'S HEMORROID PREPARATION: **TUSH!**"

The TUSH tube did a double flip toward camera and shook its hiney.

The voiceover announcer said: "Sigtoid's Hemorrhoid Preparation TUSH... no more pain in the you-know-where!"

The TUSH tube looked straight at camera and winked.

Lou liked it. He ran the video twice. The animation worked well with Vessie's jingle. The tune was catchy, the lyrics memorable. It was better than good for her first attempt. Lou told her: "It's all right. You can do better."

Lou's office looked like Lou: wool, tweedy and grey. Every space was taken up with something that was useful to him: an intercom, a tape recorder, video unit, liquor cabinet, dart board with effigies of his biggest competitors.

As soon as he stepped off the sixth floor elevator each morning into his working domain, Lou Fields was no longer a husband, father and grand dad. He was a slave driver who made it to the top by surrounding himself with talented people. He paid bare bone wages, no compliments, and lavished his peons with a tremendous amount of grief. As for the creative environment he provided —

Vessie's office looked like a piano-size phone booth. The walls were bare and the only window was in the door. A telephone sat on a small table. If she needed to call anyone other than a client she had to do it on her dime and on her time.

Remy's office was next to hers and twice the size, which made it half the size of an average office. Filled wall-to-wall with master tapes, it was really a store room with a desk. On that desk sat a framed photo of Kat, pronounced *cat*, a model who had broken his heart years ago and was his on-going excuse for not being in a relationship. She had gone on to fame and fortune and Remy had gone on talking about it.

"Ves," he would say, "she was so beautiful and just as beautiful inside. And so giving. I don't mean just, you *know*... She appreciated everything I did for her." He was referring to his gourmet cooking, housekeeping, gift giving, and on-demand chauffeuring. He was a real pet, and Kat knew a good doormat when she stepped on one.

"She just got tired of me, I guess. I wasn't beast enough for her. I told her I'd glue hair on my chest but it was no use. She fell in love with a Doberman Pincer and we never made love again."

Vessie would hit him when he said that, and they'd laugh. But there was a sadness in this handsome young man she called her friend—a sadness she didn't understand.

So, here she was in her tiny working cave smack in the middle of the fashion and theatre meccas of North America with barely enough time to change her clothes or enough money to see a play. Lou had found a good thing in Vessie and took advantage of her talent, work ethic, and underfed pocket book.

The day he announced a new jingle assignment, it was already two weeks late. He would make her write it and re-write it and re-write it for days and nights and lunchtimes and breakfasts until finally it resembled the Lou Fields Hit Jingle Formula. Then the Emperor would reluctantly bestow his personal stamp of approval, tweak the new ditty ever so slightly, and claim it as his own.

There was nothing in Vessie's life that she considered glamorous, but Smoodgie thought otherwise. Her heart would race just seeing the NEW

YORK postmark on her sister's letters, reading about the long hours at the office and her Geo nominated jingles. Sure it was great being the wife of a doctor and mother of a beautiful baby girl, but holy heck, grandma, Vessie was *making it* in NEW YORK!

For six months Vessie had taken the Lex subway home to her rented alcove on Second Avenue, one floor beneath the apartment of Rabbi Joseph Lebrovnick and next door to an all night fruit and vegetable stand.

At first she could be on a subway, bus, or crowded sidewalk able to sustain a Sanskrit hymn in her mind or silently repeat her mantra or do a breathing technique and hold on to the peaceful calm she had brought with her from the ashram. But *calm* and Vessie were becoming more and more estranged. She noticed that she had begun *sighing* a lot. Big, deep, desperate sighs that usually came after recalling something Lou had said.

"The jingle you just wrote? It's *passable.*"

Or how he'd mark up her pages like an over-zealous grade school teacher and tell an audience of staffers:

"See this? This is what you *don't* want to write."

Sigh, sigh, sigh, sigh, sigh.

Vessie got off the subway and ran up the stairs to the street. She had recently read about women who were raped on their way home from work and chose not to be one of them. She decided that if anyone grabbed her she would scream and kick to kill. She no longer bought the philosophy, "Love Thy Neighbor and Turn the Other Cheek." She believed Thy Neighbor had better prove to be loveable or the only thing she would turn would be into a *pit bull.* She never had thoughts like these in Los Angeles or Symington, and was beginning to feel stupid for being in New York.

Fly in a jar. Fly in a jar.

She finally arrived home with words and music spinning in her head and an impending deadline mentally exhausting her. Listlessly, she peeled off her clothes and dropped them on the rug. She lit a stick of incense and plopped down in a chair to meditate. But her focus kept being interrupted by the chop chopping of vegetables coming from the all night take-out salad bar next door.

I need to mediate. I need to do my levitation technique. It's been weeks.

114

It was Friday, way past sundown and the Shabbat service that Rabbi Lebrovnick had conducted ended hours ago. Now, he was upstairs directly above Vessie's head rolling around on his living room rug with his fiancé laughing and grunting.

Vegetables, Vessie's main source of food had become the enemy; and, in her tired frustrated state the good rabbi, who was entitled to a little R&R, had become a pervert.

Oh my god, what's happening to me? I hate when I get like this—such negative thoughts. Okay, Vessie, she told herself. *You know what to do. DO IT.*

She jumped into the shower, visualized washing her frustrations down the drain, jumped back out, dried herself off, took her phone off the hook, shoved it under a pillow, sat down in a full lotus by the small alter in the east corner of the alcove, and stared at the photo of her guru. She could have sworn he winked at her.

Right nostril, breathe slowly out, left nostril, breathe slowly in. Vessie did pranayama breathing exercise for a good ten minutes, then broadcast her mantra from her tiny room in a city of skyscrapers to God, the universe and everything. Her chakras spun, her life-force energy flowed, her eyes rolled up in her head. She envisioned a man running naked on a shoreline.

"Coooooooooooooooo."

TWENTY-FOUR

Vessie Queen of the Jingle

The first year Vessie lived in New York, she wrote two jingles that won the coveted International Geo Award—only the Cannes Eagle Award shared equal status. Upon receiving the slender statuette at a presentation of five hundred advertising moguls, Lou made no mention of Vessie as writer of the honored gems.

The second year she worked at Fields & Friends, Lou accepted five Geos and again made no mention of Vessie or any of the other award-winning composers. She had written three jingles that won Gold; and, two freelance composers Lou had hired won Silver.

But, the New York advertising community was discovering who she was, anyway. Remy saw to that.

Whether they were squeezing in a meal in a mid-town restaurant or standing squished at an uptown bar, Remy would find a way to spread the word. "That red-headed leggy girl, third booth down, with the sunglasses and sweater... she wrote the *Chow Chow* spot and the *You want 'em, We got 'em* jingle... Vessie VanCortland, hot, hot, hot."

At first, Vessie would blush with embarrassment and slink down into her socks; but, soon she realized that it was Remy's mission to make her a cult celeb, and forced herself to accept his efforts graciously.

One rainy March afternoon, Remy entered her office all decked out in a three piece suit—his eyes glowing with excitement. Vessie was too preoccupied to notice.

"C'mon, Ves, I'm taking you to the Russian Tea Room for lunch, my treat."

She was headlong into writing a jingle that had a four o'clock deadline and so far, this is as far as she got:

Sticky licky, never yicky
Yummy crummy want more in my tummy
Oreos, Oreos, Ore-ore-ore-ooooooooos

"Remy, I can't. I need to finish this."

He yanked the plug to her amplifier, grabbed her coat and purse, and extended his hand from the doorway.

"I know you like the dark, so threatening to turn off the lights won't work. C'mon, or we'll be late. And trust me, this is one lunch you won't want to miss."

Vessie followed like a good girl and thanked God for sending her a friend who was forcing her to take a break from her love-hate relationship with work. Even though Lou made her crazy, he did keep his promise—she was learning her craft. In fact, she was more creative than ever. She wasn't writing songs, but she was writing lyrics and melodies that hooked an audience, sold products, and generated smiles. And she loved being in the "creative zone" where time slipped away and so did Lou.

"Okay Rem, what's going on? What's with the suit and the intrigue?" she asked.

The elevator doors opened and they got in.

"You'll see," he said. "Now don't ask again. It's a surprise."

Vessie looked at Remy as if seeing him for the first time that day—his boyish good looks, handsomely GQ in a silk Yves St. Laurent suit. She had only seen him in cords or jeans and a sweatshirt. "Boy, you look handsome," she said. He smiled as the doors opened and they got out past six soggy people who were dripping like something just broke.

Outside the wind was blowing umbrellas inside out causing them to look like television antennae. People kept bumping into each other trying to avoid gutters full of water that stretched halfway to the middle of the street. Taxis hugged each other as ambulances, police cars and construction vehicles ground to a halt. Manhattan had become an obstacle course befitting a marine drill that Vessie failed when a truck splashed her from head to foot.

117

The Russian Tea Room was filled with every kind of chatter but Russian. Half of the people waiting to be seated were out-of-towners hoping to catch a glimpse of notables sucking on vodka, caviar, and borscht.

"I'm not dressed for this," Vessie snarled, "and look at me, I'm soaked."

Remy led her past a velvet roped stanchion to a table at the far corner of the room where a balding man of fifty waved to them. He too was wearing a three piece suit. Vessie's running shoes squished as she walked, her blue jeans were striped with water, and her dirt-spotted sweatshirt read: MUSIC SLAVE. She wanted desperately to dive behind a fern.

"Who's our mystery guest, you rat?"

"James Slater," said James Slater extending a thick hand. "I've been looking forward to meeting you, Vessie."

James Slater of James Slater Music? Jesus Holy Christ. He's Lou's biggest competitor! I've seen Lou throw darts at every letter of his name.

A waiter approached and asked for drink orders. Slater assumed the role of host. "Bring us a pot of caviar with our drinks. Vessie, what'll you have?"

"Orange juice straight up."

"Cute." He turned to her colleague. "Remy?"

Remy chose to sip white wine, and Slater ordered two double martinis for himself.

"Might as well get it out of the way." He looked straight into Vessie's eyes. "I want you to come work for me."

"Om-mani-padme-hum, om-mani-padme-hum." Vessie and her inner child looked like they were welded together. The inside of the Thunderbird was covered with frost, and in the darkness of her icy prison she thought about the note she had written three hours earlier:

*To whoever finds this—
forget the "shoulds" and live life NOW!*

Damn it! I hate this. My hands are numb. My feet are numb. I can't move my mouth. Oh God, I DON'T WANT TO DIE!!! Guruji, Guruji, please help me. Please come to me. Please come to me nowwwwww!!!!!.

118

"Gita."

His legs were folded in a full lotus in the bucket seat beside her.

"Do not be afraid. Concentrate on what I tell you. This technique will raise your body temperature. Close your eyes and listen carefully." Vessie tried to speak but couldn't. "Yes, I'm really here, Gita. This is really happening. Now close your eyes. Bring the color orange to the cosmic consciousness center between the eyebrows. Feel its warmth radiate to every part of your body: to the top of your head, down your back, neck, shoulders, chest, down your arms, your torso, hips, legs, feet. Feel the heat grow more and more intense. Feel it saturate every cell of your body."

Orange, orange. Yes, yes, I see it. It's glowing brighter, brighter. She visualized it radiating out to every part of her body just like Master said. The longer she concentrated the warmer she felt. *Orange, Orange.* She could feel her toes beginning to thaw. Her fingers tingle. It was working. Orange was beautiful. Her inner child woke up, still snuggled in Vessie's coat.

"Vessie, what's going on? I'm too young to get a hot flash!"

Vessie opened her eyes. Guruji was gone. "Guruji!" she said, thrilled to find that her mouth was working. "Thank you, Master. Thank you!"

Just then she heard a siren coming closer. *Oh my God, I'm going to be saved.* But the siren grew faint and Vessie clung, once again, to her mantra.

She was shocked at James Slater's offer. "But I already have a job."

"Contracts are made to be broken. Remy told me your salary is commensurate with Lou's receptionist's."

Vessie searched Remy's eyes. *How could you?*

"The truth is the truth, Ves."

Slater drained his drink. "I'll start you at eighty grand a year plus bonuses and fringe benefits, and we'll raise you from there."

Vessie ordered her first martini and Remy fell off his chair.

Oh my god, oh my god, oh my god. I can move to the Upper East Side. I can buy a car and another t-shirt. I can see Broadway shows... go to concerts...buy better food for the cockroaches. But wait. I have to give Lou a chance to meet Slater's offer. I have to. It's only fair.

"Eighty thousand dollars, are you crazy?" Lou said. "And bonuses and fringe benefits? Slater's meshuga!"

"And a bigger office," Vessie told him, "... a telephone that reaches into the real world and a promotion for Remy—ten thousand more a year and a Producer title."

Lou waited a whole week before getting back to her and agreed to everything but the telephone. He had to save face somehow.

> "Friend, you are my friend
> There is no end to all our caring."

Vessie sang Remy a new song she was working on and stopped. "That's it. That's all I've got so far. It's about us, ya know." She smiled into Remy's eyes and, in that moment, he knew he had to tell her.

"Ves... I know I can tell you anything, so I'll just say it instead of beating around the bush because beating around the bush is one thing that drives me crazy when somebody else does it and God knows I try to keep far away from people like that and I know that you would rather I just come straight out and say what I have to say instead of building up to it or defending myself in any way because you're always honest with me and I think that's what makes our friendship so special so instead of doing that I won't waste any time I'll simply tell you right now that what I'm about to say is something that I don't need to hesitate for one second saying, Vessie... I'm gay."

Vessie embraced her best friend closely. "Thank God!"

"You knew?"

"Uh-huh."

"Why didn't you say something?"

"It had to come from you, darlin'."

"God Ves, I've been in the closet so long my skin is dusty."

"Well shake it off... AND that excuse about Kat the ex-girlfriend."

"She *was* my girlfriend... my girl... *friend.*"

Vessie was relieved. *That* was the sadness she felt coming from Remy—αeep dark desperate isolation. Finally, he felt secure enough to be straight about not being straight; but, what about *her* feelings? The loneliness *she* kept hidden? The secret longing that made her cry too easily at sentimental movies and love songs? The indescribable sadness she pushed under hours and hours of too much work? Yes, it was wonderful having a close platonic friendship with Remy; but, she was a vital young woman in need of intimate love.

"Come on, we've got some celebrating to do."

She led him out the door, past Lou who was surprised to see them leave, down the elevator and around the corner to Shanty's Bar & Grille.

"A toast," Vessie said, lifting her orange juice high, "to love, laughter, and being whatever and whoever we are at all times, no matter what."

TWENTY-FIVE

Where Is Love?

Vessie always remembered the events that took place on August 9, 1974. She moved to the Upper East Side and Richard Nixon moved out of the White House.

Her new neighborhood reeked of money. Instead of pizza slices and submarine sandwiches, the take-out counters offered sole stuffed with crab meat, pork almandine, and imported truffles. Instead of alley cats and rummies, the sidewalks sported Dobermans and chauffeurs.

Vessie's new one bedroom apartment was on the twelfth floor of a beautiful art deco building. With wall-to-wall carpeting, floor-to-ceiling windows, a jungle of green hanging plants, a baby grand in the bay window and a doorman named Rodney who said, "Good morning Miss VanCortland," and "Good evening Miss VanCortland," just like the parrot she always wished she'd had—Vessie was a much happier unhappy camper.

Her new used four-seater Thunderbird was her salvation—her means of spontaneous escape from the congestion of the city. She loved taking long drives on warm summer Sundays out along the Hudson where the skyline was visible above two-story houses and lush green yards. She could breathe again and dream and watch birds fly higher than a window ledge. She would drive and drive until she found lakes and streams and woods. What joy! What happiness, sitting on a tree trunk, barefoot, feeling the cool earth beneath her hot feet, hearing birds sing different unique melodies and rhythms, watching them dive and swim, feeling the sun nip at her cheeks, a gentle breeze kiss her unkissed skin. She felt whole again. Here, her mantra came to her like a long lost lover, bringing her home, bringing her home, bringing her home.

Vessie would stay until her mind was clear of the city, Lou, and deadlines. She'd stay until she squeezed the last bit of sunshine from the sky. Until it glowed orange behind streaks of grey night. Until she could see the man again—with deep hazel eyes and sunbleached hair running beside a turquoise sea. Until she could face returning to her twelfth story apartment where she would be alone again. Year after year. Jingle after jingle. Outing after outing.

Seven years passed.

The wintry December sky was bright, the air brisk, and Vessie—toasty warm inside her Thunderbird classic. Enroute back to the city, driving past stately homes set away from the road on sumptuous wooded acreage, Vessie imagined being one of the wives cooking a meal, something out of "Better Homes and Gardens," a recipe to surprise her husband with. She could see him watch her as she entered their bright inviting kitchen and tell the maid not to bother, that she'd do it all that night. And oh! how he'd drool over her passionate Pastitsu, her beguiling Blanquette de Veau, and her sultry Soufflé Glace Au Grand Marnier. Yes, Vessie was having marital fantasies, and it surprised her as much as it did Sheila Hurt, the psychiatrist who lived down the hall.

"You're under a lot of pressure, Vessie," Sheila said after Vessie told her she was under a lot of pressure. "You're thinking of alternative lifestyles," she said after Vessie told her she was thinking of alternative lifestyles.

The short gravel-throated overly made-up woman continued her parroting until Vessie finally told her: "You know Sheila... I think being a psychiatrist means never having to say anything *original*."

Sheila snapped back: "It's important that you know I'm hearing what you're saying. That's why I repeat it."

"But I *know* you can hear what I'm saying, you're sitting two feet away from me. Wait, I'll go into the bedroom. You stay here and I'll keep talking. Then, *maybe*, there'll be some reason for me to wonder whether or not you can hear me!"

Vessie knew she was being hard on Sheila, but she couldn't help herself. "I'm sorry. I guess I'm just tired... and frustrated."

"You're tired and frustrated."

"YES, I'M FRUSTRATED! I go to work, I come home from work, sometimes I go to my health club or for a drink with Remy or I chat with you. The only time I feel any real happiness is when I escape to the country. I haven't been able to meditate in my apartment for months—my mind's always too wound up."

I won't cry. I won't cry. I won't cry. Vessie's eyes filled with tears. "It's been such a long time since I finished writing a song, a real *song.* I'm not even sure I *can* anymore. *That* depresses me more than anything."

"It depresses you."

"And *men.* I'd love to meet a great guy. But the only guys I meet are at work." So they're either musicians or the ad-pack. And so far? They're as deep as a pizza."

"Deep as a pizza."

"Either they feel threatened by my independence or they get upset when they find out the face also has a *mind."* Vessie grabbed a tissue and wiped her eyes. "It's all short term, Sheila—two weeks, two months. *That's* not a relationship—that's one long *orgasm."*

Sheila nodded.

"You know John Morgenstern, the guy who orchestrated that new Pepsi spot? He tells me to dress for dinner then shows up at my apartment and informs me that *I'm* the main course. And Chad Goodrich, the saxophonist? His idea of fun is doing cocaine and crying 'til four in the morning because John Coltrane is dead. My *boss* feeds me enough work for ten people and I don't have time to travel in new circles. My chances of meeting Mister Right? He'd probably be married or gay or stuck on an ex-lover. I'm going to be thirty, Shiela—and I'm ALONE. Fucking a-*LONE!* The sexiest thing I've done all year is lick *stamps.* I'm not frustrated. I'm *FRUSTRATED!!!"*

"So, you're feeling frustrated."

Sheila's four-foot-ten round body paced the floor on black spiked heels. She squinted her teeny rat-shaped eyes silently composing her closing.

"What *you* want," she said, "is a meaningful relationship with a single man who isn't in the music business, who has a great deal of self esteem, is health conscious, loves nature, isn't a jazz fanatic, enjoys the company of an intelligent woman, and who won't treat you like a sexual object but loves sex. Sounds like you want a middle class doctor from Scarsdale."

"A doctor?"

Sheila's words stayed with Vessie until one lonely Sunday when she found herself writing:

> Sometimes I know where I am going going
> sometimes I know where I'm going
> Sometimes I see the flower growing growing
> sometimes I can see the flower
> Sometimes I like the part I'm playing
> I like the things I'm saying, sometimes sometimes
>
> Right now I feel I'm getting closer to the place I've
> longed to be with him
> And right now, the fire's glow is warm
> and we're pretending hiding from a storm
> And right now, I know where I am going
> and *he* is where I'm going, growing, going
> I am going home.

Right now, the only place Vessie was going was *no*where. She raised her mittened fist to the sky... *correction*... to the roof of her frozen car and shouted: "As God is my witness, if I ever get out of this friggin' ice cave alive, I will *never* work for Lou Fields again!"

Her inner child rolled her eyes. "C'mon Scarlett, you can do better than that."

"I *wasn't* finished." Vessie raised her fist higher. "I'll compose music from my *soul*... I won't be afraid to love again... and I will live *authentically*."

She closed her eyes. *Authentically... authentically.*

"John Lennon lived authentically," a trembling man told the crowd. It was midnight, December 8, 1980. Hundreds of fans gathered in Central Park across the street from the Dakota Apartments where John Lennon was slain getting out of a limousine earlier that night. The cold wintry air couldn't keep them away. Nothing could. They prayed for the Beatle they knew intimately through songs he wrote that made them think, feel, and dream—who walked the talk, lived his truth, and spoke of peace.

Imagine there's no heaven. It's easy if you try. No hell below us. Above us only sky. Imagine all the people living for today...

10:50 p.m. As Vessie blew out the candles on her thirtieth birthday cake and made a silent wish—John was shot four times in the back by a young man who wished to be remembered.

Remy and Vessie held onto each other as she laid thirty long stemmed roses he had given her on the grass beside photos of John and Yoko—John, Paul, George, and Ringo.

From candles on a cake to a candle in her hand, Vessie and Remy stood with the other mourners as the candlelight vigil grew into the night.

Night night. Where the hell am I? Vessie opened her eyes. *"Noooooooooooo,"* she cried. Sirens wailed in the distance. They grew louder and louder. She listened savagely. *Oh my god, they're coming this way!* They screamed loud like freshly skinned cats. Then stone cold silence. *What's happened? Are they out there? Am I imagining this? Dreaming this? What the hell is going on?*

She couldn't bear it any longer. Vessie flew out of her body high above the car through the pelting snow. She saw an ambulance, squad cars, and rescue workers grabbing shovels and pics and hacking away at the mound of ice and snow that she was buried under. She saw Remy agitatedly talking to police and pointing to her car and talking and pointing and pointing and talking. Then *ZAP!* Vessie was back inside her car, unconscious.

TWENTY-SIX

Vessie & the Doctor

St. Agnes Hospital was miles from Manhattan but had an available bed, so that's where Vessie was taken. In the ambulance, covered with blankets and pity, she heard everything the paramedics said but was unable to respond.

"No signs of frostbite. Amazing."

"Respiration, extraordinarily low, but body temperature's normal."

"That car was frozen inside and out. I don't get it."

The main highways had been cleared enough for emergency vehicles to crawl on, but the blizzard held its own, continuing to create the worst plugged arteries the city had known. Hundreds of people filled hospitals due to accidents and exposure to the fierce sub-zero temperatures and eighty-mile-an-hour winds.

The ambulance continued to drive north to White Plains in Westchester County. Vessie remembered none of this, but while being gurneyed to a hospital bed unable to move or open her eyes, she saw flashes of light and felt grateful for being alive.

During the night she woke up horrified by images of her thirty-six-hour incarceration. Her body was warm, but she felt cold. The hospital was safe, but she felt danger. Vessie had just lived her worst nightmare—being *caged.* Like the closet she was locked in when she was a baby. Like the birds who begged her to set them free. Like the lover who locked the door and threw the key away. She felt sick. Her gut wrenched. She jumped down from the hospital bed and ran to the bathroom. She threw up again and again. Weakened and frightened she climbed back into bed and wept.

A night nurse offered her a sedative. Vessie rolled onto her side. *This is private. Personal. Please go away.* She needed to be comforted. To be taken care of. Not with a drug. With love.

She closed her eyes and saw him again—his deep hazel eyes smiling at her.

Come on, he said. *Come with me.* He turned and ran along the shoreline. A flamingo flew overhead. Sun glistened on a calm turquoise sea. She looked back and he was gone. *Where are you? Who are you?*

The morning came and with it —

"I'm Doctor Reed. How are you feeling?" His voice was velvet and Vessie wanted to paint on it.

"Uh... a little shaky. I was afraid when I woke up, you know... frost bite, gangrene. It's amazing, isn't it, that I'm all right?"

His eyes were chocolate—his hair, black silk that brushed his lashes.

"Yes, it's amazing," he said, "a miracle according to the police. They figured you must have been stuck for thirty hours or more. You don't have any secrets you'd like to share about how you survived, do you? Any supernormal abilities or techniques?"

Sheila's words echoed in her head. *What you need is a doctor.* Vessie laughed to herself. *This is one hell of a way to meet one.*

"Private joke?" he said.

"Very."

"I'd still like to know how you managed."

He was charming, warm. Vessie wasn't about to blow this one. She had learned that telling too much too soon could cause even the most intelligent man to run. She noticed that Doctor Reed wasn't wearing a wedding band and just in case he wasn't sleeping with an intern, a Swedish foot masseuse, or his dog, she was going to take her best shot at getting closer to him than on the other side of a thermometer.

"My back aches," she said, diverting his question. She sat up, tossed her long auburn hair over her shoulders and let Doctor Reed open the back of her hospital gown.

"Take a deep breath," he said, ignoring his stethoscope, penetrating his hands into Vessie's back.

Oh god that feels good, she thought. A gentle touch had been long in coming.

"Your muscles are extremely tight," he said. *My god her skin is soft.*

"And sore," she cooed.

"A nice hot bath would do you good." *She's curved like a marble whore.*

Is he flirting with me? "With incense and music," she said.

Is she flirting with me? God, I hope she's easy. His hands moved lower and stopped just above her buttocks.

He IS flirting with me. Vessie lay back against her pillow, smiled her most seductive smile and closed her eyes. When she opened them—he was gone.

"Ms. VanCortland," he said, re-entering in a huff. "Please rest up and never be a patient of mine again." Vessie's mouth flew open like a broken glove compartment. "Then I'll be able to invite you to dinner." He was gone.

What? Yesssssssss.

Later that morning, Remy brought love and flowers, and Lou brought *angst.* Remy held her hand and thanked God she was alive. Lou told her she ruined the Catflakes session and owed him an award-winning jingle. He was a man possessed. *She'll bounce back,* he thought, *but what about my business?*

"Lou, I quit."

"What? What do you mean, you quit?"

"I've had it. I want to write songs. Not jingles."

"Did you hit your head, too? Your ears not working? I need you to do this *now*!"

"Forget it, Lou. I'm *tired.*"

"No, *I'm* tired, and you're still on *my* payroll. So forget it! I don't accept your resignation! Besides, we have a contract. You're mine 'til the end of next year."

The nurse interceded and ushered Lou to the door. "I think our patient needs to rest now."

"Two days, Vessie, that's all you get!"

The next afternoon Vessie was back at home. The thirty-six-hour incarceration in her frozen car had a lasting effect. Mortality had paid too close a call. Her independent, self-reliant nature had shifted. She didn't want to be alone anymore. Didn't want to rely on her self for everything. She felt a need to be taken care of, protected. And like most girls—Vessie wanted to have fun.

"Have dinner with me tomorrow night?" Doctor Reed kept his promise.

"This is what you had in mind, doctor, when you suggested a bath during my examination?" *I love this I love this.* Vessie wiped bubbles across Richard Reed's chest.

She'll look so hot in my Mercedes.

It was four hours from the time he had dropped an escargot in his wine glass and kissed away Vessie's laughter. Four hours from the time he knew that leaving a table full of food at Chez Pascal's wouldn't make him feel guilty about the starving children in Africa. He was hungry for this auburn haired beauty with the smile of a saint.

Screw the Visa charges!

There was room enough for a party in Richard's black ceramic Jacuzzi—room for experiments which neither of them hesitated to initiate. Vessie had abstained from sex for a year but no rust was showing, no second thoughts or strained reactions. Her long legs and his strong muscular thighs were knit one pearl one—a human bridge under bubbled waters.

She sank down into the swirling water. He met her there exploring, exploring.

Lips touched, chest to breasts. Up for air. Up for more. Rhythms in sync. Sighs. Moans. Calls for time out. She was a girl with spirit and imagination. He was a guy with a house in the country and one tooth brush—he had potential. He wasn't some goof with a trombone who cried with cats 'til the birds went tweet, or a joker who bought the myth that he was the second coming of Charlie Parker. Richard Reed cared about people. He was good, decent, sweet and charming and Vessie was finally going to give herself a chance to be with Mr. Right.

The last candle burned down to a stump as they dripped their way into the bedroom. They were playing an open hand and the only thing they closed was the light.

TWENTY-SEVEN

'Til Death?

You're mine and we belong together
Yes, we belong together for eternity
You're mine, your lips belong to me
Yes, they belong to only me for eternity

Vessie loved slow dancing with Richard to oldies like Ritchie Valens' recording of, "We Belong Together," barefoot, breathing each other in, feeling *close, closer, never close enough.* Sweet smelling wood burned and crackled as they moved with eyes closed on the living room rug.

> You're mine-mine, baby and you'll always be
> I swear by everything I own
> You'll always, always be mine

Hips to hips, slowly slowly, they were one shadow, one heart. "I love you, *baby*," Richard said.

> You're mine and we belong together
> Yes, we belong together for eternity

It was Sunday. Richard was in Scarsdale playing golf. Vessie was in her apartment talking long distance to Mrs. Smith. "He loves you, Vessella? Mazeltov!" Vessie smiled. Remy sat on the chinz sofa watching his best friend share the news with her surrogate mom. "Did she say, Mazeltov?" he whispered. Vessie laughed. "She *did*." "I did *what*, Vessella?" said Mrs.

Smith. Vessie laughed again. Remy saw Vessie's green eyes glowing—a playful swish of her hair. *I've never seen you this happy,* he thought. *I'll miss you.*

And he did.

Weeks passed. One jingle after another seemed to write itself. As soon as the deed was done, Vessie was gone. Remy didn't see her. Lou didn't see her. Sheila didn't see her. She'd meet Richard for dinner, a play, a roll in the hay. He was her life-raft, her protector. He made life yellow.

Flowers bloomed beneath snow banks. Squirrels and blue jays winked at Vessie and asked, "How's your guy?" Zip-i-dee-doo-da was whistled and hummed by every junky and rip-off artist in Manhattan. Vessie's new experience of life was complete illusion and sparkling clean, like her latest lyric:

> No more mess on your dress
> All you need is WIPE YOUR WORRY
> Spray it on, spots are gone
> So go in, be in a hurry
> With WIPE YOUR WORRY

Even Lou seemed transformed in her mind: a bull terrier with wings, the devil in clown shoes. Geos shmeos, he'd get what she'd write and do with it what he might.

As for Richard—he no longer checked beneath the hospital gowns of single female patients for anything other than what was required. Vessie filled his aching moments, and in return he wooed her. Candle light dinners—kisses in corners—phone calls at work—flowers with sweet notes—hand-holding at movies, plays. His look said *your mine* at the end of the day.

It was pure folly. Vessie knew it and chose to be in denial about anything that could change it. When her inner child shouted: *warning, warning*—Vessie told her: *Go play. I love you, but for now, stay away.*

She wanted to believe it was cute when Richard would re-fold his used napkin after each meal, iron it flat with his hands and reposition it beside his plate. Or when he'd go through his house after the cleaning lady had finished and gone, and put each magazine back within a hair of its previous angle. Or pull the bedspreads tighter, straighter, until not a hint of a wrinkle could be found. Or re-straighten the clothes in his indexed closet—and dust his crown.

Of course Vessie would have to be perfect, too—always perfect. She knew human nature enough to know this was true, but didn't want to think about it, just kept wearing those glasses with the rose-colored hue.

"Come here, baby," he said, reaching out his hand. He wanted her there. Right *there* beside him where he could watch his two favorite things—Vessie and golf. A tournament was on the huge panoramic screen in front of his king size bed. A bachelor's bed. A bed that knew many women. He lay back against the black ebony headboard. Vessie placed a tray with fruit, nuts, and juices on its edge. She lay beside him. He stroked her hair—a cat in his lair.

It all rhymed. Everything in her mind. At *first.*

Richard was a romantic hedonist. He loved good food, good wine, good music, good cars, good clothes and good sex. Having a beautiful woman on his arm was part of it. An important part. Although he was a successful Internist and a physically attractive man, Richard still saw himself as the fat kid and fatter teenager from the Bronx who had many complexes and few friends. Having Vessie in his life doubled his worth. She was the payoff for those long hard years of reinventing himself as a valued member of the community. A more sophisticated community.

"Damn! I need that medical journal." Richard looked at the chintz sofa in Vessie's living room. *What the hell am I doing here? I should be home where my library is. Where my clothes are. I'm tired of commuting back and forth—running to the hospital nervous and un-rested. This has got to stop.*

"What Richard? Did you say something?" Vessie walked in, stretching into an over-size sweater.

"We've got to talk."

"Oops. This looks serious. What is it? What's wrong?"

"Nothing. Let's get married."

"Married?" Vessie wasn't prepared for the question, although she had thought about marriage. Toyed with it like a cat with a ball of yarn. Held

134

it close when she felt vulnerable. Envisioned herself as Mrs. Dr. Richard Reed of Scarsdale. She would kiss the life of jingle writer goodbye. Learn to play golf and fly south when her skin paled. And the bonuses! She would have Richard to discover every night. Richard to tease and satisfy. And when it came time to share her innermost wishes and dreams, Richard would be there. Richard would know about her secret desire to fly. Richard would encourage her to compose great songs. Richard would... *Wait a minute. Richard? Richard doesn't like when I close a door to meditate or work on a song. He'd freak out if he saw me levitate. The only thing he likes about yoga is that the physical exercises keep my body toned. But that'll change. He'll get used to it. Won't he?*

"Well, whaddya say, Ves?" Richard waved his index finger across her nipple. Vessie kissed him, trying to avoid an answer. "You're not sure are you?" He pulled away. "I thought we had something special. I thought you'd be thrilled."

"I am. I... it's just that... things are great the way they are."

"Not for me!"

Richard told Vessie that he was tired of the Scarsdale-to-Manhattan-to-Scarsdale routine and wanted *his* home with her *in* it. He was ready for marriage *now*, and if she didn't want to go the whole nine yards he was out of the game.

Vessie didn't want to be alone again. Didn't want to go back to a life of platonic relationships and flannel pajamas to keep her warm at night. She wanted to be loved. Wanted an intimate relationship that would last. A life with a good man who loved her. A chance to relax. To compose sweet music. Take part in the community. Could Richard give her that?

Vessie wanted to see what she wanted to see, so she put on a blindfold and said: *yes.*

The wedding took place at the Long Island home of Richard's mother's sister, Ricky Thornhill. It was the largest of the venues offered and the showiest. Vessie preferred an intimate setting. Richard vied for opulent. From a helicopter it looked like a hotel. From the circular drive—Tara.

It was June and the unseasonably warm weather was pushing eighty. Several women wore velvet and were sweating. Others wore organza and were grinning.

Vessie sat in front of an ornate mirror in the designated Bridal Room on the second floor of the twenty-two bedroom home. Her long white satin gown hung from the top of a door frame along with an endlessly long flowing veil. A white lace merry-widow hugged her torso pushing up her boobies and cinching in her already tiny waist. She wore French satin panties, sheer white stockings, and three inch hand embroidered rosebud brocade heels. Her long hair was neatly coiffed on top of her head in a feminine Gibson *do*. She was about to put lipstick on when Richard opened the door. Standing beside him was Mrs. Smith wearing her favorite yellow daisy print chiffon dress, all sixteen yards of it, looking at least twenty minutes younger.

"Vessella!" she cried.

They ran to each other and embraced. *I've missed you. I've missed you. Oh god, how I've missed you.* Their love was so thick that Richard suddenly felt out of place. "I'll leave you two girls alone."

"No, please don't run, Ritchie," Mrs. Smith said. "I have a question for you." She moved closer and looked him straight in the eye. "When are you going to retire my Vessella so she doesn't have to work for that shmeggegie anymore?"

Richard smiled. "As soon as her contact's up she'll be free to cook my meals." He gave Vessie a hug. "See you soon, gorgeous!" He closed the door behind him.

"He was joking, Vessella?"

Vessie heard her inner child's muffled voice. "He *better* be," Vessie said.

They walked to the window with arms around each other and looked down at the gathering below. Among white ribboned tables and lush white bouquets, wedding guests munched on savory hors d'oeuvres.

Remy looked stunningly handsome in a grey pin-striped suit and silver and white striped tie. He was drinking champagne with Jacques Bisset, the much talked about Soho installation artist who spun his heart out of control the night of the blizzard.

Lou was on a mission to find Vessie with an unfinished jingle in hand, rushing past Sheila Hurt who was telling a six foot hunk that as a female psychiatrist she could help him overcome his sexual anxieties any time around Happy Hour.

The entire Kleig family was sampling the fare: Smoodgie, Edward, and baby Everlyn-Gene who was no longer a baby, but almost a teen.

There were ties and tuxedos, high heels and pastel laces worn by cousins, patients, colleagues, and friends of friends of Richard's, mostly. Richard shook hands and received pats on the back. His teeth were white and his caps were whiter. He looked happy and clumsy spilling his champagne, bumping into a roving waiter, tripping his mother who fell into Ricky who dropped her cigarette in the caviar bowl.

"So, Vessella, you're going to be Sadie, Sadie married lady."

Vessie forced a smile, saying a silent prayer: *Jesus, I hope I can pull this off.*

Mrs. Smith gave her a kiss and left the room.

Remy poked his head in.

"Something old, something new, something borrowed and something *blue*," he said holding out something that looked *green*. "It was my mother's."

Vessie wasn't sure what she was looking at. It didn't matter. She was thrilled to see her kindred friend and opened her arms for a hug. "Oh, Remy…" *No, Vessie,* she told herself. *Be happy. Everything's good. You're about to be a bride.* She looked at Remy's offering.

"Put it on," he said.

"Underpants?"

"She only wore them *once.*"

The panties were as limp as old lettuce and about the same color. Vessie didn't know whether to laugh or cry. *Remy's so thoughtful… so sweet and caring…but yuck!*

"They were blue the day she got married."

Remy's face registered loss. His best friend would soon be part of another world. She would rhyme grocery lists and count sixty-second eggs instead of jingles. She would ride in on the Metro North and they would drink martinis and pretend they still had much in common. His hair would turn grey as hers got blonder. He would come further out of the closet as she would go in to rearrange golf togs.

He held her hands firmly. "Promise me… if Richard ever hits you or withholds your spending money… if he cheats on you or dents your car, tell me and I'll have his golf clubs broken." He turned away, forcing back tears, and turned back. "Always the bridesmaid, never the bride." Remy feigned a smile, blew a kiss and left the room.

Vessie put on Remy's mother's green underpants over her white satin panties.

Smoodgie came in, her face all puffy and pink. "Oh, Vesssssiiiieeeeee," she cried, throwing her arms around her younger sister.

Vessie was shocked. She was being clung to for support by the most self-sufficient person she knew. "What is it? What's wrong?"

Smoodgie sobbed, unable to speak.

Vessie was sure she knew what the problem was. Smoodgie was feeling a real separation from her. She was feeling older, about to witness her little sister's wedding. She must also be sad because their mama and daddy couldn't be there. Even a bit jealous because Richard was such a hunk and Edward had grown a pot belly and taken to smoking cigars.

"It's all right," Vessie whispered. "It's all right."

Smoodgie broke away, turning into an instant ice machine. "What the hell would *you* know? You were never pregnant. You never had to carry a squirming kicking kid inside your belly. You never had your tits sag and your stomach lined like a freeway. You're going to be an aunt again, and according to my husband the doctor, we're having *twins!"*

"That's great! You'll be the youngest grandmother in Symington."

"*Grand*mother? You… you… you *bitch!*" Smoodgie raised her hand as if to strike, then suddenly realized the absurdity of her action and stopped. "Good Lord! It's those damn hormones again. Vessie, I'm sorry!" She looked down and noticed Remy's mother's underpants. They were four sizes too big and uglier than hell. "What the *hell* are those?" They laughed—relieved to laugh. Smoodgie teased, and Vessie accepted as they turned their anxieties to love.

The wedding march began.

Vessie looked radiant, the epitome of the beautiful bride. Her long auburn hair, pulled up in a Gibson, her veil trailing yards behind her white flowing gown. Edward, walking beside her, looked handsome with a full-grown moustache, in a three piece tuxedo and cumber bun sash. But something was strange—the sound of the music. Synthesized sound effects that shouldn't be there, like someone peeing, lightning striking, horses destroying a corral. It wasn't the cellist Vessie had hired who called in sick with the flu. It was a keyboard player arranged at the last minute—an improvised wedding present from Lou.

Vessie and Edward walked down a path of white rose petals. Everlyn-Gene, now a smaller spitting image of Smoodgie—dark eyes, dark hair, turned-up nose—led the procession in a white organza dress, tossing the petals onto the manicured green grassy path. They walked beneath a floral-covered archway to a pulpit-on-the-green. A canopy dotted with pink throated Maui orchids completed the scene. Each time Vessie heard one of the bizarre musical embellishments she shook her head and mentally hammered a nail in Lou's coffin. *Great wedding gift, Lou.* But Vessie's dismay didn't consume her. She carried herself with serenity and grace—walking elegantly into her future.

Mrs. Smith beamed with pride. She nudged guests on either side of her and explained that Vessie was her daughter, *sort* of.

Richard fell in love all over again as he greeted his wife-to-be before God, the universe, and his tailor. His mother blew her nose causing dogs to bark, and the priest began the service. All the normal things were said, vows and rings exchanged, the kiss—and then the festivities began.

It was lush, lavish, and expensive. Fortunately for Vessie, it was a wedding gift from Richard's aunt Ricky. A ten piece band played rock and roll gems and the music grew raucous and wild. Guests in all sizes and colors got into the beat and boogied as Richard and Vessie, oblivious to them all, slow danced in an endless kiss.

> You're mine and we belong together
> Yes, we belong together for eternity
> You're mine, your lips belong to me
> Yes, they belong to only me for eternity

TWENTY-EIGHT

Unraveling the Knot

It was all a blur, meeting Richard, falling for Richard, and now being married to him. Flashes of the wedding: Remy's mother's underpants, Smoodgie's hormonal outburst, and her darling Mrs. Smith kept Vessie's lips on automatic smile as the limousine pulled into the driveway of Richard's Scarsdale home.

"It's all ours," he said, flashing a seductive grin. "I told the maid we wouldn't be needing her."

It was the happiest weekend Vessie had known. They slept in, fed each other, listened to music. Richard even canceled his regular Sunday tee time. It couldn't have been more romantic. They spent five whole days together. Then—back to work.

Lou didn't like Vessie being married. He was used to controlling her time to his advantage. He could always count on her to work late at the office—grab a taxi home. Now? Now she was a *commuter*. Now she was controlled by train schedules not him. His solution: give her more work.

Vessie's new life forced her to wake up 3 ½ hours earlier to make it to the office by 9:00. Richard liked to make love in the morning: 30 minutes. He liked Vessie to prepare the breakfast each day—french toast or croissant, eggs, bacon, freshly ground perked coffee, freshly squeezed juice: 30 minutes. Richard wanted Vessie to eat at the breakfast table and be cordial: 20. Vessie watched Richard re-fold his used napkin, crease it and iron it flat: 3. Richard insisted that Vessie leave the kitchen spotless: 15. Shower: 10. Make-up: 10. Hair: 20. Drive to the station: 15. Wait for the train: 10. Commute to Manhattan: 30. Walk to the office: 10.

Richard did jobs he knew he did best: make the bed, straighten the magazines, pens, pencils, cushions, re-fold the tea towels, bathroom towels; straighten the sky, the moon, the air. *Perfect! Perfect! Perfect!*

One morning as Richard was leaving for work he shouted: "I'll be home at six… and Vessie… make something special for dinner, okay?" He threw her a kiss that she flushed down the toilet.

Vessie was tired. This wasn't the marriage she had in mind. He wasn't the "supportive protector." *Does Richard really expect me to commute to Manhattan, work a full day, and then come home and prepare a gourmet meal for him?*

"Yes!" Richard told her, pushing a pizza away. "I expect you to be the woman I fell in love with, not a suburban house-frau. *You're slipping away. You're slipping away.* "I love you, baby." He grabbed her engulfing her mouth with his, pulling her close until they became a complete puzzle.

Vessie was disappointed but submissive. She was afraid that arguing would prove futile and determined to make their marriage work.

Then Richard fired the maid. *Oh no!*

Then Richard grew distant. *So cold.*

Then Richard snapped at Vessie. *How rude.*

Then Richard barked when she was too tired to make love. *The brute.*

They stopped going out. *Boring. Boring. Boring.*

Stopped talking. *Depressing. Sad.*

Then Richard told the truth.

And Vessie got mad.

He lost all his money on the stock market, had gambling debts, and was broke. That's why he fired the maid. That's why they stopped going out. That's why he snapped at her, was distant and always on edge. He didn't say, I'm sorry, he said: "I need you to extend your contract with Lou for at least two more years."

Two nights later, Vessie drove to the hospital to meet Richard at St. Agnes Emergency. The place was in chaos—too few staff for too many patients. Ambulances with opened back doors and swirling lights—paramedics rushing in bodies strapped onto stretchers.

She saw a young teenage boy in jeans and a blood-soaked t-shirt hunched over in a chair, shaking. She raced over to him. Asked him what happened. He didn't want to talk about it, just indicated a shoulder wound and said some doctor took a look at it and said he'd be back. "You're going to be all right," Vessie said gently. She silently stated her intention to heal the boy, held her hands just above his wound and closed her eyes. *His love goes through my hands to your wound...through my hands to your wound.*

Richard came in, looked for the boy, saw his wife doing some *weird little ritual* and went ballistic—especially when he opened the kid's shirt. The bleeding had stopped and the wound had closed up. He took Vessie aside and told her: "Don't you *ever* do that again. *I'm* the doctor. Remember that!"

TWENTY-NINE

Burn Out

One brisk October afternoon, Vessie returned to the office from a lunch break—her arms filled with groceries and vacuum cleaner bags—and fainted across Remy's desk. He thought she was pregnant and knowing how unhappy she was with Richard, grieved all the way to the hospital.

"Wake up!" her inner child shouted. "Wake up so I can tell you what a loser you are!" She stood between Vessie and the emergency room sink.

"Remy?" Vessie opened her eyes.

"I'm baaaa-aaaaackkkk!" shrieked her inner child.

"What the? Where am I? What happened?"

"*We're* in the emergency room. I had to punch your lights out to wake you up, and this time, Vessie dearest, you *better* wake up!"

"Oh my god, I *do* have bad karma."

"Hey, you're the one who's got her head in her navel."

"Help!"

"Nowwww you need help. I've been screaming at you for months: Remember who you are, Vessie. Don't lose yourself in Richard's craziness. But did you listen? Noooooooo! And now... now *matzo's* fatter than you are."

Remy came to Vessie's rescue with Doctor Melvin Grossman, a colleague of Richard's. Grossman, twenty years his senior, had a warm fatherly presence: a patch of white hair, moustache and soft feathery goatee—a round pouch that knew home made kneidlach and raisin kugel. He looked at this beautiful young creature and could see that she was coming undone. "You are suffering from acute anemia and fatigue," he said. "Richard must be aware of your condition."

Vessie felt obligated to cover for him. "Of course he is. I, uh, just hate taking all those vitamins he gives me."

Dr. Grossman knew something wasn't kosher. So did Vessie's smaller self.

"Loserrrrrrrrrrrr!"

"Pipe down!"

Grossman winced. Remy looked at thin air. *Who is Vessie shouting at?* "It's uh, you're going to be fine, Ves, fine," Remy told her.

Remy took Vessie's hand, not Richard. Doctor *Grossman* showed concern, not Dr. Reed. She knew that going home to rest was out of the question. *Richard's house isn't my house. It's my second place of work. It's where he lured me, lied to me, and asked me to extend my sentence when I'm just about to be free of Lou Fields. He wants me to pay the price for his mistakes. That's not love. That's deception and torture. My inner child is right. Richard's an ass and I'm a bigger ass for not having allowed myself to see it.* Vessie felt exhausted and resentful. She was determined to see Richard just one more time—in a court of law.

Vessie resumed residence at her Upper East Side apartment which Remy had suggested she sublet rather than give up when she married Richard. He didn't say, just in case you and Richard break up. He knew that Vessie would have thrown that idea to the wind. Instead he suggested that sometime in the near future she might want to use it as an office or a pied-à-terre. He even knew someone who needed a short-term rental. Fortunately, Vessie loved the idea. Now the apartment, empty for two weeks, was available, so Vessie could return home.

For eight days following her dramatic faint in Remy's office, Vessie remained propped up in her four-poster bed, licking her emotional wounds, repeating her mantra, and trying to figure out how the hell to move on with her life. The answer she kept receiving was: *You must look back before you can look forward.* She knew it was true and would be painful, but she closed her eyes needing to find out.

She saw herself, unhappily working for Lou shortly after starting at Fields & Friends but remaining silent, avoiding any discussion about boundaries, consistently giving into his demands. And when it became obvious that despite her efforts to change things for the better, Lou remained the same crazy-making boss he always was—she stayed there. *Fly in a jar. Fly in a jar.*

She saw Bobby sweep her off her feet and then cage her like her pet cockatiels, while she allowed it. Why? Why did she let him? Why did she wait until she learned of his betrayal before finally leaving that desperately unhappy situation? *Fly in a jar. Fly in a jar.*

And Richard. She saw herself jump into *that* relationship blindfolded. She may as well have been playing Pin the Tail on the Donkey. By not honoring herself, *Vessie* turned out to be the ass.

Rose incense wafted from Vessie's apartment to the outer hall as Remy stepped off the elevator armed with flowers, groceries, and home-baked bread. He was thrilled to have Vessie back in his life, to spend time with her, care for her, share thoughts and feelings with her. Jacques didn't mind. In fact, he welcomed it. It gave him more time to work on his new art installation. And besides, the happier Remy was, the happier he was.

"Bublichkie!" shouted Sheila Hurt marching toward him like a pit bull. With her lack of height, two thick sweaters, a long woolen scarf, double twisted belt, and boots that climbed to her neck, she looked like one of Santa's helpers in drag. Loud and demanding, Sheila was responsible for the second *s* in the word as*S*ertive.

"So what's with the incense? Vessie's becoming a *monk*?"

Remy kept walking.

"She's got to talk about it. She experienced a major trauma."

Sheila pulled a box of strawberries from the grocery bag. Remy tapped her on the wrist. "She needs help. I'm a psychiatrist." She took the cellophane off the berries and popped one in her mouth. Remy grabbed them and shoved them back in the bag. "I know all about her and Richard," she said.

"Down girl."

"Tell her I want to see her."

Remy backed into the apartment and kicked the door shut. He was not pleased. He had assumed the roles of Vessie's nursemaid and secretary, and Sheila was not on the A-list. She was on *some* list— Laundry or Garbage. He couldn't put his finger on why he disliked her. She was loud and abrasive but so were a lot of people he *liked*. And although it seemed a shallow reason, he thought her bright red lipstick had something to do with it, the way it surrounded her lips, ambushing the natural flesh line. And her hair cut at angles attempting the likeness of a China doll. She was a short person with a nose like a plum and a chin that was hiding and no amount of paint and paper was going to change it.

"And stop screening her calls," Sheila yelled through the door. "What are you, her mother?"

Remy growled as he put down the groceries. A pungent fragrance drew his attention to numerous flower arrangements resting on the baby grand in the bay window. *Now who's that one from?* He walked over to an enormous bouquet and read the card: *Lou again.* "Aaa aaa aaa aaachooooo!" He grabbed a tissue and called to Vessie. "Honey, I'm ho-ome!" No answer. "Ves? Vessie?"

Vessie was sitting on her bed in a full lotus. Her eyes were closed and her lips softly whispered: "Hi."

"Hi back." Remy entered the room and sat on the edge of the bed.

She slowly opened her eyes and took a few deep breaths as she came out of meditation. "I was just thinking about Lou."

"Lou, what a joke," he said. "The living room looks like a funeral parlor, thanks to him. If he sends you any more flowers we'll have to hire a corpse." Vessie laughed—her eyes alive again—her earthy sound, music to Remy's ear. *Yes,* he thought. *Laugh...laugh past the pain.*

Vessie's eyes withdrew back to the memory of Lou.

"Ten years ago," she said, "I'm working at The Hole in L.A. I'm playing one of my songs and this guy walks over to me and gives me a song and dance about how great my music is. Next thing I know, I'm in New York, writing jingles for him. *Jingles! Schlock. Crapolla.*"

"Well, at least they're *good* schlock."

"They're schlock?"

Remy high-tailed it over to Vessie's message machine wanting to avoid *that* can of worms. "Have you listened to your messages lately?"

"I'm the Schlockmeister of the Crapolla industry, Remy!" Vessie grabbed a tissue and dried her eyes. Remy hit the Play button.

"Hello Vessella. Remy told me you're much better and that you're flying to St. Lucia tomorrow. Just make sure you bring sun screen with you and shmise it all over. I love you, my precious."

Beep! Another message.

"Hi Sis. Just checking to see how you are and if you're still flying south tomorrow. Listen , you're gonna be fine, so don't go doing any of that booga-booga yoga stuff again, okay? I mean, there's no need to get all weird on us again."

Beep! A message from Lou:

"How's the best little jingle writer in the whole wide world. Okay... *universe*?"

"You're intergalactic now," Remy said.
"Did you get my flowers?"
Remy blew his nose. "Yeah, and a hayfever attack in October, thank you."
"Keep gettin' better, will 'ya? I need you here."
Then Lou sang to the tune of "Strangers in the Night":

"Geo's in the night, da-da-da-da-da,
Geo's in the night, da-da-da-da-da."

Beep!
"The Schlockmeister awards?" Vessie said. "They're seven friggin' months away!" The doorbell rang. "I'll get it."
"No, *I'll* get it." Vessie was determined and raced Remy to the front door. She opened it and Sheila Hurt stomped in.
"You look terrible."
"Thanks."
"You should be in bed. What's with the incense?"
"I should be in the sun. What's *wrong* with the incense?"
"What are you, becoming a monk or something?"

147

"You and my sister," Vessie said. "Look Sheila, I'm really busy right now. I'm flying to St. Lucia tomorrow."

"Tomorrow?"

"Tomorrow."

"You're flying to St. Lucia tomorrow?"

"Yes, Sheila, tomorrow."

"Tomorrow."

"To-mor-row!" Remy shouted. He put his arm firmly around Sheila's shoulder and forced her toward the door. "Now off you go. Vessie's got things to do. Stay in touch. By mail, dear. Registered. On second thought, carrier pigeon." He shoved her out the door and slammed it shut. "The bird will never make it."

"Vessie, don't go into denial over this!" she yelled.

Vessie took a deep breath. "I used to like her," she said. "Now I like her less than cancer."

The two best friends toasted orange juice and protein powder to Vessie's two glorious weeks away. Richard would still haunt her, but he would soon fade in the tropical sun. She would float on crystal clear water, feel warm sand between her toes, watch flamingos fly overhead and imagine she was one of them. She would luxuriate in the freedom of halter tops and shorts. She would be herself again, not a woman whose desire for happiness had gotten confused with fantasy and myth. And when she returned she would complete her time at Fields & Friends and move on. She would follow her heart, not another sales pitch from a man like Lou. *Just because a wolf shows up at your door doesn't mean you have to let him in.*

Remy asked Vessie if Lou knew she was going to St. Lucia.

"Only if you told him."

"Of course not. He still thinks you're coming back to work on Monday."

"Damn. I really should tell him."

"Sure, if you want him coming over here and chaining you to your piano."

"C'mon, he'll understand."

"Then why haven't you told him?"

"Okay. I'll call him right before I leave, when the limo driver gets here."

"Perfect. That way he won't have a chance to sway you. Better yet, phone him from the airport." Vessie didn't answer. "Vessie!"

"Alright!"

THIRTY

Suckered Again

Vessie awoke to the sound of wind rattling the fire escape outside her bedroom window. She smiled. She felt energetic, excited. She would be away from the city for two magical weeks. Her inner child jumped up and down on the bed. The healing process had begun.

She ran to the bathroom, turned on the shower, and stretched her way out of an oversize t-shirt. She looked pale in the mirror and mentally splashed herself with tan. She slinked into the spray. *Clear me now. Clear away all negative thoughts and feelings. Clear Richard from my mind and straight down the drain.*

The water obeyed licking her body, spitting out frustration and anger into the swirling wetness below. Vessie was not about to recoil from the experience of a failed marriage. She would enjoy life and be open to love with more awareness next time. But first, she would fill herself with the person she once knew—*Vessie.*

Ten minutes later, she heard her inner child calling. "Come on, let's go!"

Vessie laughed as she stepped out of the shower and grabbed a towel. "Hey, I'm excited too, but we've got plenty of time. Trust me, Little One. We will be on the island today." *Plenty of time,* she thought, remembering something she had promised herself she would do—begin writing a journal. It was there waiting for her. Right there in the living room. The white cloth covered book resting on the small oak table beside the chintz sofa—its empty pages waiting to be filled. And right now, it felt not only appropriate, but a necessary Right of Passage. Vessie towel-dried her hair, put on a terry robe, curled up on the sofa and wrote:

October 25, 1984.

*I remember something Guruji said: **Accept your lessons as blessings.**
I think I'm beginning to understand what he meant. I've learned that
marriage does not make a person whole. Wholeness is the unity of body,
mind, and spirit. It's an individual journey that can be shared with someone
but attained by one's self alone because, it's about self. It's what Guruji
taught, but which I'm only now beginning to understand. I've learned that
it's not selfish to set boundaries in order to protect my own well-being. To
let others take responsibility for their actions. To ALWAYS listen to my inner
child—my intuition—my higher self. I've learned never to allow traumatic
experiences to handicap me, make me afraid, and lead me to making poor
choices. And, I'm beginning to see what happiness means to me: being
myself at all times, doing what I love to do, and living authentically. Right
now it means getting the hell out of Manhattan and smelling the mangoes.*

At half past nine Vessie was ready to go: bags packed, light timers set
to confuse burglars, and plants soaking in the tub. She stood in front of a
full length mirror wearing sunglasses framed with pineapples, bananas and
flamingos, and held a floral print bathing suit against her traveling outfit.
The limousine was due to arrive any minute. It was time to phone Lou.

"Lou? It's Vessie. I, uh, I'm not ready to come back to work."

"What?"

"I'm going to the Caribbean."

"The Caribbean? Are you crazy? I need you here!"

"I'd be no good to you, Lou. I don't' feel myself yet." Vessie winked at
her inner child as she took off her sunglasses and put them in her bag.

"When are you leaving?"

"Any minute."

"Stay there. Don't move. I'll be right over." *Click.*

"Jesus! He's coming over!"

Manhattan being Manhattan, Lou knew he would get there faster on a
mule than in a taxi so he ran, pushing people out of his way for ten straight
blocks. Vessie's inner child broke into tears.

"You promised. You said we'd go!"

"Damn, where the hell is that limo?"

Minutes dragged like months. Then: *bzzzzzzzz*. Vessie ran to the intercom and pushed the "Listen" button.

"Airport Limousine Service!" shouted a scruffy voice.

"Thank God. Come on up!" She could feel her heart beating again.

The limo driver took his hand away from the intercom and heard the door lock buzz. So did Lou who raced in just as the driver was about to enter. He pushed the man aside and ran into the lobby forcing the door to shut between them. An elevator ride later, Lou was in Vessie's apartment—flushed, out of breath, and looking half-crazed.

"I was going to tell you on Monday. We've got a shot at the Tropical Fruit Punch account."

"That's what you came here to tell me?"

"We need this bigtime."

"Liar!" screamed her inner child.

"You're unbelievable," she told Lou.

"Look, I won't burden you with my financial problems, but if we don't get this account..."

"Lou, this does not feel good. I don't need this. I don't want this. You'd better go now."

"Please, Vessie. You're my number one."

A knock at the door caused their heads to turn and Lou to ramp up his plea.

"Look, we're in a lousy recession. I don't blame you for dropping the ball. You needed to give your marriage a shot. But Vessie..." Lou turned away. His shoulders shook, his whole body vibrated. "Whether you like this business or not, I believed in you. I gave you a chance. Now I need..." He broke into tears. "I need... your *help*."

Lou sobbed into a handkerchief. Vessie was shocked. This big menacing crazy-making power-hungry bag of hot air was as vulnerable as a pup. Or was he?

"You're not doing the old onion-in-a-hanky routine, are you Lou?"

"Jesus, Vessie!"

The knocking grew louder and Vessie ran to the door and opened it.

"You have luggage, m'am?"

Vessie looked over at Lou who was holding the hanky to his eyes, tears streaming down his cheeks—then back at the driver. "Yes, I do." Lou's eyes pleaded: *help me.* "But it's staying. How much do I owe you?"

"No, I'll get it," Lou said, walking toward the door.

The limo driver recognized him as the asshole downstairs. "A *hundred* bucks."

"What, are you crazy?"

"Is there a problem?" Vessie asked.

Lou thought it best not to explain, and sorely pulled two fifties from his wallet.

"Much obliged," said the driver, smirking a goodbye.

Without a beat, Lou shifted gears. "Thanks, babe. I'll make it up to you. I promise. Monday, 8:00 a.m. sharp. Be there!" He spun out the door before she could blink.

"Oh my god, it's happening again," Vessie told her inner child. "What the hell did I just do? I *need* a vacation."

Halfway down the hall, Lou unwrapped the hanky filled with chopped onions, dumped the tear-inducers down a garbage shoot, and grinned all the way to the office.

Vessie's smaller self was pissed. "What did you *do*? You put *HIM* first, just like you always do. And it's not just Lou, you do it with *every* man in your life."

"I do NOT!"

The child stood staring at her.

"Oh my god," Vessie said. "I DO!"

"Yeah, you DO! I'll tell you what *you* need. YOU need a *barometer*!"

"A barometer."

"Yes, a simple one-question barometer. Just ask yourself: Does it feel good? If it doesn't... DON'T DO IT!"

"Does it feel good? Hey, a lot of choices I've made felt good at first, but they turned to rat poo and hurt!"

"What I'm telling you is—as soon as they start to hurt, that's when you need to DO something about it. Like you did with Roy Thatcher. You jumped off that near-disaster immediately."

152

"I *did*...but not with Bobby or Richard. Why? What was it? What happened to me? Oh my god... SEX! It was *SEX!* SEX changed the dynamic."

"So, what's your excuse with Lou?"

"Insanity?"

"No, really."

"Do you charge by the hour, doctor?"

"Come on, you can figure it out. What is it, Vessie?"

What is it? What is it? Meditate, Vessie. Close your eyes... quiet your mind. You've got the answer... find it. Vessie closed her eyes and took several slow deep breaths. "Om-mani-padme-hum, om-mani-padme-hum."

Her inner child closed her eyes and joined in. "Om-mani-padme-hum, om-mani-padme-hum."

Finally, when the second hand on her flamingo clock did ten full cycles the answer came: *Daddy. Daddy? Lou and Daddy have about as much in common as Bambi and Godzilla.* She closed her eyes and repeated her mantra. "Om-mani-padme-hum, om-mani-padme-hum."

Vessie's eyes popped open. "Lou is the same age Daddy would have been."

Her inner child opened her eyes. "And you met Lou right after you said goodbye to another man you loved—Guruji."

"Oh my god." Vessie finally *got it.* "Daddy's death left a big hole in my heart—and it went straight to my head."

"Ding ding," said the little one. "Epiphany time."

Vessie grew silent. So did her inner child.

"I know you won't believe me," Vessie said, "but I swear... if I ever find myself in a relationship or situation with someone who tries to devalue me, disrespect me, or control me in any way, I will stop it right then and there. You are going to be proud of me, Little One, because I'm going to put *us first.*"

Monday morning Vessie walked into Remy's office. He was sitting behind his sleek black desk. *Oh Ves,* he thought. *Another canceled vacation. What am I going to do with you?*

"You phoned Lou from your apartment, didn't you?" he said, shaking his head.

"I don't want to talk about it. I just want you to know—it will *never* happen again." Vessie made a beeline to her office before Remy could say a word.

Lou was a new man. He whistled, smiled, and made everyone want to puke. His exuberance lasted nine minutes—Remy clocked him. That's when he screamed at Vessie.

"No songs! I don't want songs! This is the jingle business. You want art? Go to a goddamn museum!" He was furiously waving a jingle she had just written. His agitation completely countered the tranquil turquoise sea and white sandy beach in the poster on Vessie's office wall directly behind him.

She sat at her electric piano watching Lou vent and saw the man in the poster come to life and run along the shoreline. *It's him,* Vessie thought. His deep hazel eyes smiled at her.

"Wow!"

Lou winced. "What?"

Vessie snapped back to the present. "Lou, listen to it again." *Take the safety cap off your brain, man.* "The market's changing. The jingles that are hot are written like songs, not four bars of repetitious tripe."

"Tripe? Are you calling what I built this business on *tripe?*" *Bitch. How dare you.*

"It was *in* then."

"And sophisti-fucking-cation is in now, is that it? Then what about the Catflakes jingle… and Da-da-dats-a-Daddy-wafer, huh? Huge successes!"

"Some still work, but the trend is…"

"Trend shmend. You write it the way I taught you and that's that." He walked to the door and turned. "You having a tough time getting comfortable here again? I'll get you what you need. Two slaves and a fan? A tub of martinis? Just give me what I want, okay, Vessie? OKAY? ALL RIGHT?" He shouted so the others would know he was back to abnormal.

Giving Lou what he wanted wasn't always easy, but now it felt impossible. Now that she had outgrown a musical structure that was just about as exciting as Mr. Rogers. Vessie looked at the poster.

"*We've* got to get away," said her inner child. "The sun, the sea… blisters on your tush, salt water on your flippers. Remember, Vessie?"

Vessie opened her arms wide and her smaller self ran in for a touchdown. Determined to get her work out of the way, she whipped off one idea after another hating them all. At half past four she walked into Lou's office and told him:

"Get me an appointment with the client. I need input on this one. I'm stuck and I promised you, so you'll get what you want, but I need them to help me nail it down."

Lou was taken aback. This was a Vessie he hadn't seen before.

"Just who the hell do you...?"

She stopped him cold. "My terms, Lou, or forget it!"

The subway ride home was crowded with people wearing raincoats, down-filled jackets, woolen scarves, and gloves. It was nearing November and a cold front reminded Vessie of a winter she was determined to escape. Rain-soaked streets would be icy in the morning. But for now she could walk home from the train without falling on her butt.

She turned, sensing somebody staring at her. It was Sherman Frankel, a patient of Sheila Hurt's. *Oh god, please don't talk to me,* she thought. *I'm not up for you today.*

"Bessie... Bessie!" he shouted moving beside her. "Aaa... aaa... aaachooooo!"

Right in her eye.

"Oh brother."

"I know, isn't it awful? I feel absolutely misera... ahh... ahhh." He sneezed again causing onlookers to comment. Sherman was oblivious to it all. "You remember me, don't you? Sherman Frankel? I'm a patient of your neighbor's Sheila Hurt? We met in the... aaa... aaa..."

He sneezed on her again.

"Hey, Sherman, you sure you got enough on me? C'mon, sneeze again. I'll open my mouth this time."

"Sorry, it's a bad cold."

"Really? I thought it was a bonding ritual."

The train came to a stop and Vessie headed for the door.

"Hey, this isn't your stop!"

"It is *now,* you jerk!

THIRTY-ONE

Vessie Learns to Fly

"You are what I call a suck!" Remy stomped out of Vessie's kitchen wearing a flouncey pink and white polka dot apron over his trendy trousers and shirt. "I warned you not to phone Lou. Now you're stuck here 'til this job is over and then you'll be stuck again." He bent down and pulled Vessie's wet boots off of her soaking feet. She was a child, over-tired and helpless. "He'll come up with something else to wrench your tender little heart."

"I told you, this is the last time."

"Right. I warmed up some barley vegetable soup and you're going to eat it. Go take off those wet clothes and get into bed. I'll bring it to you there."

"Giving you a... aaa... aaa... achoooo! Excuse me," she said, reaching for a tissue, "... a key to my apartment was the smartest thing I ever did. Being born was the dumbest."

Remy shouted from the kitchen. "You'll get no tears from me."

"What? You think I want to be here? I want to honor my contract?"

"Your contract entitles you to a vacation! Lou owes you, how many? Five? Six? Besides, remember what James Slater told you? *Contracts are made to be broken.*"

"Yeah, well I looked into it. It could cost me my entire savings to get out of it. But I swear, as soon as I finish this jingle I'm *going* to St. Lucia."

"You'd better, because next time you'll need more than a baby sitter to help you."

"What's that suppose to aa... a... aachooooo! mean?"

Vessie was now in her flannel pajamas and terry robe climbing into bed as Remy entered with a food tray. "It means there's just so much stress one person can take."

She ate her soup like a good girl, burped twice and said goodnight. *He's so wonderful,* she thought. *God, I'm lucky.* But then a tsunami of sadness came and claimed her. *I need to get out of here. I need to get away.*

Vessie shoved the food tray aside. She knew what she had to do. She climbed out of bed and hurried over to the bookcase. *Where is it? Where are you?* She thumbed through her spiritual books: "Tantra Sex & Kama Sutra," "Hatha Yoga," "Yoga: Body, Mind, Spirit." *Nothing. Damn.* Then she remembered. "Right!"

Her inner child appeared. "Right? Right what? What are you doing?"

Vessie pushed a chair over to the open closet, climbed up, then reached as high as she could feeling around blindly. "Ah!" She pulled at a ribboned box. "Aa… aaaaachooo!"

The box fell to the floor. She jumped down and grabbed it. "We've got a chance now, kid."

Vessie climbed back into bed with her smaller self right behind her. She untied the box and lifted off the top. There, inside, was a framed photo.

"Gurugi," she murmured. Just saying his name made her feel better. She gently held it in her hands, then placed it on the night stand beside her. She looked back inside the box and saw the sari she wore at the ashram. She held the white sheer cloth to her face and inhaled its still pungent aroma of sandalwood.

Finally, she found what she was looking for—the book her guru had given her the day she left the ashram—"Light on Yoga" by Paramahansa Bramananda." She lifted it out of the box and held it *hoping hoping.*

In the silence she remembered her Master's words: *When you totally believe and know that you are one with pure universal energy and not separate, you will be able to fly.*

Her inner child cuddled close. *I'm ready, Guruji.* She opened Bramananda's book and thumbed down the Table of Contents to Chapter Seventeen:

BODILY TELEPORTATION THROUGH DEMATERIALIZATION.

157

"If I can't get to an island by plane," she told her inner child, "I'll get there… aa… aa… achooo! without one." She turned to Chapter Seventeen and read:

> He who knows himself as the omnipresent spirit
> is no longer subject to the rigidities of the body
> in time and space. Free of matter-consciousness,
> a Master teleports his body of light beyond the elements
> of fire, water, earth and air to his chosen destination
> where he presents himself again in the physical.

Vessie continued to read and sneeze and sneeze and read, her nose getting redder as used tissues filled the basket beside her.

> … and so, when first beginning this practice a material
> object must be chosen which clearly suggests the
> destination desired.

The destination desired, hmm. Okay, I want a lush green tropical island. She scanned the room looking for an object that would meet that criteria. *Hmm… island… lush… green.* She spotted a palm leaf vase that Smoodgie had given her for a wedding gift. Her inner child jumped out of bed and dashed straight to it. "It's great! Very island-ish."

"Yep, it should work," Vessie said. She headed for the vase, put it on the bureau in front of her bed, then continued reading the instructions.

> You must also choose an object to keep on your body for
> use as your means of return.

"I know!" said the little one. "Your apartment key."

"Perfect." Vessie ran to her shoulder bag, fetched a key on a long red satin ribbon, put it around her neck and hopped back into bed.

> Upon reaching the deep meditative state, focus on your
> object, being careful that no other thoughts enter your
> mind or your destination may be altered.

Vessie stared at the palm leaf vase. *Okay, I've got a material object to get me to my destination and*—she clutched the key around her neck—*one for my return.*

> If the energy connection is broken at the place of origin you can be pulled back from your destination.

> If the energy connection is broken at the destination, you must enter a deep meditative state and focus on your material object in order to return.

Vessie's heart raced. She finally had the information she needed. She was so excited she closed the book without reading the last two lines. *Yes I'm going to do this, I'm going to fly!* She was pumped, primed and ready to go. *Better travel light,* she thought, and took off her pajamas. She closed her eyes, grounded herself, then visualized pure energy flowing in through the top of her head and into every cell of her body. She kept running the energy, feeling it clear away knots of tension. Twenty minutes later she felt relaxed and ready.

Four elements. There were four elements Guruji said I needed to remember in order to fly. What were they? What were they? Another twenty minutes went by and she had them all: (1) intention, (2) lack of fear, (3) connecting to pure energy, and (4) believing you can do it.

The "on button" is intention. Okay, I will declare my intention. My intention is to dematerialize from my bed in Manhattan and rematerialize on a beautiful lush green island in the Caribbean. Two—lack of fear. I am not afraid to teleport my body by dematerializing. Three—connecting to pure energy. I will repeat my mantra and become one with pure energy. And four—I believe that Guruji's technique will work because I've seen him do it. So, let's go!

Vessie repeated her intention, focused her eyes on the palm leaf vase and repeated her mantra: "om-mani-padme-hum, om-mani-padme-hum." So did her inner child. "Om-mani-padme-hum, om-mani-padme-hum."

She stayed with the mantra, re-stating her intention, focusing on the vase, bringing the mantra back every time Lou or Sheila or Richard popped into her head. The longer she concentrated the more it began to assume the physical properties of a real palm leaf. Now, it was surrounded by light.

159

"Om-mani-padme-hum, om-mani-padme-hum "

A tropical breeze blew through the room and the palm leaf swayed. So did everything else including Vessie. "Om-mani-padme-hum, om-mani-padme-hum." Now *Vessie* was surrounded by light. She could feel herself becoming free of her body, no longer limited by time and space. She was a vessel that housed a powerful energy—one with everything everywhere.

The palm leaf shot into a tree as the breeze grew more powerful. Vessie's body grew fainter and fainter, fading, disappearing completely from sight.

"What the hell are you doing in my bed?" Smoodgie was shocked by Vessie's appearance and upset for being interrupted right in the middle of reading her Cosmopolitan horoscope for the month. Plus, her belly was enormous. The twins were due in a couple months, and Vessie was practically on top of her!

Vessie on the other hand was thrilled. "Fantastic! It worked. It really worked... well, sort of. Sorry, Smoodgie, I... aa... aa... achoooo! Excuse me." She reached over her sister's belly and grabbed a tissue from the night stand. "I guess you must have slipped into my thoughts while I was meditating... and the instructions said if something like that happens, I mean because you were thinking about something else—the destination could get mixed up. Well, *hellooooo!* You see, you gave me that palm leaf vase and I guess by association..."

"What the *hell* are you talking about?" Smoodgie had no patience for booga- booga as she called it. All she knew was that her strange sister was stranger than ever appearing from nowhere, clad in nothing, and sitting beside her in *her* bed.

"Put something on before Edward sees you."

"Are you okay, honey?" he called from the john.

"Hurry, Vessie, grab my robe."

Instead, Vessie closed her eyes, repeated her mantra, and was about to focus on the apartment key around her neck to get the hell gone when someone knocked on her apartment door and *snap!* the energy connection broke and she was pulled back to her apartment in a nano-second.

Vessie couldn't believe it. Symington to New York in a snap, or rather—a knock. She was ecstatic and so was her inner child.

"You did it! You did it! You're not metaphysically challenged after all!" Vessie shouted, "Who is it?"

"It's Sheila!"

"Look kid," Vessie told her smaller self. "I love you, but you'd better do your disappearing act."

"Don't worry. Sheila won't see me. Only another inner child can do that and hers is so under-developed, the only thing it would recognize is a *gnat*."

Vessie wanted to tell the whole world what just happened, and if it had to begin with Sheila, so be it. She ran to the door as Edward ran to the medicine cabinet to get smelling salts for his very faint wife.

"For God's sake, put something on," Sheila said. She had never seen Vessie naked before and her playmate body made her blush. Vessie ignored her request.

"Come in, come in. Oh my god, I have the most amazing news!"

Sheila thought Vessie was high on something and walked in cautiously.

"You'll need to sit down for this."

Sheila obeyed, unable to imagine what Vessie could be so excited about.

"You're the first to know..."

"Let me guess. You're *naked*."

"I just dematerialized!"

"Oh boy." Sheila mentally booked Vessie onto her couch for at least a hundred sessions.

Vessie told and Sheila listened and when they finished, Sheila made her promise not to tell anybody else. She knew that Vessie was over-worked and depressed about canceling her trip. The problem was obvious: Vessie was on the verge of a nervous breakdown. Not wanting to frighten her, she suggested that she tell her about these experiences as they happened and, in the meantime, to take a tranquilizer to help her cope with the excitement. Vessie passed on the drugs, but accepted the invitation to share updates on her teleportation breakthroughs.

Sheila wasted no time. She went straight back to her apartment and placed a long distance call to Vessie's sister, who was still feeling faint and unable to come to the phone.

161

THIRTY-TWO

Garlic Therapy

A flamingo stood in front of the twelve story Tropical Fruit Punch building—thirty feet high, hand-carved and painted pink, shading the sidewalk like King Kong in drag. In the foyer stood phony palm trees, papier mâché flamingos, Birds of Paradise, murals of oceans and sunsets and long sandy beaches. Vessie was in a virtual paradise. *How ironic,* she thought. *Here I am staring at the very place I want to be, on my way to a place I dread—another schlock jingle meeting in outer suburbia.*

"Yeah, bummer." Her inner child unbuttoned her matching coat. "Hey, check out the guy in the mural."

Vessie looked. There was no *guy.* Then she saw him—the guy she had dreamed of for years—running, as always, naked along the shoreline. "I'm crazy, that's it! I saw him yesterday in the poster at my office."

"You're not crazy. You want to meet a guy like him, that's all. You still believe…"

"In the Tooth Fairy, clean air, and global peace," Vessie said. "Now, vamoose Little One. I've got business to attend to."

And with that, her inner child disappeared.

The weight of her coat made Vessie's shoulders ache. But, as she slipped it off she began to feel liberated, free of restraint—a tall woman in a short mini.

Vessie took the elevator to the top floor where Bill McBain, Jennifer Watson, Dick Claremont, Judy Finestone, and Jack Cruthers greeted her. They looked *golf-ish.*

The men sported wrinkle-free polyester slacks and shirts in red, yellow and green, and the women wore copy-cat shirts and a-shape skirts. They reminded Vessie of a Sears summer catalogue. She thought they would be wearing Hawaiian shirts and sarongs—*something* that reflected the Tropical Fruit Punch brand. But, *nooooooo*—it was corporate shmorporate!

"We're accepting submissions from other jingle houses as I'm sure you know," Bill McBain told her, "but give us what you gave Da-da-dats-a-Daddy-wafer, and you've got our business."

Vessie's jaw dropped. She wanted to sell them on the idea of writing a *song*.

Jennifer Watson handed Vessie her card. "You're too humble. It's absolutely inspired."

"Stellar work," chimed Judy Finestone straightening her too-tight skirt. "My whole family sings it." She warbled:

> "Da-da-dats-a-daddy-wafer
> Yeah yeah lots of yummy flavor
> Da-da-dats-a-daddy-wafer for me."

The others applauded. Vessie cocked her head to one side. *Here we go again.*

Bill McBain took the reigns. "So you *do* understand the direction we want to go?"

"Absolutely. Da-da-dats-a-Daddy-wafer, everyone's favorite, except with flamingos and fruit."

The team smiled. It would be a success.

Now I really need inspiration, Vessie thought.

"If there's anything we can do to be of assistance."

"Well, actually, Mr. McBain." Vessie batted her eyelashes.

"Call me Bill." He was suddenly Manly-Man, straightening the waistband of his royal blue polyesters.

"There are a couple aa… aa… aachooo! Excuse me… objects on display in your lobby that I'm sure would help me give you… aa… aa… aachoo! Everything you could want in the *jingle*." She lowered her eyes and swung her long hair over her shoulder. "Can I show you the ones I mean?"

All the way down in the elevator Bill sweated, coughed, and smiled nervously. He was happy that his teeth were clean and his deodorant was working.

"Ah... there!" She pointed. "Those palm trees... and that bird on the wall."

"The flamingo?"

"Yes, the flamingo. Can I borrow them? I'd like to keep them at my apartment for inspiration."

"Uh, yes, of course... *Vessie*," he said, tip-toeing on her name, careful not to over-step his boundaries. "If you like, I'll send some scenery to your office as well. Whatever I can do to help."

Vessie smiled her best smile, winked her best wink, sneezed her best sneeze, and left via the double doors draping her winter coat over her shoulders, leaving Bill McBain wiping sweat off the back of his neck as he watched her strut to the parking lot. What he couldn't see was Vessie's inner child strutting along beside her. Vessie looked down.

"Hey, was that your idea?"

"The props? Natch."

She loved the drive from Yonkers back to the city—the blue sky, clear laneways. It was cold but sunny and dry; and, Vessie took the good driving conditions as a good omen.

She and her inner child sang camp songs all the way to a specialty store where she bought six feet of track lighting and four sunlamp bulbs. From there, they drove to a local ice cream parlor and shared a root beer float. It felt good enjoying her own company again until her sneezing returned with a vengeance.

"Don't worry," she told her smaller self. "We'll get to that island, and we'll...aa...aa. aachoo!... get there soon!"

That night Vessie's sneezing could have fuelled a plane, thanks to that subway ride home with no-boundaries-sick-as-a-bow-wow Sherman Frankel. Her eyes ran a race with her nose so *she* ran out for supplies, right down the street to an all-night fruit and vegetable stand owned and operated by Joe Chang.

164

"Bad cold, eh? You know about ginger root and garlic?" Joe's eyes sparkled beneath the brim of his well-worn Yankees cap. "Ginger chopped and boiled make good tea. Good for cleaning nasal passages. Garlic good for cleaning blood. The more you eat, the cleaner you blood look. You want try?"

"I want try." Vessie grabbed a bagful.

"You sure goin' for it."

"I've got to get rid of this cold, Joe. It's putting a cramp in my *travel* plans."

"I got something for cramp, too."

Vessie was determined to make her flying technique work and it was near to impossible when she kept sneezing all the time. She bought an arsenal of supplies including six boxes of Kleenex, and headed home.

She did what Joe told her to do. She spread three diced cloves of garlic on buttered bread and popped it under the broiler. Her inner child was livid.

"I thought you loved me... that you wanted me to be happy. Where's my licorice and Ovaltine? Where are my Oreos and Ding Dongs?"

"Hey, hey, hey! You want us to get down south? Then this body has got to get better so I can focus on my technique." She bit into the garlic toast. "Damn, that's hot!" She knocked it back with a mug of boiled ginger water. Cough cough—even hotter. The combination was killer but Vessie felt victorious. *Those germs don't stand a chance. I'll keep coming at them with garlic and ginger until their little white flags unfurl.*

In the morning, Vessie felt great, but her pores exuded a smell similar in no way to Chanel. The problem was—she didn't know it. She went about her business showering, drying her hair, and eating more garlic. Then she left for work.

"Hold it please!" Vessie yelled to a woman getting into the elevator.

One floor up, the woman lifted her purse to her nose and sniffed. "Sorry, that horrible smell must be coming from my new leather bag."

A woman standing on the other side of Vessie sniffed the air and said, "No no, it's garlic. I definitely smell *garlic.*"

There was no way Vessie was going to open her mouth to comment.

At half past ten, props arrived at Fields & Friends from the Tropical Fruit Punch marketing team. Attached was a cassette of Hawaiian love songs and a letter that read:

Dear Ms. VanCortland,
Here are the props you requested. More will be delivered to your residence. Hoping this proves inspirational, I am, Yours Truly,
Bill McBain
P.S. If the jingle doesn't meet with our team's approval, will you sleep with me anyway? Just kidding... wink wink.

Surprise surprise, she thought, not being the least bit surprised at Mr. Testosterone's testicular request. Vessie grabbed the plastic bananas from her booty and hung a string of them around her neck—then more around the window frames. She placed two papier mâché flamingos on her piano, hung straw from the ceiling like crepe paper; then sat back in her well-worn chair and stared at the golden-tan man running down the beach in her favorite poster. *God, you're fabulous,* she thought. Looking at him always filled her hope and wonder. She popped Bill McBain's accompanying cassette of Don Ho into a tape player, as Remy entered the room.

"Carmen Miranda, right?" *You are too funny,* he thought.

"No. Ma Kettle. You want some garlic toast?"

"Garlic toast? Ah, so *that's* the culprit. I didn't want to say anything, but I've been keeping my distance, in case you hadn't noticed. Is there a reason for the quarantine or do you just vant to be alone, dahlink?"

Vessie explained the garlic therapy which caused Remy's eyebrows to shift. She wanted to tell him about her dematerialization technique and how she wound up in Smoodgie's bed in Symington, but Sheila's warning rang loud and clear—*Don't tell anyone or your next jacket will be white with long sleeves that strap in the BACK!*

Vessie couldn't wait to go home. She knew more props would be waiting for her that might help her get to an island. Finally, at six p.m. she entered the foyer of her apartment building and was greeted by Rodney the doorman.

"Oh, Ms. VanCortland. Some pretty strange equipment came for you today. I let the delivery guys in like you said. You giving a party or something?"

"Thanks, Rodney." Vessie's adrenaline shot through the roof. She ran to the elevator just making it inside. Standing beside her was a broad shouldered man in a dark blue jump suit, black baseball cap that shaded his eyes, and a tool belt hung low around his thick bulging waistline. Somewhere between the sixth and ninth floors he took off his cap, pulled a ski mask over his face and forced the elevator to stop. No alarms went off except in Vessie's head. He stopped her mid-sentence.

"Fight me and you're dead."

She took a whack at him, then another. Before she knew it, her wrists and ankles were tied, her mouth taped shut, and her blouse ripped open.

"Eeeeoooooo... what the? You smell *disgusting!*" His erection shrunk to a question mark, then a comma, then a period. "Damn you, bitch!" He hit the elevator buttons, and it jolted down one floor. "Jesus!" he shouted, gagging from the stench. He attacked the panel again, yelling and cussing. The elevator jolted again, stopped, its doors yawned open, and he ran out.

Oooooomph! It climbed up five floors, shuddered, and the doors opened again.

Sheila stood there about to get in, wearing dead animal skins and fumbling with a shoulder bag half her size, when she saw Vessie, bound and gagged, on the elevator floor.

"Vessie!" She flew inside, knelt beside her neighbor, and quickly removed the tape from her mouth.

Tears streamed from Vessie's eyes. "I can't even get raped in this town."

"Raped? What are you talking about? What's going on? And what in God's name is that sickening smell?"

"It's *me*. It's garlic. That's why he didn't rape me."

"Who didn't rape you?"

"The guy in the elevator. He said he'd kill me if I fought him. But I smelled so bad—he *ran*."

"A guy was going to rape you but didn't because you ate garlic?"

"Ironic, isn't it? If I hadn't been doing garlic therapy..."

"Garlic therapy?"

Sheila untied Vessie's wrists and ankles.

"Yes. If I didn't smell so rotten there's no telling what he might have done."

"And where did this man go? Did you see him get off the elevator?"

"He just went. I don't know. Isn't it bizarre? I mean, can you believe it?"

No. Sheila couldn't believe it. She believed Vessie created the fictitious attacker out of repressed sexual frustration and anger.

"I better call the police," Vessie said.

"No, Vessie, they'll never believe you."

"What do you mean? Why wouldn't they? Because the guy left? But I *do* smell disgusting. You said so yourself." Vessie reflected on what she just said. "You're right. They'll think I'm a nut case. But he could still be in the building. What if he comes back?"

"He won't," Sheila said, convinced he was never there in the first place.

"You mean, some screwball can just show up, slap me around, threaten me, and make *me* look like the weirdo? I can't let him get away with that. It wouldn't be fair to me or anybody else."

"I'm telling you, Vessie. Your intentions may be honorable, but the police would never believe you. And you don't want to be put on their *Weirdoes to Watch List*."

Vessie knew Sheila was right, but that didn't ease her anger any.

They entered her apartment and saw two phony palm trees that touched the ceiling adorned with papier mâché flamingos and plastic bananas, and a hammock strung between them. Above it was track lighting with four sunlamp bulbs, and beneath it all was sand in a six inch deep box, framing the simulated island.

"It's perfect," she told Sheila. "Now I'll be able to dematerialize and get to a *real* island."

That was it. Sheila knew she had to reach Smoodgie this time and explain that her sister's condition was critical. She backed away from Vessie's Manhattan Jungle as she told her: "I think I'll be going now. I, uh, have some paper work to finish and, uh… if anything else *exciting* happens, don't hesitate to knock." Sheila was gone.

Right, I'll keep you as posted as a glueless stamp, Vessie thought. Her gut screamed: *Sheila didn't believe a word I said.*

Vessie heard weeping. It could only be—"Come out come out wherever you are." Her inner child popped up from behind the sofa.

"That man in the elevator was scary."

"Come here, I need a hug." Vessie held her inner child close, needing to calm that part of her that longed for some TLC.

Why was I chosen to be a victim of some sick person's whim? What am I doing wrong? Why are abusive men manifesting in my life? A pressure-demon boss, a soon-to-be ex-slave-master husband, and now a goddamn rapist? She decided to take action. *Whatever the cause, I've got the cure.*

She turned on the sunlamps, lit incense, took off her clothes, and lay down in the hammock. She looked at the palm trees supporting her, the flamingos, the bananas. Vessie closed her eyes, grounded her energy, visualized pulling pure universal energy in through the top of her head and moved it to every part of her body. She repeated her mantra over and over until she was able to get the creep who attacked her out of her mind. *The Four Elements,* she thought: *(1) Intention, (2) lack of fear, (3) connecting to pure energy, and (4) believing that you can do it. My intention is to dematerialize in this hammock in Manhattan and rematerialize on a lush green tropical island.*

"Om-mani-padme-hum, om-mani-padme-hum."

"Om-mani-padme-hum, om-mani-padme-hum," echoed her inner child.

Moments later, all that was subjective became abstract—all that was eternal, clear. Fear was not present. Pure energy flowed from the crown chakra at the top of her head down through her body. *Ahhhhhhhhhhhhh.* A wave of sweet gold.

As you reach a deep meditative state, focus on the object, being careful that no other images enter your mind or your destination may be altered.

Vessie slowly opened her eyes and focused on the papier mâché flamingo in the palm tree before her.

"Om-mani-padme-hum, om-mani-padme-hum... om-mani-padme-hum, om-mani-padme-hum..."

A breeze blew through the room. The palm trees swayed. The bananas rattled. "Om-mani-padme-hum, om-mani-padme-hum." Her eyelids grew heavy and closed. A white ring of light surrounded the flamingo. Vessie remembered the flamingos she had seen last summer at the zoo. "Om-mani-padme-hum, om-mani-padme-hum."

The sunlamps were no longer warming her body. The hammock was empty.

Vessie was gone.

THIRTY-THREE

Oops! Wrong Turn

Vessie hugged her naked body. The only thing that covered her was squawking sounds. Flamingos, parrots, and other brightly colored birds gathered around to see the new spectacle.

"Who's the weirdo in the skin suit?" they asked.

"The zoo?" Vessie was incredulous. Her inner child touched the glass enclosure that separated them and the squawkers from the observation area at the Tropical Room. "I'm sorry. I love this place and must have pictured it without thinking."

Vessie put her face against the glass spreading her features like warm Brie.

The birds fussed louder causing the night watchman to run in waving a flashlight before she could reverse the technique and escape the locked enclosure. He saw Vessie's face and then the rest of her. "Holy Mother of Jesus. Ain't never seen no bird like *you* before."

At the Manhattan Precinct, the key around Vessie's neck was confiscated. Without her object-of-return she was caged once more. Wrapped in grey woolen blankets, she sat in a holding cell between a prostitute whose long legs were covered in black thigh-high vinyl, and a wild looking woman whose steely grey hair was in total disarray. The wild woman kept moving her jaw in and out.

"I'm from the moon, ya know."

The lady of the night spit a wad of gum in her hand and stuck it to a corner of the metal bench.

"I'm from the Bronx, myself."

"Okay, VanCortland, come with me," shouted a hefty female officer. The cell door opened and Vessie hobbled out.

"Holy Mother of Jesus. You *de*materialized and then *re*materialized at the zoo?" Remy didn't know what to think. Here was his best friend sitting wrapped in blankets in a downtown New York Precinct telling him a totally bizarre story.

"Yes, that's how I got there. I couldn't get back to my apartment because there was no time to meditate. Then when I got here, they took the key I needed to get back. Remy, you believe me, don't you?"

You're my best friend and I don't even know you, he thought. "Vessie, whatever you do, don't tell that to the police. They won't believe you. Just say you got drunk and don't remember how you got there. Okay? Otherwise, I don't know. They might put you under observation or something."

"Seems I'm hearing a lot of that lately. Look, I'm fine. I'm not crazy. What I told you really happened. And quite frankly, I'm pretty excited about it and wish you would be too."

Remy's eyes couldn't hide his concern. He loved Vessie and was afraid she was losing it. Not knowing what else to do, he put up bail and took her home.

Vessie put on her jammies and told Remy how her yoga technique worked. She showed him where she laid in the hammock, where the papier mâché flamingo was perched, the key around her neck to be used as her object-of-return, and Bramananda's printed words. She wanted desperately for him to believe her, to share her excitement and lose his concern that she was a prime candidate for basket weaving at the Mount Sinai Mental Health Center.

"I'll show you. I'll do my technique and you'll see for yourself."

"No no no… that's quite all right." He was afraid that if he saw her disappear he would be the one in need of a shrink. "Just don't screw up next time, okay? Get your ass down south and bring me back some good cheap rum. That's all I ask. No zoo. And no… wherever the hell *else* you could end up… like at the Geo presentations in your Sunday suit."

Vessie laughed. "They're not for another six weeks. By then I'll have the technique down pat." Remy looked at her helplessly, wanting to protect her but not knowing how. She was determined to get to an island at any cost and he hoped it wouldn't cost Vessie her sanity.

For several hours after he left, Vessie sat at her piano and did her homework assignment.

Tropi-Tropi-Tropi-Tropical Fruit Punch
Lazy, hazy days inside a drink
Tropi-Tropi-Tropi-Tropical Fruit Punch
Grape, orange, lime, and cherry-pink

She let Lou's direction guide her: *Structure. Keep it simple. If you want art go to a goddamn museum.* She felt sick about it and was determined to fly south in the morning.

Vessie opened her eyes and for a second, thought she was back at the zoo; but, one look at Guruji's photo on the nightstand beside her offered instant relief. She climbed out of bed, walked over to the window and drew back the curtains.

A grey pall hung over Manhattan like dirty soup. The clouds huddled en masse calling silent plays against the sun. They were too dark for snow clouds and if they were to produce heavy rain there would be three mile islands of flooded streets. It was a dismal day and Vessie couldn't wait to escape. This time she would take no chances. She put on a two piece flamingo-print bathing suit, pulled her hair back in a Hawaiian print scarf, and smeared sun screen on her pale skin.

"What about me?"

Vessie looked at her inner child. She was wearing the same flamingo-print bathing suit and had flippers on her feet.

"What do you mean, what about me? You know you're always with me."

Vessie turned on the sunlamps, lit incense and climbed into the hammock strewn between her beloved phony palm trees. This time she would focus on the flamingo and not let anything enter her mind except a magnificent island illuminated by warm sultry light.

THIRTY-FOUR

Vessie Meets Johnny

What's that? Splashing sounds? Vessie opened her eyes and had to squint. She looked around and realized she was on a sandbar fifty feet from a white sandy shore. The splashing grew louder. Rising from the turquoise sea was a perfectly formed male body wearing nothing but a smile. *Oh my god, it's him—the guy in the mural, the poster, my dreams. That's it, I'm dreaming. I'm in my apartment on my hammock, I've fallen asleep and I'm dreaming.*

He stood over her blocking the sun, dripping. She was Thumbelina. He was the Jolly Nude Giant. She didn't know whether to float away in a walnut shell or spread her legs and introduce herself.

"Are you alright?" He gently kneeled beside her presenting a face carved for a Gillette razor. His thick sunbleached hair said: *Play with me.* His deep hazel eyes said: *Come inside.*

"Am I all right?" Vessie said. "I'm perfect."

"Yes, I can see that. What happened? Were you on a cruise ship or something?"

"No." *Silly dream,* she thought.

"Was there an accident?"

"No."

"Are you a sky diver?"

"No." *Oh boy.*

"An Olympic swimmer?"

"No."

"Then I give up. How'd you get here?"

"I dematerialized in New York and rematerialized here."

174

He laughed. "Right, that's what I thought. I'm having a sexual fantasy, which makes perfect sense considering I've been alone on this island for over a year." He looked at Vessie claiming her with his eyes.

"Now just a darn minute, buddy."

"Johnny," he said.

"I have rights, even on this sandbar… even in this dream."

"I don't believe it. I'm hundreds of miles from civilization and I create a feminist?"

"Yeah, you and fifty million other guys."

"But you're my fantasy. I can make you say and do anything I want."

"Excuse me… *you* are *my* fantasy!"

"You are hot!"

I better shut up. He's bigger than I am and if he tries making love to me, the worst that could happen? I might leave a wet spot on the hammock…mine.

"Say to me, I'd love to go down on you right now, but I don't even know your name."

"But I do. It's Johnny."

"Johnny Century. Okay, okay. Say to me… I want romance in my life. I need time to fall in love with you. I want to know your mind. I want you to know mine. Sex is fine when it reflects genuine caring. Let's get to know each other and see what develops from there."

I'm definitely dreaming because I sure as hell have never met a guy like him before. Not only is he physically yummy, he's intelligent, sensitive, and has values to write home about. Why can't he be real?

"Let's swim to the island," he said, taking for granted that she could swim. "I've got so much to show you." Vessie followed like a guppy.

"Oooooooo," she cooed, entering the sea, feeling the water envelop and push her toward shore. She wanted to tell everyone she knew what was happening in this dream. Mrs. Smith would be kvelling. Smoodgie would be salivating. Remy would be uncorking champagne. Vessie couldn't help herself. The sea was delicious, he was delicious, and she wanted more.

Johnny watched her water ballet performance hoping she would be different from the women he had known. *Will you be happy without Saks Fifth Avenue, Bergdorf's and Regine's?* he thought. *Will a good book hold your interest? Will conversation be something to explore? Yes, of course it*

will. You're everything I want you to be. How could you be anything else?
I created you!

Vessie finished the grand finale: The Submarine. She floated flat on her back treading water with her hands, extending her left leg straight out in front of her and bending her right leg at the knee. She pointed the toes on her right foot skyward, then slowly lowered herself into the water, treading, treading—then forced herself back up. Esther Williams she wasn't, but happy she was. Finally, the water ballet lessons Erlinor had insisted she take were paying off. She opened her eyes and saw a tiny version of herself swimming alongside, gurgling.

"I *like* it here." The child turned her little body around and swam toward shore.

The sun glistened on Vessie's wet skin like crystals. Her long wet hair ribboned against her smooth toned back. Her high cheek bones and green eyes glowed in the light. She thrust her body forward with each step away from the sea toward the six foot two chiseled dream man who stood in knee-deep water applauding her. She felt no embarrassment as he touched her body with his eyes.

He led her away from the beach toward a long sandy path. "I own this island as much as a person can own anything," he said.

You own this island? she thought. *I'm renting 400 feet of mouse space in Manhattan and you own an island?* She gazed at Johnny Century's paradise. *It's more beautiful than I had imagined. Oh my god... mango trees? Banana trees? Avocado trees?*

Hills of pure white sand climbed high to the sky where lush green trees stretched and shimmied. Bluffs curved along the shoreline and jetted out into the sea where a flock of flamingos flew overhead. Johnny watched Vessie take it in like ambrosia, as light reflecting off his shiny bronzed face made her knees go weak.

"May I hold your hand?" he asked.

You can hold any part of me, she thought.

Vessie held out her hand and felt Johnny's warm strong fingers curl around hers and —*snap!* the toilet flushed in the upstairs Manhattan apartment and she disappeared. They were both left in a state of *wha?* Johnny, on his island, doing a 360-degree scan searching for his fantasy girl; and Vessie in her living room hammock, spinning her head around,

176

looking for her dream man among papier mâché flamingos and phony palm trees. That's when she heard squawking sounds.

I must still be dreaming, she thought. *This is one totally weird frigging dream. I'll probably get up from this hammock and be swarmed by a pack of flamingos.* But the squawking wasn't coming from real birds, or any bird, it was coming from a tiny body dressed in a flamingo-print bathing suit who was complaining loudly.

"That salt water's itchy. Itchy itchy itchy itchy itchy."

Vessie began to scratch. *Huh?*

She jumped off the hammock and ran to the hall mirror. "My face..." she gasped, "...it's sunburnt!" She pulled her bathing suit away from her skin. *Tan lines?* Her eyes shot straight forward. *My hair is WET?* "Oh my god oh my god oh my god!"

Lou Fields was ecstatic. "They loved it. Didn't I tell you they'd love it if you did it *my* way? You did it, kid. You got me the Tropical Fruit Punch account and I owe you. Now, *I* owe *you!*" Lou was beside himself which left very little room in Vessie's office.

"Terrific, Lou," she said, silently thinking: *Disgusting, Lou. Artistically average shouldn't be valued as great.*

"We're on a roll—next one, Soulmate Cologne. It's a natural for you, Vessie. Soulmate. Crunchy granola sixties. Do it like you did..."

"The Catflakes jingle."

"Nah... Tropical Fruit Punch. They'll eat it up."

Vessie couldn't do it. Enough was enough. She would feel better about herself hustling her body at Times Square than writing another piece of garbage. "I can't Lou. Not anymore. Not the same formula. I just... *can't.*"

"What do you mean, you *can't?* You just did. You did hundreds of times. And each time it made my accountant very happy. What is it with you? This isn't a case of artistic integrity. This is *sabotage*, quirkiness... your menstrual period? Hey! Why don't you go home early? Rest up. Tomorrow you'll feel different. Go home, Vessie. I'll phone you later with some ideas I have." *Damn you, Vessie. You probably just need to get laid.*

"Sure, Lou." *You'll phone me with the same old stupid crap.*

Vessie got into the over-heated elevator. The meeting with Lou was still fresh in her mind, and her gut wrenched. *This is not good. Not good at all. I've got to switch gears. Got to.*

She breathed deeply. *Soulmate cologne. Soulmate. Soulmate.* Another deep breath. *Hmm. It could be an opportunity to say something significant. Soul mate. To meet my soul mate. What would he be like? What would make him different from other men?* She looked around the elevator at her immediate choices and couldn't find any answers there. But she knew. *There would be a synergy, a communication beyond words. A caring, nurturing, sharing, understand-ing, love and trust. Independence and yet, closeness. A feeling of unlimited freedom within a heart-felt commitment.* Vessie was getting totally jazzed thinking about it when she felt a tug at her coat sleeve and looked down.

"And he'd be a great playmate for me."

That afternoon as the waves broke along the shoreline, Johnny, now *half-naked* in floral trunks and bare chest, showed Vessie his island. It was straight out of a Tarzan movie. Natural waterfalls surrounded by rocks and wild orchids. Coconut, pineapple, banana and mango trees, ginger palms, bamboo, Birds of Paradise, long feathered cockatoos and brilliantly colored macaws and flamingos. But the house that John built wasn't resting in a tree. It stood on a hill, proud and majestic looking out at the sea—its wings reaching out like the wings of an eagle.

"It looks like a magnificent bird about to take flight," Vessie said.

"You can see that?"

"Of course."

She's fantastic. I love my fantasy! "I had it in mind for years. So, when it came time to put it on paper it was easy."

"You're an architect?"

"Was…in New York."

"And you gave it up to live here?"

"Yep."

"Because?"

"Long story."

"Try me."

"You're compassionate, too?"

Vessie smiled. "That *is* what you want me to be, isn't it?"

Johnny met her smile, then grew serious. "It was about… corruption… greed…*lies.*" He rubbed his hand against his face vigorously, shifted his weight from foot to foot. "I'd spend months, sometimes years working on a project thinking, this is going to be beautiful… *this* will enrich people's lives. And then deals were made. Corrupt deals, totally out of my control. Sub-quality materials, sub-quality crews. Let's just say, bad things happened. *Very* bad things." He turned away.

Vessie thought she had better change the subject.

"So… here you are on this gorgeous island."

"With you. I'm so glad you're back. I thought, man, that fantasy I had was *way* too short."

"Johnny, I'm not a fantasy."

"Right."

"I'm not."

"C'mon, I see you appear and disappear. What do you call *that*?"

There's time. There's time. Don't blow this, Vessie. "Okay, you win. So, I uh… was going to ask you if you ever get lonely?"

"Obviously… *you're* here."

Oh boy. "Why'd you come to the island alone?"

"I didn't."

Vessie's heart jumped. "You mean there's someone living with you?"

"When I first came here I brought a woman with me. But she left."

"How could she? It's so beautiful here."

"Poor girl had charge card withdrawals."

They walked up to the house and stood looking out at a magnificent sunset—broad splashes of orange, red, and a wash of grey. Vessie looked at the vast blue water and could see no other island in sight.

"Johnny, do you ever get bored?"

"Bored? When you were a kid were you bored?"

"Never. I was too busy being weird according to my sister." Johnny's brain went tilt. *Her sister?* Vessie saw his reaction. *Too much information,* she told herself. *You're his fantasy. Stick to the program.* " I uh… swam… climbed trees… played the piano," she said.

"The piano?" He grabbed his fantasy's hand and ran toward the house. Vessie skipped every other step to keep up.

A panoramic view through ceiling-to-floor windows was the backdrop for the sunken living room: earth tone sofas, large throw pillows in cream-colored textures and weaves, antique wood hutches and tables mixed with modern sleek glass and marble stands and shelving, deep cushioned chaise lounges, a stone fireplace with a massive hearth, a painting above of it: The House That John Built, and the pièce de résistance—a magnificent baby grand piano.

Vessie ran over to it—its thick black shiny veneer and perfect frame, an irrisistable magnet. "What a gorgeous old Steinway," she said. "Do you play?"

"No, my mother did. It was hers."

"May I?"

"Of course.

Vessie sat down on a delicately embroidered piano bench and improvised a melody that gave romance a new high. *This feels good. So good.* Her fingers were in love again. So was Johnny.

I love my fantasy, he thought. *And that music. It's beautiful.*

"When I was a kid," Vessie said, "making music was pure joy... no pressures, no limitations."

"That's what it's like for me here. That's why I never get bored. I do everything I liked to do when I was a kid, only bigger. In New York, I had nothing but limitations. Now, I create exactly what pleases me. Even you."

Vessie's eyes widened. Her hands froze on the keyboard. Standing beside Johnny was her inner child. She had forgotten that Johnny couldn't see her.

"Oh no!"

"No? You don't like that? You think it's..."

"No no... I think it's fantastic!"

"Whew! I thought you were going to say... stupid or self indulgent."

"I like this guy," said her inner child.

"Keep it to yourself. I mean... keeping it to yourself is *wrong*. We've got to embrace our inner child. Get over here!"

Johnny walked over thinking Vessie meant *him*. "You are definitely the best thing I ever created." He put his arms around her, sandwiching her inner child between them.

"I can't breathe," said the wee one.

Vessie looked down. "You love it!"

"That's for sure," Johnny said. He led Vessie to the east side of the living room for a look at a whole new vista. "Tell me what do you see."

She peered through the massive wall of glass. "Sandcastles? You built all those sandcastles? *Of course he built them, who else would have built them?* "They're fantastic!" *He's too good to be true—a grown man who builds sandcastles.* "But, what if it rains? What if a strong wind knocks them down?"

"I'll build more. I like knowing they're temporary. It reminds me to enjoy them *now* because, hey—you can't take it with you."

Vessie grabbed his hand, wanting to take him with her to see them up close—to show her appreciation for his childlike spirit. But, Johnny didn't budge. He pulled her close with a mixture of gentleness and strength searching her eyes for a name other than *darling* or *sweetheart*.

"Vessie," she whispered. "My name is Vessie."

Johnny met Vessie with a kiss, encasing her lips with his, saying hello with his tongue, moving his body slowly against hers, inviting her to do the same. *Claim me, Vessie... claim me.* The sandcastles could wait. Their desire to be closer couldn't.

They were Zen lovers—he the candle, she the flame. He listened and watched like an Indian in the bush. He moved his hands above her skin feeling the heat of her emotional scars, the coolness of her spiritual centers. He burrowed his head into her curves enlivening her flesh. *She is me and I will please her as I wish to be pleased.* She *oooo'd* and *ahhhh'd* as he attended to her every desire.

Vessie turned onto her stomach, folding her arms like wings. Johnny combed her hair with his fingers. He squeezed her fingertips gently between his, then moved along her arms licking them like stamps. Her neck was blocked with knots of tension. He stretched and kneaded them until they relaxed. His tongue unzipped her spine finding her buttocks. He bit gently like a baby bird then molded her flesh in his hands following her signals for desired intensity. He pushed the blood in the veins along her legs with his fingers, forcing a feeling of well-being to flow through her like warm scotch. He moved each toe delicately in circles, spread the soles of her feet, dug into the thick skin with his thumbs until it turned crimson. And all the time he focused on her like a mantra, silently repeating: *I love you, I love you, I love you.*

Johnny found a place on the bed far enough away where he could look at his fantasy and not disturb her tranquil state. She moved toward him wanting to give back, needing to satisfy him. Their eyes locked. Their mouths locked. Their tongues found molars they never knew they had. Time slipped and tumbled. Their hips joined. Their chests mowed each other down. Legs climbed. Arms clung. Johnny entered Vessie like the coming home of a missing piece. They shot through space with each thrust landing on Uranus, sucking the Milky Way, breaking into shooting stars that sprinkled the heavens and wet Johnny's sheets.

He was different. He didn't fuck Vessie. He made love with her. He didn't ride her manically trying to leave in her, his anger and fear. He didn't use her, or unload in her, or tear her apart. He mended her, nourished her, followed and guided her, comforted her, stroked her, worshipped her, enjoyed her, shared with her. Johnny shared his happiness inside of Vessie. And when she left that day, she left whole. No part of her was left to be auctioned off or notched on a gun and forgotten. Vessie knew that she had met her like, and his name was Johnny Century.

> As we look into each other's eyes
> we are one, we are one
> As we move into each other's arms stars come out
> And as the night again turns into day
> we look at the sun and become again, one
> And we know love, and we know love
> and only our love survives us… *soulmate*
> You are my SOULMATE

Vessie handed in the new Soulmate jingle; and, it was received on deaf ears.

"I'll pretend you didn't write what I just didn't hear," Lou said. "I'm not trying to get a record deal, Vessie, so stop with the goddamn uptown stuff and give me what I can sell. That's not asking too much, is it? IS IT? Because I'm NOT going to ask you again!"

His toxicity filled the room just short of making the walls buckle.

Vessie dug in her heels and knocked out a catchy corny rhyming ditty that pleased Lou so she could go home.

She peeled off her winter coat, kicked off her boots and headed to the phone. "Remy, I have something to tell you." She couldn't wait. She had to tell him about Johnny and the island.

"Sounds serious. Don't tell me. You've been *flying* again," he teased.

You're teasing me about flying? This isn't funny. This isn't a joke. This doesn't feel good, Remy. Rather than jump into telling him, she grew silent.

"You *have* been flying? Jacques!" he yelled, "Vessie's been *flying* again."

Jacques grabbed the phone. "Vessie, what happened? What have you done *now*?"

Vessie's stomach clenched. Something was telling her to keep it to herself, *for* herself. Jacques wasn't Remy. And besides, they were both making her feel like some kind of freak show. *Nooooo. Johnny's real and he's mine.*

"Sorry, Jacques…Remy misunderstood. I just called to say, uh… goodnight."

THIRTY-FIVE

Island Romance

Later that night, Vessie and Johnny slept on the beach hundreds of miles from New York. The moon lit them like stars in their own Broadway show. The night was their backdrop, the ocean waves their musical score, the swaying trees their chorus, their laughter and whispers their story.

In the morning, Vessie watched him work on his tree house constructions. He referred to them as *play areas.* Five were already completed and the sixth was underway.

"I love them. It's where I read, write poetry, draw... play with myself," Johnny said. "What do you think?"

"I think I'm the luckiest girl in the world."

Johnny practically skipped away, hammer in hand, whistling a tune and looking back at her just to make sure he was dreaming. That's when Vessie saw Johnny's inner child. He skipped alongside of him, tiny hammer in hand, happy, mindless—the spitting image of her lover, only twenty-five years smaller.

Vessie's inner child was over-joyed. Now, she could have a playmate. She picked up a sea shell and threw it, hitting him in the back. He turned and without a beat ran after her with gleeful vengeance. Johnny turned and without a beat ran toward Vessie and planted his lips on her belly. It tickled. He did it again. She squealed with laughter.

"Is there anything I don't love about you?" he said.

Later that day, Vessie swam beneath the ocean waves exploring the magic of a world where star fish, sea turtles, and translucent gilled sea creatures waved spots and stripes challenging her to do the same.

The sun baked her like lasagna, but she didn't care. Nope. No care in the world in Johnnyland. Not today, not tomorrow—*snap!* Pounding at her apartment door caused Vessie to disappear.

Back in the hammock again, Vessie's first thought was: *Damn, I hate when that happens.* She searched her brain for the cause. *If the energy connection is broken at the place of origin you can be pulled back to your destination.* She thought about Johnny. *This is getting serious. He's got to believe I'm real.* The pounding grew louder. *Who the hell is pounding like that?* She threw on a robe. "Okay, I'm coming, I'm coming." She looked through the peep hole. "Lou?"

He was fuming inside a muskrat coat.

Vessie opened the door. She could have been naked or standing on her head and he wouldn't have noticed.

"I've been trying to reach you all day, but your goddamn answer machine was on. Why the hell aren't you at the office?"

"I finished the Soulmate jingle. You said you loved it."

"Yeah, well… they *hated* it." He walked in, saw the palm trees and hammock and didn't even comment. "Vessie, I need the first version you wrote. Where is it?"

"Oh, you mean the…if-you-want-art-go-to-a-goddamn-museum version?"

"Okay, okay, you were right. Now where is it?"

"What did they say, Lou? Specifically."

"You're gloating."

"They said you're gloating?"

"No. I'm telling you that you're gloating and you look ridiculous."

"Specifically, Lou. What did they say?"

"They said it was corny, outdated, and had nothing to do with the sensuality of their product. There. Are you happy? Now will you give me the goddamn music so I can save our asses?"

Vessie stood with her arms folded unmoved by Lou's plight.

"You were right," he said. "I'll shout it so the whole world can hear. *VESSIE VANCORTLAND WAS RIGHT AND LOU FIELDS THE MESHUGA* was wrong! Okay, I was wrong. Now, where's the goddamn jingle?"

Vessie sloooowwwwly made her way to the piano and picked up the piece of music. Lou could see her smiling from the back of her head. She was thrilled. Finally, it was her turn, her *time*. Now, the teacher would be taught. She held it out and he grabbed it.

"Thanks. They'll love it. But what the hell do *they* know?" Lou slammed the door behind him.

The following afternoon, Fields & Friends was blessed with a contract. The heat was off. Lou had two major accounts and could keep the wolves gnawing at somebody else's door. He also had the jingle he needed to submit for this year's Geos.

Remy broke the bad news over dim sum dumplings. "Lou submitted the Tropical Fruit Punch jingle for the Geos. Soulmate surpasses it artistically... and I must say I did a *splendid* job producing it."

"Fabulous," Vessie said.

"But what can you do? Lou's taste is in the crapper."

Vessie dropped her chopsticks. "Damn! It's the only jingle I've written that I'm proud of."

"It's a radio spot, Ves. You know he only submits for television. Besides, you've won enough awards and citations of merit to wallpaper Grand Central."

"But they were all for lousy spots. Spray and Play... Salties... Elasio's Wines. Any two-bit song hustler could have written that junk."

"But they didn't, Ves, *you* did."

Her heart sank.

"Hey, those companies made millions because of you," Remy said.

"Please, don't rub it in."

"Well then, submit the Soulmate jingle. Lou doesn't have to know. If it wins, he'll know and he'll be happy to take credit for it. Submit it, Ves, what have you got to lose?"

"I should, you know. I really should."

"Sure, you can use an alias."

"Remy, you're a genius."

The best friends played with names until they were jasmine-tea'ed out. Vessie decided to use the last name: *Flamingo*, in honor of the effigy she

186

used as her key to the island, and of her inspiration—Johnny, who Remy still knew nothing about.

"Flamingo suits you," he said. "Vessie *Flamingo.*"

"I'll just put *V.* Flamingo on the entry form."

From a hilltop, Vessie could see Johnny bend his long solid legs, muscular torso and forearms, and delicately dribble beads of wet sand onto his newly crafted sandcastle. His inner child dribbled along with him. He was immersed as if nothing else existed. *Like when we make love,* Vessie thought. *Like when I write music and time disappears.*

Vessie watched a group of gulls fly in tandem toward the tall sandy cliffs that curved along the shoreline and stretched into the sea. High, higher and beyond, clusters of lush green foliage reached for the sun. *Johnny and the island are one—wild, open, free. With Johnny, it's Anything Goes played in my key.*

At sunset, he chased Vessie up the hill and into the house, still wet from a swim, laughing, out of breath, their bodies tanned from a full day in the sun. His bathing trunks hung low on his hips. A cut-off t-shirt soaked with sea water was saran against Vessie's breasts. She ran for the couch as he grabbed her and turned her, falling together in a heated embrace.

The sky caught fire as Johnny entered Vessie slowly, growing inside until she moaned. They were off again, in another dimension, no longer feeling ecstasy, but *being* it—their bodies floating, minds exploding. They were Fred and Ginger dancing naked in the clouds. Popeye and Olive rolling wild on a bed of spinach. They were every hit song yet to be written and every romantic lyric ever sung. Together they transcended heaven and earth traveling beyond the speed of light.

Later that night, as Johnny stoked the fire illuminating the living room, Vessie sat at the piano in a thick plush robe playing a beautifully melodic song.

"Johnny, do you mind me disappearing all the time?"

"Do I have a choice? You're my fantasy."

Vessie froze. *I've got to tell him. I may be his fantasy lover but I'm not a fantasy.*

"Please, keep playing, Ves."

Tell him. Tell him. You've got to tell him now. Vessie mustered her courage, took a few deep breaths and began to play and sing a medley of her greatest hits:

> "Da-da-dats-a-daddy wafer
> Yeah, yeah, lots of yummy flavor"

She segued into another as Johnny turned to her in horror.

> "Take a Catflake to Breakfast
> And you'll have a thrill
> Take a Catflake to Breakfast
> And I'm sure you will"

"Stop, stop that!" he shouted.

> "No more ouchy
> No more grouchy
> Now you can sit all day on your couchy"

"Vessie, stop that right now!"

> "You-know-what will feel so ooey
> Like when you're in love, all gooey gooey"

Johnny walked over to Vessie as if sniffing the devil.

> "It's so soothing, you'll feel like mush
> SIGTOID'S HEMORROID PREPARATION: **TUSH!**"

"You *know* those commercials?"
"I wrote them."
"No... no, you didn't write them. I never would have wanted you to write them. I used to hear them all the time in New York and I *hated* them!"

Vessie's back stiffened. "They happen to have made my clients millions of dollars. And they're not called commercials, they're *jingles*! I'm not a fantasy, Johnny. I told you that when we first met but you wouldn't believe me."

"But, you can't be. You... you... I keep seeing you disappear." He was horrified and backed away.

"It's a yoga technique. I concentrate on an object, repeat a few words and..."

Johnny fell back onto the couch; then jumped up onto the cushions. "You're a witch... a goddamn witch! Go away. Get off my island."

"Look, I hate those jingles, too. I can't rationalize creating garbage anymore just to make money. That's why I keep coming here. *This* makes sense to me. You, me... time to just *be*."

Johnny's head was swimming. *If she's human, then she's responsible for writing the worst music conceived of in the twentieth century. Mother wouldn't have approved. But fuck mother, she's dead.*

"Vessie... a yoga technique?"

"Yes, I'll show you."

"No. No please... just sit. Don't move."

Johnny jumped down from the couch. "Do you know how many times I passed on women who were *into yoga?*" Vessie smiled. "They were flakes!*"* he said. Vessie's smile widened. "But not *you,* right?" Vessie nodded. "God! You really are something." He was drawn to her, but this time, with a sense of caution. Vessie threw her arms around him throwing caution to the wind. They kissed from the couch to the bedroom.

Moonlight filtered in through the window onto Vessie's sleeping face. The other half of the bed was empty.

Johnny walked ponderously along the shore. Vessie, being human, changed things. She had a history. She lived in the same city he had. They may have known some of the same people. She may have slept with one of his friends. She had a personality that he could no longer control. She would get old one day and have sagging tits. She could also be the best playmate he ever had, the best friend he could hope for, the best mother to their children. Jesus! There was no place to buy Pampers. Johnny wrestled with old fears of failed relationships. He walked in the moonlight kicking shells with each remembered face, hoping that Vessie wouldn't be there when he got back, then needing her desperately. He juggled every emotion he ever had and finally came up with this: *Vessie is the best thing that ever happened to me and I never want to lose her.*

"Johnny, Johnny!"

He turned. Vessie ran toward him, the moon painting her naked body white. Breathlessly, she knocked him down on the sand. He laughed and rolled her like a cigarette.

"I love you, you weirdo." He took her in his arms and kissed her with urgency.

"Johnny, I never want to leave you. I love you."

That was it. Johnny's libido shot starch into every inch of his manhood.

"Yes, yes," he said, ravaging her. "Stay with me Vessie. Stayyyy with meeeee!"

Lou was frantic. Almost a week had passed and no sign of Vessie. She didn't phone, didn't write—no word, no jingles, no nothin'. Not even an answer each time he knocked on her apartment door. Remy's attempts also proved futile. Together they feared the worst.

"Rodney, have you seen Ms. VanCortland?" they asked.

"No, sir."

"Sheila, have you seen or heard from Vessie?"

Sheila told them she tried reaching her several times, but got no answer. Remy and Lou decided to brave it and enter her apartment with Remy's key.

"You go first," Remy said.

"Me? But she's closer to you. Look, maybe we should get the police to do it."

"No. If Vessie's in there, she'd want us to be the ones to find her." Remy's heart was in his throat. *Where the hell are you, Ves? What the hell have you done?*

They entered the apartment with Sheila sneaking in behind. The sunlamps were glaring and a table lamp was on. The quasi tropical motif appeared to be not kitsch or funky—but an act of a desperate woman.

"Jesus!"

"Check the closets," Lou shouted.

Remy opened them like a madman. "Everything looks normal."

"Look. Her purse is here," Lou said. "And her wallet... money, credit cards."

"Let's see if her makeup's here." Sheila made a beeline to the bathroom. "My god, it is!"

"She can't be far," Remy said.

"She's probably gone too far," Sheila countered. "We better call the police."

High tea at the Grand Hyatt lounge was in full swing. Sheila made room on the small velvet settee for a very pregnant Smoodgie. "Charlene, I'm so glad you could come."

"Edward didn't want me to fly, with my due date just a couple months off, but..." She reached out to Remy who sat in a chair beside her. "Oh Remy! Our girl's in trouble." She could hear her own voice crack. She threw her arms around him letting go of the controlled façade that enabled her to get from Symington to New York without falling apart. Tears escaped, igniting an emotional release from Remy. Together they tried in vain to wish Vessie back, to believe she was safe. Without any corroboration, they feared she was either suicidal or raped and, when found, would be either a mental case or dead.

Sheila sat quietly waiting for the hysteria to subside. She knew what had happened and they were *wrong*.

"As you know, the police are looking for her, and I have every reason to believe that Vessie is alive and well, physically. I say, physically, because her actions over the past several weeks have been dangerously irrational. I've asked you here to discuss my observations and ask for yours. Vessie's in trouble—*psychological* trouble. Right now, she could be walking the streets not knowing who or where she is. And if we are fortunate enough to have the police find her before she comes to any harm, then it will be up to us to take drastic measures on her behalf."

THIRTY-SIX

Living Authentically

A warm wind pushed against the white sails moving the thirty foot cruiser along a smooth crystal sea. Johnny's island was no longer in sight—another took its place after a six hour early morning sail.

From the open cockpit he proudly manned the vessel in his bright floral trunks —pointing, smiling, waving to fisherman, scuba divers, and islanders swimming, sunning, washing clothes beside sleepy weathered docks. Vessie waved, too. These would be her new friends, her new neighbors who lived in the houses and huts that dotted the lush green hillside.

The sun had bleached streaks into Vessie's long hair and it waved in the wind like a light auburn flag. Her skin had turned dark honey; her body—*electric*. She was a bird in flight without leaving the ground.

Two small bodies—one in a bathing suit that looked like a miniature version of Vessie's—the other in bright floral trunks—played tag on deck laughing and yelling, then climbing down to the cabin below.

The sun beat down—a glare you had to look away from. It was half past noon when the boat pulled into dock.

A man of fifty, barrel chested with a ruddy complexion and strong-like-bull demeanor despite a game leg, limped toward the boat. "Hey Century," he yelled. "We thought you were dead. Where the hell have you been?"

Johnny grabbed the mooring line and attached it to the dock "It's *her* fault, Clifford me boy," he shouted, beaming at Vessie. "She kept me prisoner in me own home."

The men laughed heartily—Clifford Stout admiring Johnny's magnificent jailer. The pink-faced Irishman offered Vessie his plump red hand and she jumped onto the dock with Johnny a beat behind.

A gaggle of children appeared yelling: "Sandcastle Man! Sandcastle Man!"

"Well my boy," said the Irishman to Johnny, "looks like you're still in demand."

Johnny yelled to the kids. "Next time. I'll build you one next time." A great collective "awww," ushered forth. He smiled warmly, offered a well-intentioned promise; and the small fan club, once again hopeful, skipped away.

Johnny, Vessie, and Clifford Stout headed up a hill toward a street lined with small shops. A handsome woman in her mid-forties with long black waist-length hair, eyes the color of coal, and skin like wine-dipped olives stepped out of the largest shop with an apron around her waist, beaming with delight.

"John Century, you dog," she yelled. "We thought you'd met your maker!"

Clifford piped in: "Gisela, look what the dog brought in."

"I see, old man—and she's a vision."

Gisela Stout came right up to Vessie and gave her a big welcoming hug.

Wow. I never got a hug from a stranger in New York, Vessie thought. *I like this.*

They entered beneath a sign that read: STOUTS GENERAL STORE.

The shop was filled with canned goods, frozen beef, chicken and fish, fresh eggs, bread, flour, coffee and a decent range of packaged goods, fabrics, sewing supplies, automobile and household products. It was an all-purpose store the likes of which Vessie had never seen before.

The Stouts loved their lifestyle. It was just ten years since Clifford had lost his leg in a skiing accident and left the London brokerage firm of Grist, Oswald and Stout, married Gisela who had been his secretary and lover for years, and moved to the island to begin their new life.

"The regular, Johnny?" asked Clifford.

"Yes, and whatever Vessie wants."

The Stouts wanted to know more about his new love interest and insisted they stay for lunch.

During a meal of fresh baked bread, warm oozing Brie and Clifford's favorite—Kinsale Irish lager—they learned that Vessie was a composer and, according to Johnny, "a wicked pianist."

Gisela's eyes glowed. "Would you consider teaching, Vessie? We're a bit culturally deprived on the island and I'm sure the parents would be thrilled to have a musician of your caliber teach their children to play."

Teach kids to play. I LOVE kids. Images flashed across her mind—the church in Symington—accompanying the children's choir—the Nativity play. Something was happening. Something warm and sweet and scary. Could this be what Guruji meant by *attracting that which is your like?* And, *sharing your love through music?* Could it be that she had seen glimpses of her future all these years and now she was in it? Could this finally be the "home" she longed for—this life with Johnny? She never felt connected to Symington despite her position as Church Organist. Now, for the first time, she could see herself being part of a community. It felt familiar, somehow—comfortable and good. She turned and saw her inner child nodding *yes.*

"Yes, I think I'd like that," Vessie told Gisela.

Johnny beamed and put his arm around her just a little more proudly.

The wind shifted and with the additional power of the boat's engine, the lovers arrived back at the island just before midnight.

The next day, Vessie and Johnny picnicked in his favorite tree house—the one with the winding stairs and a deep cushioned floor. Johnny lay back reading Lord Byron, his head resting on Vessie's lap, as Vessie read Johnny's mind.

"Cool fresh water," she said. "Ahhh, the waterfall."

He dropped the sonnets and lifted his arms pulling her down for a kiss.

"I was just thinking that."

The natural pool of water bubbling from the crystal clear waterfall sprayed, teased and welcomed them. Johnny pushed Vessie in, then dove in after her. They found each other beneath the whirlpool and emerged touching and feeling their way into an embrace as the water bubbled around them.

Off to the beach, they ran and laughed—their inner kids trailing behind.

And, as the sun set that day, they looked at a sandcastle they had just built and knew what they had to do. They gouged it with their hands, grabbed great fistfuls of wet sand, and threw it at each other in a playful down and dirty mud fight.

It was midnight, May 20, 1982. The moon shone so brightly that Johnny lost all track of time and was still working on a new tree house. Vessie lay at the water's edge asking herself some serious questions.

"Are you happy?"

"You know I am," said her inner child. "I'm just scared."

"Scared? Of what?"

"Of you screwing up again. I want to *stay* happy. I like it here."

Vessie rolled over on her back and faced the moon. So did the little one.

"Do you know why you like it here?"

"Are you playing shrink with me?"

"No... *friend.*

"I like it because I'm not afraid here."

"You just said you were scared. Make up your mind."

"I'm scared of *dying.*"

"Dying?"

"Whenever you fall in love, you lose yourself, and each time you lose yourself, I die a little."

"That's how I felt with Bobby and Richard." *Ding ding.* "That was YOU?"

"Of course it was me. And I don't want it to happen again. Vessie, there's still so much you don't know about Johnny."

"Like what?"

"Are you kidding? Like *every*thing. Look at him. He's a recluse. Sure he goes out for groceries once in awhile, has lunch with a couple friends, but what happens when you want people *here on the* island? *Your* people, *your* friends: Mrs. Smith, Remy and Jacques, maybe even Smoodgie and baby Everlyn-Gene. What if he's a homo-phobe? What if he can't stand it when you want to be alone to meditate or when he sees you practice your

195

yoga techniques? He told you he avoided women who were *into yoga.* Is he going to freak out again? And what about your music? What if you want to spend time composing instead of playing with him? That's what I'm afraid of. I'm afraid you'll let me die, Vessie, and this time it'll be for good."

"I'd never do that." *I'll never let you die. You're my touchstone—my heart.*

For the next three days, unbeknownst to Johnny, Vessie put him through a series of tests.

DAY ONE:
Vessie told Johnny about her life in L.A. and her close relationship with Mrs. Smith.

His reaction: "I'd love to meet her. Let's get her to visit us. Stay here awhile. We'll spoil her rotten.

She told him all about her best friend Remy.and he said: "He sounds like a great guy." And about Remy and Jacques. "Love is love." And about Jacques' art installations: "The island's perfect. Look at all the room he'll have to play with."

DAY TWO:
Vessie gave up sailing with Johnny to stay home and work on her music.

His reaction: "Can't wait to hear it." And when he returned at sunset and found her still at the piano, he blew her a kiss and busied himself until she invited him in.

She still hadn't played the SOULMATE jingle because she knew how much he hated her other ditties. But this one was different. This was a piece of music that meant something to her, and that she was proud of. If Johnny hated it, *that* could be a problem.

Vessie sat at the keyboard about to find out. "Johnny, listen to this."

"As we look into each other's eyes
we are one, we are one
As we move into each other's arms stars come out
And as the night again turns into day
we look at the sun and become again, one

196

And we know love, and we know love
and only our love survives us… *soulmate*
You are my SOULMATE"

His reaction: He kissed her tenderly. "The words… that's how I feel about you, about *us*. And the melody is beautiful, Ves. It reminds me of one of my favorite classical pieces—Erik Satie's "Gymnopédies."
Oh my god oh my god oh my god!

DAY THREE:

It was time for the most crucial test of all. Johnny awoke to the sound of cooing. It wasn't like any cooing he had ever heard—it was oddly human. The other half of the bed was empty. He didn't like that Vessie wasn't there. "Ves?" No answer. "Vessssieeeeee!"
"Cooooo."
He jumped out of bed and followed the sound to a bedroom in the far end of the west wing. The door was closed and a sign was posted that read:

MEDITATING. PLEASE DO NOT DISTURB.
Love, Vessie

I don't like this, I don't like this, I don't like this, I don't like this, I don't like this. This is my house and I don't like being shut out!
"Johnny?"
Johnny looked down. It was his inner child.
"Don't be a dickhead. Vessie's not shutting you out. She just wants some privacy. And, by the way, it looks like she's living here now, so stop with the *my*-house ownership crap."
"Yoga shmoga."
"Cooooooo."
"Why can't she be normal like other women?"
"Did you hear what you just said? Did you? Did you?" Johnny's inner child was shouting. "You love Vessie because she *isn't* like other women.

197

And if doing yoga is part of what makes her special, then wake up and smell the incense!"

Johnny needed to get his thoughts straight. He walked outside around the property until he came to a spot where he could see into the far back bedroom of the west wing. *Oh my god—she's hovering three feet above the floor!*

"She's amazing," said his inner child. "So what's the problem? Knowing you can't control her? Fearing that she's more powerful than you are? Or is it that she doesn't *need* you?"

Vessie opened her eyes and fell on her tush. Like Lester-Anil, she still hadn't learned to control her landings. Just then a gull flew straight into the window and fell to the ground. She ran outside and found it fluttering in circles trying to lift off, but held back by a broken wing.

Vessie grounded her energy, raised both hands to the sky, stated her intention to heal the bird, then lowered her hands as close to its broken wing as it would allow. She repeated silently: *His love goes through me to your wing, through me to your wing.*

Moments later the bird relaxed and lowered itself into a clump. Vessie gently put her hands on it repeating her intention. She picked the bird up and held it in her lap as she curled her legs beneath her. She closed her eyes and went into deep meditation. Thirty minutes later she opened her eyes, lifted the bird up, opened her hands and watched it fly away.

Johnny witnessed the whole thing.

He didn't say anything to her about it. He didn't tell her how he felt when he saw the sign posted on the door, or when he saw her hovering three feet above the floor. He didn't explain his confusion and upset and horror and absolute thrill when he saw her heal an injured bird. He just told her that he loved her more than he ever believed be could love anyone and to ignore him if he ever acted like a dickhead.

What do you think of him now?
I think he's...
What? What?
I think he's... a keeper.
Because?
Because he loves me for who I really am.

Vessie and Johnny lay on the sand by an open fire as cinders burst like fireflies. Words from Shakespeare's Romeo and Juliet fell from his lips:

"But, soft! what light through yonder window breaks? It is the east, and Juliet... I mean, *Vessie*... is the sun. Arise, fair sun, and kill the envious moon, who is already sick and pale with grief, that thou her maid art far more fair than she."

Oh my god, I love you, Vessie thought. She kissed him gently as the moon splashed its light, and time passed in silence along the sleepy shore.

"Johnny," she said, "you know that song I played for you the other night—the one that reminded you of Erik Satie's *Gymnopédies*? I submitted it for this year's Geos. You know, winning a Geo is like winning the Oscar in my field."

Johnny's heart sank. *She isn't finished with New York. She isn't finished there.*

"Artistically, it's everything I've been trying to achieve. If it wins it could set a new precedent... raise the bar on jingle composition... open doors for new composers. We've *got* to get beyond writing meaningless *tripe*."

Johnny did something selfless. "Vessie," he said, "you've got to go back."

"What?"

"You've got to be at the Geos to find out what happens with Soulmate."

"My *soulmate's* right here. Are you trying to get rid of me?"

"I want you to go so you'll be sure you want to stay."

"You've got to be kidding."

"Ves... Marjory, the girl who came here with me? She said she loved me, loved the island, wanted to stay with me. Three weeks later, she was gone."

"I'm not Marjory!"

"This song means a lot to you. If you don't find out what happens, you'll kick yourself, especially if it wins." Vessie's gut wrenched. *Those were Daddy's words: If you don't find out what happens, you'll kick yourself, especially if it wins.* "Ves," Johnny said, "I don't want you to end up resenting me and resenting being on the island."

"Johnny, I don't care enough about winning to leave you." *Oh my god,* she thought. *That's what I said to Daddy!* Blood raced to her head.

Marjory, Vessie, Vessie, Marjory. Tell her. Tell her, Johnny thought.

Johnny, Daddy, Vessie thought.

"Ves, listen… maybe you need to go back. Maybe once you're in New York you'll find that there are still things you want to accomplish there and…" *spit it out, John* "… that you really don't want to be here."

Vessie was horrified. "What? Oh my god. You don't want me!"

"Of course I do. That's *not* what I said."

She jumped up, her mind spinning. The pain of loving her father so deeply, then losing him. She couldn't bear losing someone she loved so deeply again. She was trembling. Heat raced through her body as words flew out from a place of denial and fear.

"It was great when you thought I was a fantasy," she said, "but now… now I come with responsibilities," she said. "How could I be so stupid? You're a bachelor from Manhattan—the only futures *you* know are on the *stock* exchange." Her eyes welled with tears. "What a cheap way to end it."

"*End* it?"

Vessie ran down the beach.

"You're wrong," he yelled, running after her. "I want you here more than anything. I just want you to be sure, that's all."

I can't bear it. I can't bear it. She dug her feet into the sand. "I'll go back to New York," she shouted, "but you will never, *ever* see me again. *Images of Everend lying face down in the vestry.* "That, I can promise!" Vessie grabbed the key around her neck and began to focus on it when someone pounded on her apartment door and *snap!* she was gone.

A bottle of Halston left her hand and hurled toward the apartment door.

"Son of a bitch!" she yelled.

Crash!

"Vessie! Vessie are you alright?"

She pushed the door open.

"Ves! Thank God." Remy threw his arms around her and drew her close.

"He used me, Remy. I was nothing but a playboy bunny." She broke away. "I'm a goddamn bunny rabbit!"

"You're one helluva *tanned* bunny rabbit." Aside from her angry outburst and tears, Remy hadn't seen Vessie look this radiant in years.

She grabbed a tissue and threw herself on the sofa. "I'm a goddamn rabbit."

Remy sat down beside her. His tone was gentle. "I'd offer you a carrot, but I'm afraid I'm all out." He carefully peeled her out of a fetal position and held her close. "Ves, where have you been? I've been worried sick about you."

Remy, oh Remy. Vessie told him that she had dematerialized to an island. "That's where I've been all this time. I wanted to stay with him but he insisted I come back."

Remy looked up at the sunlamps glaring from the ceiling, then back at Vessie's tan. The *he* and the *where* of her story were too vague to understand. The *how* filled him with despair.

If you don't find out what happens you'll kick yourself—especially if it wins. Something was making her deny the truth. Something was forcing her to believe Johnny didn't love her. "Johnny said I'd never be satisfied there until I was successful here," she told Remy. Her whole body shook. "I told him about the Geos and he said I have to be here to see how Soulmate makes out."

"Smart guy, this Johnny."

"He just said it to get *rid* of me."

"Ves, it's probably his way of saying, please don't hurt me—if you come back, make sure it's for keeps."

"If I come back he may be dead!" *Oh my god, what did I just say? Where did that come from?*

"Dead?" Remy said.

Then she saw it. *This isn't about Johnny. It's about Daddy.* She turned to Remy. "I keep being triggered by old feelings about my father!" she said. Now Remy was *totally* confused. But Vessie understood. She got the connection. When she came back to the church after the song competition, Everend was dead. He didn't send her away because he didn't love her. He sent her away because he *did.* She wasn't responsible for his death. It was *his time.* And why in the world, when she finally found a man who loved her as selflessly as Johnny did, would she not take the chance of losing him one day? "Idiot. That's what I am," she told Remy. "Johnny loves me! And I'm going back to him right now."

"No!" Remy said. He had to stop her from leaving again, and immediately flew into high gear. After arduous mental and verbal gymnastics, he finished pleading her phantom lover's case. "You need to be here to find out what happens with Soulmate."

"Okay," Vessie said, "I'll go to the Geos, but as soon as they're over, I'm going back to Johnny." Vessie ran to the bathroom and threw cold water on her face.

The bathroom door closed and so did Remy's eyes. He cried for his friend. *She's gone. Too much pressure. Vessie's checked out of the real world and into Fantasy Fucking Island.*

Vessie lay in her bed. *Johnny Johnny... I'll make it up to you.*

"You better!" said her inner child, miserably unhappy to be back in the city away from her playmate.

Vessie gazed at the curtains that hid the iron fire escape—not the panoramic star-filled tropical sky. She listened to sirens wailing in the streets—not cockatoos screeching in nearby ginger palms. She felt the cold empty space beside her—not her lover's warm gentle touch.

Her inner child cuddled close.

"We're going back right after the Geos," Vessie said. "I promise."

Via taxis, subways, and walking on cement in well worn running shoes, Vessie revisited her old haunts: Greenwich Village, the Indian area at Lexington and Twenty-eighth, the Oyster Bar at Grand Central Station and her health club on the Upper East Side.

There, middle-aged matrons sucked in their bellies and spit out their envy as she exposed her toned body and sun-streaked hair.

Vessie kept to herself as they watched her leave the change room, re-enter after a swim, then again after a sauna and shower, and paint her face like a porcelain doll. The finishing touches: a gold beaded floor-length gown and French silk brocade heels. The apartment key on the red ribbon was now on a gold chain around her neck.

Vessie said goodbye to the ladies, not having said hello, but knowing full-well that they had been watching her every move. And they said goodbye, remembering the gowns they used to be able to fit into, the heels they used to balance on, the dreams they dreamed when they were fresh and young and believed that anything was possible.

Vessie was off to the Geos.

THIRTY-SEVEN

Breaking Through

Glasses clinked and faces shined. Tuxedos smelled of moth balls and rental bags and gowns took precedence over conversation. The Plaza ballroom was at its elegant best—all chandeliered and floralled.

Attendees from major international advertising agencies, design firms, and jingle houses sat at round tables with pink numbered cards on tall metal stands.

On stage, THE 21ST GEO AWARDS FESTIVAL was emblazoned on a large center screen. Just below was a line that read: TELEVISION & RADIO.

Vessie turned heads as she entered the ballroom in a long gold beaded gown that clung to her like baby seal skin. James Slater sprang up like a James-in-the-Box, said hello, gave her his best smile, and made her promise to "do lunch" with him *soon*.

Lou couldn't believe his eyes—she looked radiant. *How can this be?* he thought. Remy had given him a heads-up about Vessie's delusional island story. How could he get through the evening without asking her where she had been? What she was doing? And all the time pretending she was all right? *Look at her—she looks like she fell into a vat of chocolate.*

Forks and knives clicked and clacked against fine porcelain as various courses were consumed on automatic pilot. Anxious attendees faked social pleasantries and drank too much while thinking: *Just get to the goddamn awards!*

Finally, the band played an introduction and a disembodied voice announced:

"Ladies and Gentlemen, please welcome the Director of the Geo Awards Festival, Michael Carafello!"

"Alriighhtt!" Lou said, angling his chair toward the stage along with five hundred other people.

"Ladies and Gentlemen, it's my pleasure blah blah blah… tremendous response from over one hundred and twenty countries blah blah blah… over two hundred awards this year, blah blah…"

Lou was not pleased and his third double scotch let everyone know.

"Two hundred frigging awards? I'll be *dead* before this turkey's over."

Carafello continued: "Only the Gold, Silver, and Television Hall of Fame awards will be presented tonight. The Bronze winners will receive their honors by mail—we only have the hall 'til midnight, ha-ha."

Lou-three-sheets-to-the-wind Fields, Vessie and Remy sat through the cavalcade of honors applauding and offering congratulations to everybody else.

"What about *us?*" Lou said. "Where's *our* award? Why aren't *we* up there?"

"Our category isn't up yet, Lou," Remy reminded him.

Finally, Carafello announced: "And now for our Geo award winning *jingles.*

Fresh applause rang out.

On and on, winners were announced: Gold award winners, Silver award winners and none of them Fields & Friends. Not the Tropical Fruit Punch jingle Lou had submitted or Vessie's Soulmate jingle. Vessie and Remy hugged each other. "You did good," Remy whispered. "We tried," Vessie said. "We lost?" mumbled Lou.

He was about to slide off his chair under the table when the orchestra blasted a fanfare. Carafello was back at the podium. "It's not over 'til the fat lady sings," he said. "And this year she's singing: There's a *Grand* Geo in the spotlight tonight!"

Lou, now *five*-sheets-to-the-wind, slurred: "Lezzz gedd owda here."

Vessie grabbed his arm. "We can't, Lou. We're the only ones standing. Just hang in there. The fat lady's almost dead."

The Director puffed out his chest and continued: "Tonight we are about to make Geo history. As you all know the Grand Geo is the most prestigious award…"

"Blah blah blah," Lou moaned. He plunked down into his seat.

Carafello continued: "… and has always been awarded to either a television commercial or television campaign. This year, however, our panel of fifteen top international Creative Directors have unanimously awarded the Grand Geo to a Single Radio *Jingle* entry… *"Soulmate"* entered by its composer… V. Flamingo of Fields & Friends, New York."

"Oh my god oh my god oh my god!"

"Huh, wha, WHAT?"

"You did it!" Remy shouted.

"We did it," Vessie said, throwing her arms around him. "C'mon, Lou." She grabbed both men's hands and led them to the stage.

The large screen read:

THE GRAND GEO
U.S. RADIO JINGLE: "SOULMATE"
FIELDS & FRIENDS, NEW YORK.
MUSIC & LYRICS: V. FLAMINGO
PRODUCER(S): REMY BARTELLS, LOU FIELDS

The jingle blared over loud speakers as they made their way through handshakes and applause.

"As we look into each other's eyes
we are one, we are one
As we move into each other's arms, stars come out
And as the night again turns into day
we look at the sun and become again, one
And we know love, and we know love
and only our love survives us… *soulmate*
You are my SOULMATE"

A handsome usher stood at the foot of the stairs and offered Vessie his hand.

Suddenly, he looked like Everend and said: "Your music's beautiful, darling girl." Then Lou pinched her on the butt and Everend was once again the stranger who told her: "Congratulations, Ms. Flamingo. Great work."

A young woman with pink hair shoved a statuette in Vessie's hand as she moved to the microphone. Five hundred pair of eyes stared at her, waiting for her to be clever.

"Do you like my new name… *Flamingo?*"

The audience went wild.

"I'm so happy. This is more than just an award—it's an opportunity to celebrate change. Soulmate came straight from my heart and took me to a musical place that was different and risky. And you liked it!"

More applause.

"I'd like to thank the judges, personally… kisses on all four cheeks. And I'd like to thank this man right here… Lou Fields… my boss and tormentor for ten long painful years." She turned to him. "Thank you, Lou, for not only pushing me to the edge, but pushing me *over* it." She gestured to Remy. "And thank you Remy Bartells for all your love and support… for being the best friend a girl could have… and the best producer a jingle writer could hope for."

The audience rose to their feet as the pink-haired girl handed Lou and Remy matching Geos. They all knew Lou Fields—the old-school taskmaster who, despite his gruff personality, earned their respect. And Remy Bartells, whose solid producing skills were receiving industry nods.

Lou stepped to the microphone. "This comes as more of a surprise than you know. Thank you very *verrrrry* much." It was Remy's turn. "Thanks to you I was able to stop lying to my folks in Washington about how well I was doing in New York. That was years ago. Thanks *again,* Geo judges!" He held up the statuette. "And thank you Vessie *Flamingo* for writing one hell of a beautiful *song."*

Applause was lavish. Vessie took the microphone again. "One last thing… to those of you who have wanted to experiment and hesitated—go for it! Oh, and Johnny…I'm coming home!"

Vessie turned toward the stairs when she heard someone shout.

"Vessie! Vessie!"

Standing in the wings was—"Smoodgie?" She couldn't believe it. She flew to her sister and embraced her with urgency.

Smoodgie burst into tears. "Oh, Vessie."

"Why didn't you tell me you were coming in? Look at you. You look like the twins are about to pop."

Sheila cut in.

"Sheila?"

"Vessie dear, congratulations. What a tremendous honor!"

Warning. Warning. Alien body. This does not feel good.

Before she could say another word, Vessie was swept away by two large men in all-weather coats. "Come this way Miss VanCortland…"

Halfway up the extreme right aisle of the ballroom, Vessie chose not to be pushed and dictated to. "Wait a minute. Who are you?" She yelled to Sheila who was pulling up the rear. "Sheila, who are these guys?"

"You'll see. It's a surprise, dear."

"Forget it. I'm staying here."

She started to head back toward Smoodgie, Lou and Remy when Sheila shouted:

"Grab her!"

The two men forced Vessie up the aisle as she kicked and shouted to let her go. Several guests took notice and, believing it was a stunt, roared with laughter.

Smoodgie couldn't bear it. She ran after them. Remy ran after her. Lou grabbed a shot glass from an empty table and drained it.

Vessie struggled as the burly men carried her to the corridor.

"You're going to be all right, Vessie. Trust me," Sheila shouted.

The men forced her into a straightjacket and strapped it down as colleagues laughed and remarked: "You're too much, Vessie." "Hilarious! What's it going to be next year? Two guys in ape suits?"

"Smoodgie!" Vessie screamed. "Tell them I'm not crazy. Tell them it's a yoga technique. You saw me do it. You saw me appear and disappear in your room. Smoodgie, please—don't let them do this to me. I'm your sister. Smoodgie, pleeeeeeaaasssssse!"

One of the men stuck a syringe into Vessie's thigh. She passed out as Smoodgie fainted in Remy's arms.

Lou felt sick. Somewhere in his gut he knew this was his fault. He dropped into a chair remembering things—things that stung and burned—as hangers-on chatted in high-pitched tones. *How many times did she tell me? Lou, I can't do this anymore. Lou, I'm tired. Lou, I need to get away. And what did I do? I pushed, I prodded, I lied, I schemed. I even showed up at her goddamn wedding with work for her to do. Schmuck! What was I thinking?*

"Hey, Fields!" He didn't look up. "Congratulations," said James Slater, extending his hand. Lou took the statuette, put it in Slater's hand, and walked out.

Remy arrived at Jacques' loft, pale and trembling. He couldn't believe what had just happened—the vulgarity of it—the inhumanity. Jacques had never seen him so upset.

"She pleaded: *Please* please stop this—and I just stood there. She's my best friend and I did nothing. Jacques, Ves has always been there for me. She's always accepted me completely. And how do I pay her back?" He couldn't bear it. What to punch? Who to hit? He paced the floor beside the yellow couch where Jacques sat watching.

"When she told me about this flying thing she could do—about this guy, Johnny, and an island, I was devastated. I thought: She's completely lost it! I never even considered it a possibility. She *showed* me the book her guru gave her—the page of instructions, the props she used to make it work. She even wanted to do it for me so I could see for myself—so I'd *believe* her. But did I let her? Did I let myself see this *thing* she could do? No!"

He looked at Jacques, his face twisted with self-condemnation. "What does that say about *me*? What the *hell* does that say about me?"

Jacques smiled. "You may be gay, honey, but you're just like everybody else—scared to death of the unknown."

The stewardess was about to place a third gin and tonic on Smoodgie's tray when she ran to the restroom and threw up.

Ten minutes later, she was staring through the airplane window at memories of herself and Vessie as children. She saw Vessie heal things: a hamster, birds, stray cats and dogs. She saw her answer the door before someone appeared—run to the phone before it rang. And how she hated her for it. Hated her for being different. And the more Vessie loved her, how she even hated her for that.

Smoodgie's gut wrenched. *Maybe that wasn't a dream I had about Vessie appearing in my bed that night. Maybe it wasn't a dream.* She closed her eyes. Old hurts resurfaced. *Vessie got all the attention. So pretty. So talented. Jesus, Daddy, don't I exist?*

She drained her gin and tonic trying not to think; but the two burly men flashed across her mind, trapping Vessie like an animal, strapping her into a straightjacket as she pleaded with her to make them stop. And there *she* was allowing it, knowing all the time it was happening because of the medical certificate Sheila signed, and her own familial consent.

Dear Lord! What did I do? Why did I do it? Then she remembered: *She's sick. Vessie needs help.*

Is she Smoodgie? Is she? The truth shouted to be heard. But how could she admit that Vessie wasn't crazy? That she *could* dematerialize? That would mean admitting her sister really *was* special. That Vessie *could* do things she wasn't able to. It would also leave her with no excuse for years of unwarranted cruelty to Vessie, and now—having her institutionalized.

THIRTY-EIGHT

Fly in a Jar

Vessie came to in a room that was not much bigger than a prison cell. The window was wired and so was the one in the door. At first she didn't know where she was. Then she remembered. *Oh my god oh my god oh my god!*

She grabbed for the key around her neck but it was gone. The gold beaded gown was gone. The delicate French brocade shoes were gone. All of her personal belongings had been stripped away. A green hospital gown hung on her lifelessly, reflecting its surroundings.

Be calm. Don't freak out, she told herself.

"What? Are you crazy?" It was her inner child. "I take that back. We're in an asylum."

Their eyes locked.

"Don't you dare start crying," Vessie said, her eyes welling with tears.

Johnny stood staring at the piano. *Vessie, I did this for you.*

"Man, are you deluded," said his inner child.

"Piss off. I *did* do it for her."

"Did not. You did it because you were afraid."

Johnny rubbed his face furiously.

His inner kid continued: "Afraid that one day she'd kiss your ass goodbye—so you speeded it up."

"YOU ARE SO FULL OF... " He couldn't finish. He knew it was true. *Jesus! What did I do?*

Vessie's door opened. Standing over her was a six foot amazon pretending to be a nurse—short slicked-back hair, bulbous nose, and dark fuzz that surrounded her mouth and chin.

"I'm Nurse Clemments. And you're Vessie VanCortland. I know all about you, and you better know this about me—I don't take shit from no-bo-dy. So behave yourself or I won't be nice to you. Un-der-*stand*?" She left the room locking the door behind her.

All about me? What could she possibly know about me? And what's wrong with her? Why is she so damn mean-spirited?

If Vessie slept that night she didn't know it. Sounds cracked, bumped and banged. She lay like a corpse on a narrow worn out cot—a strip of moonlight ribboning across her tightened body onto a green enameled wall. *What did I do to deserve this? What was so horrible?* She tried to make sense of the past six hours—the incongruity of winning and losing the same hand. *Who did I hurt? Is somebody bleeding in a gutter? Mangled on a train rail? Whose life did I ruin by being me?*

Vessie had everything she desired and was happy for the first time. No longer could her inner child accuse her of not living authentically. No longer was she agreeing to play, "The Brand Message Challenge." Johnny and the island—love, nature, unlimited creativity, love, laughter—that was it for her. She was finally clear about who she was and what she wanted. She had it all and watched Smoodgie, Remy, Lou and Sheila take it away from her.

They trapped her like an animal, stripped her of her freedom, her life, her happiness. Why? What had she done that they found so threatening? Was it that she disappeared and returned happy and healthy and clear?

What was it? That she didn't make things convenient for them? That what and who she was *scared* them, so they had to make her wrong? No, not wrong—they made her SICK, demented. Surely they saw her smile? The light in her eyes. Was she shining too brightly? Was that it? Was her smile too pervasive so they thought something had to be *wrong* with her? Nobody else glowed like that in Manhattan except maybe nutcases? Was she crazy to give up what they considered "success"? Crazy for choosing a lifestyle that didn't include bus fumes, the Internal Revenue Service and rapists?

Johnny, she cried.

Vessie, he sighed.

Tears dominated her anger as morning came.

Doctor Victor Chambers, Director and Chief Surgeon of the Margaret Trust Asylum sat behind his oversized walnut desk. Anything would have looked oversized next to him: a thick book, a fat sandwich. He was small. His bulgy grey eyes were not. They peered over his bifocals at another rejection letter:

> … and therefore, on behalf of the National
> Psychoanalytical Practitioners' Medical Journal, I regret
> to inform you that our esteemed panel of adjudicators
> find your theory on Prenatal Neuroses Transference
> lacking substantive data and, therefore, we are unable to
> offer publication of your proposed paper.

He crumpled the rejection letter into a ball and screamed every profanity he could think of. When he ran dry he made some up: "You flatulent piece of dog smegma. You fart dead people. I hate you and hope you DIE!"

Doctor Chambers straightened his bowtie and pushed a button on the desk intercom.

"Nurse, send in the next patient."

Clemments clapped her hands. Vessie's response?

"Thank you, thank you, you're too kind."

The amazon seethed. "Get your ass into Doctor Chambers chambers."

Vessie laughed nervously. "Chambers *chambers*?"

Her inner child tugged at her hospital gown. "Stop screwing around. She'll *eat* us."

Clemments was turning red. "Nowwww!"

Vessie marched into Chambers chambers. This would be the first meeting with her key source to freedom. She would explain the whole mistake. What a fiasco. How unfortunate and ridiculous. He would see that of course she was sane. They'd laugh. Have tea. He'd phone for a taxi.

They'd wave goodbye. He'd shout: "See you!" knowing he'd never see her again.

"Vessie VanCortland," he said, reading her name off the file. "Do you understand that you are here under observation for the next seventy-two hours? That your behavior has created great concern for your family and friends? And that if we find that it is in your best interest to extend your stay, we can do so?"

Her words flew at him like bullets. "Doctor Chambers I'm not crazy I really can dematerialize, I use a yoga teleportation technique, I know it may sound crazy but I can prove it, I'll do it for you now but I can't travel as far as I normally can without my flamingo."

He looked at her over his bifocals then wrote down: *flamingo.*

Scribble scribble. Listen to me. "If I concentrate on..."—*choose an object, quick, Vessie, think*—"...on that *wall* directly across from me... I can disappear from where I'm sitting and reappear on that side of the room." She had never attempted short in-house trips before, wasn't sure she could do it, but was desperate.

He wrote down: *delusional.* "Tell me Ms. VanCortland..."

"Vessie."

"Ms. VanCortland. After you perform this... this..."

The words *yoga teleportation technique* wouldn't come out. To Chambers, any practice that had a guru attached to it was about as credible as sticking worms up your nose.

"Yoga technique," Vessie said.

"... yoga technique, yes... and if I tell you that you never left that chair, will you believe me?"

Vessie saw his game and was sure she would win. She *would* leave the chair, he *would* see her do it, and that *would* be the end of it.

"Yes, I'd believe you." *Lord, don't fail me now.*

She settled into a green leather chair. *Johnny Johnny, this is for you, for us.* She closed her eyes, grounded herself, visualized pulling pure universal energy in through the top of her head and moving it to every part of her body. She repeated her mantra over and over until she was able to clear her mind of the two men that forced her there—of Sheila, Smoodgie, Lou and Remy who just stood there doing nothing to help her.

The Four Elements, she thought: *(1) Intention, (2) lack of fear, (3) connecting to pure energy, and (4) believing that you can do it. My intention is to dematerialize from this chair and rematerialize on the opposite side of the room.*

She repeated her mantra and focused on the green wall directly across from her. "Om-mani-padme-hum, om-mani-padme-hum." *Mantra mantra... wall wall.*

Chambers looked at his watch—almost eleven thirty. Pastrami sandwiches danced in his head. Polish dills did the Salsa. He looked at Vessie. She was surrounded by *what? Light?* A strong breeze blew through the room blowing papers off his desk, forcing the aluminum blinds to rattle. *What the? She's? She's fading? But she can't be.* He looked again. She *was* fading. Her image was growing fainter and fainter.

"Ahh!" he gasped. Vessie VanCortland was gone.

"Ahh!" She reappeared on the opposite side of the room. Vessie was excited and relieved. Now he would let her return to the island and Johnny.

"See?" Her grin was obnoxious. "I told you I could do it!"

Chambers had to think fast. He turned away, caught his breath, then turned back.

"Sit down, Ms. VanCortland." He appeared calm, almost stern. Inside, however, he was jumping up and down, jerking off seeing his name in print, accolades showered upon him by the best medical journals; offers of grants pouring in from institutions, government agencies, and private foundations. He would be on the covers of: The New England Journal of Medicine, The American Journal of Psychiatry, Time, Life, GQ.

This woman, this phenomenon was going to put Doctor Victor Bartholomew Chambers on the Adulated Psychiatrists Map of the Fucking World. But how? What would he do? *Come on Victor, think of something.*

"You remember what I told you before?" he said.

Vessie was anxious. "Yes, but you saw me. You were watching weren't you?" *What the hell is going on?*

"You never left that chair. My eyes stayed on you and you never left that chair." *Come on, VanCortland, believe me woman.*

"But I did! Of course I did. Why are you saying I didn't?" *You little shit. You bug-eyed dickhead.*

215

"You never left that chair," he repeated firmly.

Vessie was incensed and stood up. "I did NOT WALK over there!"

"That's right. You never left that chair. Now sit down, PLEASE."

Vessie didn't budge. "What is it? Are you afraid to admit what you saw? If you do, it'll mean you're crazy. Is that it? Then bring somebody else in. Bring in your entire staff. I'll do it as many times as it takes to make it all right for you to admit that I'm NOT CRAZY!"

Chambers' blood raced as he summonsed Nurse Clemments.

Nurse Clemments gasped when she saw Vessie dematerialize. She gasped again when she saw her reappear across the room. And when asked what she had seen, Clemments told Vessiee: "You never left that chair." She was victim of the If-I-Profess-to-Seeing-It-I-Must-Be-Crazy syndrome.

Vessie bolted toward the door shouting profanities and threats. Once again, she was punched in the thigh with a syringe and taken to her room.

Clemments and Chambers were alone in Chambers chambers.

"VanCortland *did* dematerialize," he told her. "She's as sane as we are, but in possession of a phenomenal mind. In the name of science it is my duty as a psychiatrist and surgeon to investigate. She must be studied, tested, all data documented. But, I can't do it alone."

Clemments' beady eyes searched his.

"I need a strong, dedicated assistant. Someone who understands the importance of moving the mental health field forward even if it means foregoing certain uh..."

"Rules, doctor?"

"Yes. VanCortland mustn't know why she's being tested. She's got to believe I'm searching for the cause of her *acute schizophrenia*. And no one, including her family will be the wiser."

Doctor Chambers turned, looked up a whole twelve inches into her face and said:

"I need you, Clemments."

Always the consummate nurse waiting for her chance at immortality, she gladly accepted the appointment as Doctor Victor Bartholomew Chamber's comrade in depravity.

THIRTY-NINE

On a Wing and a Prayer

Vessie became a guinea pig. She was poked, prodded, hooked up to machines and drugged. But no chemical abnormalities were found. No unusual brain scans. Chambers tried taking her back through her prenatal experience. Nothing. *Nothing? There's got to be something,* he thought. *What about my paper?*

Yes. What about the discovery that would make him seven feet tall and the victim of low doorways?

There's got to be a way, he thought. *Everything can be explained scientifically. I've got to prove myself to the American Medical Association. But what am I to say? Patient "X" molecularly deconstructed by means of a yoga technique? YOGA SHMOGA!*

In need of more time, Dr. Chambers informed Dr. and Mrs. Edward Kleig that Vessie VanCortland had been diagnosed with acute schizophrenia disorder and needed to be kept at the asylum for further treatment.

Smoodgie was beside herself and told Edward: "Acute schizophrenia? Hogwash. I've got to get her out of there."

"You've got to stay right where you are."

"She needs me, Edward. There's no telling what's going on in that place."

"It's too risky, Charlene. You're too far along."

"I'm fine. I'll be fine," she said, and ran to the bathroom and threw up.

Vessie was angry. *I won't be guinea-pigged anymore. No more demonstrations. All Chambers ever says is: You never left that chair!*

Chambers was desperate. His tests proved inconclusive. He couldn't admit to Vessie that he knew she was sane without being forced to release her from the asylum. He hoped that by observing her in the process of dematerialization and rematerialization he might find some clues that would point him to the source of this psycho-physical phenomenon. "Just a few more times," he told her. "I'll concentrate harder. I'm sure I'll see it this time." What he felt like saying was: *Pleeeeeeaaaasssse! Do it and I'll buy you a house. I'll give People magazine your picture instead of mine. It'll be YOUR glory, YOUR story."*

"Get me my flamingo and I'll do anything you want."

Chambers was ethically-challenged, but he wasn't stupid. *Oh sure. You'll get your key outta here and that's where you'll go—out of here!*

Vessie sat with her legs crossed, arms crossed, lips pursed. So did her inner child. *I will not be humiliated again.*

Chambers ordered two orderlies to take Ms. VanCortland away. She sat in a full lotus like a rock and that's how they removed her.

"Nurse Clemments," said the little man. "I've been left with no choice. We've got to operate."

"But doctor!"

"I know. I realize the implications, but I've tried everything else. The answer must be in the brain itself."

"But, that could be dangerous."

"Indeed."

"Her mind…her memory. She could be rendered…"

"Enough!"

Johnny stared at the sea. It may as well have been black and murky for all he cared—the sky, grey and polluted—the fish, belly up—the tree houses torched. Without Vessie, his Technicolor world had become Film Noir.

"Look at me."

"Go away."

His inner child sat crossed legged on the sand right in front of him.

"I want my playmate back."

"What is this, a sit-in?"

"I want my playmate back... I..."

Johnny put his hands over the kid's mouth. "I want her back, too. But she obviously doesn't want me or she'd be here. So shut up, will ya?" He pulled his hands away.

"Then change her mind. Fight for her. Beg her to come back."

Johnny didn't budge.

"Johnny Johnny Johnny, what am I going to do with you? YOU'RE supposed to be the *adult*."

"But she could turn me down."

"THAT's the spirit. Oy. I'm not even Jewish and I'm saying, oy."

The kid put his hands on Johnny's face and made him look straight at him. "You've got nothing to lose and Vessie to gain. Come on, Johnny. Up you go."

The kid pushed his body against Johnny trying to force him to stand. "Come on... hiney up, leg's uncurled. Atta boy. Come on, boy, you can do it."

"Fields & Friends," Johnny said springing to his feet. "They'll know where she is." He looked down at his smaller self: "Come on kid. What the heck are you waiting for?"

Johnny sailed to Nassau, then took the first plane scheduled for New York. He made sure to leave a note for Vessie in case she returned while he was gone. It lay against the piano music stand and read:

I've gone to find you.
Don't leave.
Ever.
Johnny

Smoodgie, Mrs. Smith, and Paramahansa Bramananda sat in his little hut down the winding path from the ashram temple in Malibu. There was no furniture, just cushions, and Mrs. Smith had a hard time getting comfortable. She ended up having to lounge sideways.

Bramananda sat as always with his feet curled beneath his orange dhoti. "The teleportation technique is valid," he said. "Gita had the ability to perform it but was not yet ready during her stay here. She must have perfected it on her own. You must go back. Explain to the authorities what I have told you."

"They'll never believe us," Smoodgie said. "Psychiatry and yoga aren't exactly best friends. They'll think we're as crazy as Vessie, uh, *Gita*."

Incense permeated the room causing Smoodgie to wheeze.

"Her friend Remy told us she uses *props* to teleport?" Mrs. Smith said. "A paper flamingo and a key?"

"I see," said the guru. "Then that is what she needs. When Gita has needed me, she has called to me. I have not heard from her in a long time."

He took a flower from a small vase beside him and handed it to Smoodgie. "You must bring Gita the objects she needs for her technique so that she can free herself from that prison."

Mrs. Smith turned to Smoodgie. "I'll go. I'll do it. You need to tend to the kinder."

Smoodie didn't understand.

The elder woman patted Smoodgie's belly. "Kinder—the *children*."

"Oh, that's very kind of you, Mrs. Smith, but only immediate family members are allowed to see her."

"Well, they won't be able to say no once I'm there. What? I don't look like a mother?"

Smoodgie didn't want to be rude, but not only didn't Mrs. Smith resemble Vessie—she was old enough to be her *grand*mother.

"So, I'll tell them it was a second marriage and her father had a thing for older women. I'll think of something. Don't worry, dahlink."

It was Tuesday, and unbeknownst to Vessie—one day before her impending operation.

"I'm Mrs. Theodora Smith VanCortland, Vessie VanCortland's grandma-ma."

Mrs. Smith said the "ma-ma" with a quasi-English-Bostonian accent that she had once created for a part in a Hadassah play. The problem was, the character was from East Texas. Smoodgie had chosen an appropriate suit for her to wear, Mrs. Smith held an attractive coat over her arm, and her performance was sterling.

Doctor Chambers listened to her spiel, then practically waved her away.

"Impossible," he said. "Ms. VanCortland cannot receive visitors. I'm afraid her condition is too delicate at the moment. Any form of excitement could prove damaging."

You arrogant little putz, she thought. "I flew all the way from Los Angeles and I'm not leaving until I see my granddaughter. If you wish to proceed in forcing me to leave, you will give me no choice but to consult the authorities. And I warn you, the District Attorney for the City of Los Angeles who is my step-son would refer your behavior to the District Attorney for the City of New York, who is my nephew."

I can't afford any bad publicity, the little man thought. "Alright," he said. "You can see the patient for ten minutes. But *I* warn *you*—anything you say could trigger another seizure."

"Seizure?" *At least he's an imaginative putz.*

"Yes. As you know your granddaughter has been diagnosed with acute schizophrenia. Psychic seizures are common to this disorder."

"Oh dear."

Vessie entered the visitor's area and saw her precious Mrs. Smith stand up with open arms. "It's GRANDma-ma, darling. It's GRANDma-ma!"

"Grandma-ma! Vessie yelled, running toward her.

Nurse Clemments was right behind her. "Easy VanCortland. One foot in front of the other. Slowly, slowly."

Vessie broke her run. She reached Mrs. Smith and threw her arms around her, breaking into deep sobs.

Mrs. Smith was incensed. Her beautiful girl was distraught, thin, her eyes glazed. *What have they done to you?* "It's going to be all right," she whispered. "I brought your flamingo and the key. Remy gave them to me when I told him what your guru said."

Vessie smiled through her tears. "Guruji? You spoke with Guruji?"

Chambers was watching. *What's going on? What's VanCortland telling her? Calm down, Victor,* he told himself. *The woman has clout.*

Mrs. Smith went on: "Smoodgie and I met with him. He explained the whole thing."

"Smoodgie knows I'm not crazy?"

"Yes, Vessella."

221

"And Remy and Lou?"

"Yes, my dahlink. Now listen to me because we don't have much time. When I go to leave, make a fuss, a *big* fuss, okay?" She pulled away, straightened her suit, patted the coat that she held over her arm.

Clemments approached like a commando. "Visiting time is up, VanCortland. Come with me."

"No! I'm staying with Grandma-ma." Vessie turned to Mrs. Smith. "Grandma-ma, don't let her take me away. Please, please."

Nurse Clemments came up behind her and with steely intent. "Walk away now or I will drug you."

"Vessie, take this darling, so you won't be cold in there." She handed Vessie her woven coat. Clemments tore it from her hands.

"It's not allowed."

Doctor Chambers called to Clemments and nodded to let VanCortland have the coat. *Damn him. How dare he humiliate me like this.* She felt like ramming her horns into a wall but instead, pushed VanCortland back toward her room.

As soon as the door was locked behind her, Vessie opened the coat. Attached to the satin lining in a large plastic bag was the pink papier mâché flamingo. *No time to lose. I have to dematerialize before Nurse Clemments comes back.* She put the coat beside her on the cot, curled her legs beneath her, sat the flamingo on her lap and closed her eyes. "Om-mani-padme-hum, om-mani-padme-hum."

The door creaked open. *Shit.* Vessie shoved the flamingo under the coat as Nurse Clemments hovered casting a long shadow.

"You know, that *is* a pretty coat," she said. "*Darn* pretty." Her smiled twisted. Her eyes narrowed to slits. "I've always wanted a coat like that." She grabbed it from Vessie causing the papier mâché flamingo and the key to fall to the floor. *Clink.* Vessie grabbed the flamingo. Nurse Clemments grabbed the key. Her face brightened. She looked at the bird. "A toy? You were hiding a *toy*?"

"Give me back my key."

"How sweet. *Pink*, my favorite color." Clemments tried to snatch it from her and a tug-of-war ensued. Before Vessie knew it, her tormentor was tossing the flamingo in the air.

"Please let me have it," Vessie said. "It was my *mother's*."

Clemments caught it just before it hit the floor.

"Sure it was. Hey, I'm not stupid. Doctor Chambers told me about your pet *flamingo*. You just want it so you can break outta here." She held up the key. "This part of your voodoo, too?"

"Then you know it works. You know I can dematerialize."

"Alls I know is—the *rules*. And the rules state: NO TOYS ALLOWED."

Clemments threw the flamingo on the floor. "Oh look, it fell." She stomped on it until it was nothing but flattened newspaper and paint chips.

"You sadistic bitch!" Vessie's foot shot out in front of her and kicked Clemments so hard she fell back against the door. "Youuuuuu!" she threw herself on the enormous woman and pounded her with her fists.

Clemments pushed an alarm embedded in the wall. Two orderlies rushed in, grabbed Vessie and stabbed her with a syringe.

"Johnny! Johnny!" she cried, feeling herself reel into oblivion.

The behemoth stood over her. "We're gonna cut your head open tomorrow and you ain't *never* gonna see your *Johnny* again."

Johnny's tanned face looked odd among the pale-skins seated in the waiting area at Fields & Friends. He approached Chrissy, still Receptionist Goddess Numero Uno.

"Is Vessie here?"

"Vessie?"

"Vessie VanCortland."

Ooo, who is Mr. Yummy? she thought. "Who can I say is here?"

"John Century."

"I'm sorry, Mister *Century*. Vessie isn't in."

"Do you know when she's expected?"

"No."

"Do you know where I can reach her?"

"No."

"Is Lou Fields in?"

"No."

"Well, there must be *someone* who can tell me how to reach Vessie!"

"Vessie?" Remy had entered just in time to catch that last bit. "You want to reach Vessie?"

"Yes. It's urgent." He extended his tanned hand. "John Century."

Remy couldn't believe it. "*THE* John Century? The guy from the island?"

"Yes. You know me?"

"JOHNNY!" Remy hugged him off his feet.

Vessie didn't fight when they came to prepare her for surgery—she didn't want to be drugged again. She wanted to be conscious so that she could think of Johnny before surgery would take him away from her forever. She watched herself being strapped onto a gurney and wheeled down a hallway toward the operating room. She remembered having watched similar scenes in television dramas; but this time she wouldn't be able to get up during a commercial break. This time there would be no Eyewitness News Brief interrupting the climactic scene. No friendly visit from Remy, stealing her away to a neighborhood bar for a drink.

How ludicrous, how ironic and bizarre. After thirty-three years of searching, she finally found happiness. Finally knew who she was and what she wanted and wasn't willing to compromise anymore. And the payoff? Punishment, for being just a little too different.

The gurney pushed open the doors to her future.

Cold and stark, it looked more like a morgue than an operating room. The only thing that Vessie found even remotely patient-friendly were the lights glaring down on her, reminding her of the sunlamps strung above the hammock in her apartment.

Nurse Clemments hovered with a sneer that made the Wicked Witch of the West look like Mother Teresa. Even the green cloth surgical mask couldn't hide the pleasure she took in Vessie's pain.

Vessie lay there as her mind spun out of control. She saw Bobby Rich—his bandaged wrists. Lester at the ashram. Bramananda's penetrating eyes. Mrs. Smith, embrace her. The blizzard's pelting snow bury her inside her car. Smoodgie yell: *you're crazy!* Everend, call her: *my darling girl.* Erlinor, yell: *You blashphemous harlot!* Lou, rail at her: *You want art? Go to a goddamn museum.* The GEOS: the crowd, the applause, the betrayal—straight-jacketed and forced away as Smoodgie, Lou, Remy, Sheila watched and did nothing. She saw Johnny chase her past ginger palms—push her into a cool natural pool—brush her hair away, kiss her smile, splash, caress, enter her gently beneath the waterfall, under the stars. *Johnny! Johnny! Come to me. Be with me!*

She could hear Nurse Clemments and Doctor Chambers move closer. *Please dear God. Make this a dream. Make me wake up. MAKE ME WAKE UP!*

Vessie's inner child appeared.

"Haven't you learned *any*thing? All those yoga techniques...those spiritual books. Vessie, *stop* being a *fly in a jar!*"

"I can't help it. How am I supposed to transcend *this?*"

"You know how. You know the only way *out* is *IN!*"

Nurse Clemments cut Vessie's long sun-streaked hair down to the skin where it would soon be cut with a knife. Tears streamed down Vessie's face.

Johnny told Remy how he and Vessie met and fell in love. Remy told Johnny that Vessie was being held at the Margaret Trust Asylum as a schizophrenic because nobody believed her story.

"You're her only hope."

Johnny immediately placed a call.

"Doctor Chambers is unavailable. He'll be in surgery all morning."

"I've got to speak to him. It's an emergency!"

"I suggest you call back tomorrow."

"Listen, his patient Vessie VanCortland is sane. I can prove it."

"You'll have to speak with Doctor Chambers about that and as I've already told you, he is unavailable to take any calls."

Johnny slammed down the phone, fraught with concern. "I'm going over there." He shook Remy's hand and ran out the door.

"I'm coming with you!"

Midtown traffic was manic. So was Johnny. He jumped in front of a taxi, waving his arms.

The taxi driver slammed on his brakes. "Asshole!" he shouted.

Johnny ran to the window and shoved a hundred dollar bill at him.

"Get in."

He and Remy lit into the back seat. "The Margaret Trust Asylum, and step on it!"

Vessie closed her eyes and silently repeated: *Om-mani-padme-hum, om-mani-padme-hum. Om-mani-padme-hum, om-mani-padme-hum.*

Nurse Clemments blew into surgical gloves checking for invisible tears.

Om-mani-padme-hum, om-mani-padme-hum.

Chambers secured his surgical mask.

Om-mani... Suddenly, Vessie heard Bramananda's voice as clear as if he were in the room. *Gita, why did you not read the last two lines of my instructions?*

Nurse Clemments placed the last of the surgical implements on a tray beside Vessie. "Ready, doctor."

Eventually you will no longer need a material object to dematerialize. You will simply need to visualize the object and know and believe that you are one and not separate with all that exists. And if it is your true heart's desire to remain at your destination, then nothing can force you to return.

Johnny and Remy kept banging into each other at every turn—a case of New York City taxi driving at its worst. And they felt grateful.

Visualize the object, Vessie, see it, feel it, be it. Believe. Know that you are one and not separate... believe... believe...

Johnny and Remy ran past the Admitting Nurse at the Margaret Trust Asylum.

"Stop! Stop!" she yelled. "You can't go in there!"

They threw open the doors marked: DO NOT ENTER.

Visualize visualize, Vessie told herself. She could see her arms become wings—her neck grow long and arched—her hair transform into long magnificent feathers. *I am... I am... I believe... I believe.* Light surrounded her. A strong breeze blew through the room rattling surgical instruments—moving medical equipment around. There was no time.

Doctor Chambers wanted celebrity and nothing was going to stop him now. He lifted the razor-sharp surgical knife and brought it down on Vessie's head.

"Waaaaa—waaaaaa!"

"It's a girl!" announced a white-haired obstetrician lifting the first of the twins for Smoodgie and Edward to see.

"A girl!" Edward shouted, thrilled and relieved. He gently took his first-born in his arms as Smoodgie pushed out baby number two.

"And here comes…" the doctor said, "her… her… *sister!*"

Smoodgie's heart wrenched. "Vessie!"

Johnny and Remy burst into the operating room as three burly orderlies grabbed them. Nurse Clemments fainted to the floor. Chambers stood frozen, staring hard at the operating table—straps secured in place—Vessie, gone.

FORTY

A flamingo flew over a sandbar fifty feet from a white sandy shore—the flutter of its wings, the only sound in the late afternoon sky. The turquoise sea, calm and clear, rippled behind the thirty foot cruiser as it pulled into dock.

Johnny was frantic. *Are you here? Vessie, be here.* He cut off the engine, grabbed the mooring line. *Forget it, can't wait.* He tossed it aside, jumped from the boat to the dock and down onto the sand. He ran along the water's edge past sandcastles and sea turtles, his footprints filling with the tide. He ran as Vessie had seen him run hundreds of times… in a poster… a mural… her dreams.

"Vessie! Vessie!"

Cockatoos screeched as she ran down the hill away from the house past ginger palms and sweet smelling mangoes.

Johnny! Johnny! She could see him, touch him, feel him. Her mind exploded. Her back arched, arms opened wide. Her feet kicked back and lifted higher higher. She flew toward him—a magnificent she-bird in a sheer white dress. *"Yessssssssss!"*

She was home. Finally, home. And nothing could force Vessie away again.

ACKNOWLEDGEMENTS

Deepfelt thanks to those who have helped me birth this labour of love in numerous caring ways.

To Paul Lima for a great first edit—eye of an eagle, patience of a saint.

To Araby Lockhart, Harry Lewis, Bette Lewis, Marguerite Matteo whose continual love and support proves there really is a God.

To Cynthia Marion, Amira Cuttler, Hagan and Danica Beggs, Vern Kennedy, Marilyn Harding, Vicki Loftus, Cayle Chernin, Rebecca Couch, Dean Noblett, Lisette Lefevre, Allan Wilbee, Stephen Woodjetts, Adelle Steinberg, Denise Fergusson, Doug Chamberlain, Gord Crossland, Mari Trainor, Judy Pomerantz, Rita Montgomery, Millie Szerman, Adele Viani, Michael Lennick, Lyn Mason Green, Alan Patterson, Karen Ligier—for ears of steel and hearts of gold.

To Bruce Kimmel, Ron Bowles, and Jenn Handy for making the publishing process painless.

To Allen Kalpin, Xiaolan Zhao, and Marty Begin for balancing my **id**, my **Qi**, and my **oy!**

To my sister and brother-in-law, Rozann and Bill Newman, my brother, Joel Zetzer, and niece and nephew, Laura and Phil Newman for being there despite the difference in our time zones.

To my mother, Lee Heineman, who taught me the power of a smile, the love of a song and, to go for it!

To Eckhart Tolle, Paramahansa Yogananda, and Marharishi Mahesh Yogi whose words continue to inspire me to say *yes*.

And, to my son, Omie, for his love, support, honesty, and insight into the use of the words: prune danish.

Jerelyn Craden started out as a singer-songwriter in Los Angeles, joined Rachel Rosenthal's "Instant Theatre" ensemble, then moved to Toronto where she wrote and performed for theatre, television, film, and radio. As a top voiceover, jingle and animation performer, her credits include: "Inspector Gadget," "X-Men," and "C.O.P.S." A recipient of Canada's ACTRA award for Best Television Variety Writer, network credits include: sitcom, family/adventure and animation series. As Creative Director, Writer of event marketing projects for Fortune 500 companies in Canada and the United States, her credits include: IBM's "Right at Home" presented at the Presidential Inaugural, and Union Pacific Railroad's, "Delivering America's Dreams," presented at the Democratic and Republican national conventions. *Vessie Flamingo, Outshining the Moon* is her first novel.

To order Vessie Flamingo, Outshining the Moon
online go to:
www.vessieflamingo.com